Praise

MW01124662

It seems an almost impossible task for writers not born and reared in Ireland to realistically convey the Irish idiom of the English language, but Cindy Thomson has been more successful than most.

–Irish Emigrant

Thomson's Brigid convincingly embellishes the few known facts about this 5th century national heroine into a compelling Celtic Christian tale…

—Dr. Mark Stibbe, vicar of St. Andrews, Chorleywood, England, and author of the bestselling book, Prophetic Evangelism, Christianity Magazine

The strength of the novel lies in the richly-woven narrative and sensitive evocation of the faiths of Ireland. I certainly feel that Cindy Thompson is an emerging talent and would read her next book, projected also to be set in ancient Ireland. Recommended for both adults and young adults.

–Susan Cook Historical Novels Review 2007-02-01

It's hard to believe this is a first novel. Cindy Thomson did a fabulous job of researching her topic, capturing even small details about ancient Ireland to bring this story to life. The book is so well written you feel transported to another time and place–and it's easy to get lost in Brigid's story. The unexpected ending is both beautiful and unforgettable. From start to finish, this book is a wonderful read.

– Christy Award-winning novelist Ann Tatlock

OTHER BOOKS BY CINDY THOMSON

Brigid of Ireland, Book 1 of the Daughters of Ireland Series

The Roots of Irish Wisdom, Learning From Ancient Voices

The Ellis Island Series
Grace's Pictures
Annie's Stories
Sofia's Tune

Three Finger: The Mordecai Brown Story, with Scott Brown.

Pages of Ireland

Daughters of Ireland Book Two

CINDY THOMSON

For Sandy

One

"For the test of the heart is trouble."

Irish saying

Áine had the book under her cloak in less time than it took the scribe to light the candles in the scriptorium. Clinging to the shadows like the soot on the stone hearth, she edged slowly along the length of the outside wall. She dared not breathe as she crept outside. A rush of satisfaction hit her when the night air finally brushed her cheeks. She'd done it, and now she would escape with the book.

Using the North Star as her guide, she headed toward the Church of the Oak—Cill Dara they called it. There was a woman there she'd met long ago, a woman with the power to protect the book, and she would shelter Áine as well. The Uí Náir tribe might have mighty warriors, but no one had greater power than Brigid. Aine knew this because, as a child, she had been whisked from the clutches of a painful death. And it was Brigid, speaking to the heavens, who had saved her.

She stubbed her toe on a mass of tree roots hidden on the dark forest floor. The lonely cry of an owl sounded in the distance, but no wolves were about so far, thank the gods. Ignoring the throbbing in her foot, she continued on. They'd discover the theft soon, and then they would find her gone. Daithi himself might come after her, claiming he'd have the right to because he was her betrothed. Who did he think *she* was? No slave, that's for sure, and she wouldn't be treated like one.

She scrambled up one rise and then another, the early evening stars giving only faint light, and the clouds threatening to cover even that. She should have waited for a full moon, but there hadn't been time. Daithi had threatened to destroy the book. Her foster father would approve. They underestimated the wondrous magic she had learned it contained. Even though the book was the clan's sacred property, they would throw it into the bog if it meant they could control her. She couldn't wait for fear they'd do it, and soon.

Word was Brigid had built a sanctuary, a place of safekeeping where Daithi and his clan could not enter and take her back. It wasn't too far, she reasoned, judging from the condition of the traveler who had stopped by her foster father's kitchen yesterday and told all about it. "I've just come from Cill Dara," he had said, "and no finer house for God was ever built."

Aine had asked him what he meant, and he had told her that a woman named Brigid had acquired land from the king of Leinster by asking for only the territory that her cloak could cover.

"Then a miracle happened," the man had said. "The cloak was raised up by the wind, and it grew and grew, making the king fear he'd lose all his land to this lass. 'Put it down!' the king shouted, and then he granted the land. Brigid built a dwelling and a church, right there under the sacred oak."

This had to be the woman Aine had met when she was only a girl, the very one who had healed her. Who else performed such acts of wonder? And since the fellow looked as though he had not been on a long journey, Cill Dara could not be far away.

Aine pushed brambles aside and continued on. She wished for a torch, but did not want to risk being discovered. Her foot found a path, and she glanced up. The North Star was still in sight, so she followed the trail, gripping the parchment tightly underneath her long cloak. Even though she had tied it in place with her belt, she clung to the codex as though it were a valuable jewel. It *was* priceless, of course. Not many tribes had a book like this. It seemed alive in her grasp, a breathing entity, and she was aiding its survival. The thought was not just in her head, however. The book actually throbbed against her ribcage. At first the sensation frightened her, but soon she thought of it as affirmation of her plan.

The book needed her. She needed it.

With a flat path to follow, Aine quickened her pace, glancing backward from time to time even though she could see nothing but shadows in the darkness. With any luck, the hapless scribe would not notice the treasured book was gone. He'd push his straw broom over the dirt floor and send the mice scampering about, as was his nightly custom. He would never suspect the book was missing, at least not until he'd made his way to the north end of the room where it was kept. She had time, but still she quickened her steps.

Daithi had retired as he always did—the moment the rooks began to roost in the elm outside the window of his sleeping chamber. Always weary from work, that one, and with a fine measure of mead in his stomach, he would sleep like a dog. She had instructed his servant to see to it.

Daithi would be angry once he awoke and came to call on her, though. No one in Aine's household had ever paid attention to her whereabouts, but once she had agreed to marry the handsome Daithi, her freedom flew from her like so many doves through an open window.

May the gods protect her from his wrath and from that of the whole tribe when they discovered what she had done.

The moment she'd heard of her mother's passing, she knew she could not stay with Daithi's tribe. She would save the book from destruction by those who didn't even understand how magical it was. Her mother would have hoped for deliverance. It might be too late for her, but Aine could bring it to her people.

She glanced down the darkened path before her. She must go. There was no other place on the island that could shield her.

As she approached the territorial crosses, she spotted dark figures scampering along the walkway toward the watchtower. Some slowed and turned her direction. They had spotted her and would soon open the iron gates—at least she hoped they would. Running now, she soon arrived within earshot of the watchman.

"A visitor approaches," he called out.

The sound of hurried footsteps, like a doe scampering along a stone path, came from within the gate. With a metal-against-metal wailing, the gates flung open. Aine propelled herself inside Cill Dara's welcoming arms. She had made it. Another creaking groan, then a heavy thunk, and the gate closed behind her.

Hooded people—she wasn't sure if they were men or women—gathered around her like menacing vultures.

"Male or female?"

"Friend or foe?"

"News? Bad or ill?"

She wasn't sure who to answer first.

A white-cloaked figure approached her.

Aine tightened her arms around the concealed book.

"I am Brigid, Abbess of Cill Dara. We welcome you, traveler. You come without a torch, so we assume you seek sanctuary here. You have found it."

Aine hadn't realized she had been holding her breath until that moment.

Lowering the cowl from her head, the woman's hair flowed freely in the night air.

"'Tis you, Brigid! I knew it!"

Brigid clutched the arm of the woman standing next to her as she spoke to Aine. "God be with you, child. There is welcome here for you." She narrowed her eyes in the dim light. "Do I know you?"

"I do not blame you for not remembering. I was just a girl when you healed me on the road to Aghade. We learned to read together, remember? My Uncle Cillian taught us."

Brigid brought a hand to her mouth. By the light of the torch held by one of Cill Dara's sisters, Aine detected tears forming at the corners of Brigid's eyes.

"Aine? You are so grown up now." Brigid reached for the girl and gave her a tight squeeze.

Too late Aine remembered the book. The abbess must have felt it beneath her clothing.

Brigid stepped back. "Come to the refectory. We will give you something to eat, and you can tell me stories about that uncle of yours. Although he and I exchange manuscripts every fourth moon, 'tis done by couriers. I haven't seen him in years."

The woman closest to Brigid cleared her throat. "I'll take care of the sisters' beds, darlin'."

Aine recognized the distant look in the woman's eyes. She was blind, and because of the endearing way she spoke to the abbess, Aine realized this was Brocca, Brigid's blind mother.

The abbess steered Aine in the direction of the refectory where a fire sent smoke through a hole in the roof. "It will be warm there," Brigid assured.

The broth she was given was thin but flavorful. When Aine finished, Brigid dismissed the cook, and the two of them sat alone in a building so cavernous it could have held at least a hundred cattle.

A lone tallow candle smoked and sputtered atop the refectory table where they sat staring at each other. After a moment, Brigid's sea green eyes sparked. "What's Cillian up to these days?"

Aine smiled and shook her head. "I'm afraid I have no news from Aghade. I have not been there myself since Samhain last."

Brigid tilted her head but did not ask Aine to explain. The abbess was an extraordinary woman and never judgmental, just as Aine remembered her. Perhaps it was the policy at Cill Dara not to ask folks why they sought sanctuary. Aine would not tell. Not yet.

But the silence was as uncomfortable as a stray pebble in a shoe. She had to remedy it somehow. "I have never forgotten, Brigid, what you did for me when I was young."

"You mean what God did for you, child."

Aine drew a hand through her hair and caught her fingers in the tangles created by her exigent travel. "All I know is that my very own father was going to throw me to the wolves and you saved me. You are a mighty force, escaping even the evil druid, Ardan. So my uncle told me."

Brigid took Aine's hand. "Jesu worked wonders. Tell me, child. Would you have done the same for another?"

Aine hung her head. Brigid's condemning question pierced corners of her soul she hadn't explored. "I don't know, Brigid. 'Tis hard. 'Tis quite hard."

Life truly was. Hadn't the abbess had friends to help her through tough times? Tales had been told of a royal poet who was Brigid's aide. Aine wondered if he was among the community now. No one had been on Aine's side back in Daithi's tribe. Thankfully, she now had Brigid and her powers to protect her.

The abbess didn't ask what was troubling Aine. She just kept patting her hand while the fire burned low. Aine did not wish to endure the silent questioning another moment. "Do you have a sleeping spot for me, Maither Brigid? I will not take up much room."

"Oh, child. We believe that by showing travelers hospitality, we are opening our home to Jesu himself, so indeed we do. We've an entire guesthouse for women. I'm afraid you'll not find much company there right now. People come and go, and there aren't many visitors at Cill Dara at the moment."

Aine sighed much louder than she meant to, but at least this gesture would tell Brigid she wished to be left alone. "That is very kind of you, Maither Brigid."

"'Tis kind Jesu we seek to emulate."

As they walked together down the lonely monastery path, Brigid held a torch against the wind. She shouted to be heard over the sharp gale that continued to blow as it had when Aine entered Cill Dara.

"The bell will ring for prayers, but you are not obligated to attend, at least not at night. We would be happy for you to join us in the morning."

Aine raised her voice as well. "I have never understood why you all wake yourselves at night."

"If it makes us uncomfortable, we turn our thoughts to Jesu's suffering and the fact that He does not call us to a comfortable journey in life, Aine."

Aine shrugged. She would not wake for prayers, but she might rise for something else. With everyone engaged at the church, she would be free to find a hiding place for the book. Brigid likely knew she hid something and would probably find out what when Daithi or someone in the tribe inevitably came demanding its return.

Shadows shimmied through the shutters and under the door like spindly dark fingers summoning her. She shivered. The tribe might come for her as well, as though she were a rare heifer stolen from within their rampart boundaries. She sucked in a breath. The laws punished cattle theft more readily than runaways. And besides, she was now under Brigid's protection. Aine need never go back to a place where she held no significance.

The book, though. Ah, the book. Brigid might send it back, if she knew of it. Aine would not let that happen. She would protect it in secret.

Two

"A troublemaker plants seeds of strife;
gossip separates the best of friends."

Proverbs 16:28 NLT

Aine couldn't sleep. She tossed the lambswool cover from her legs and rose from her cot. The guesthouse was vacant, save for her, and the quiet left her alone with her thoughts—thoughts of Daithi, angry, his red face accentuating bulging eyes. She covered her face with her hands and wept. Why were men always angry with her?

Before long, the call to prayer rang out its jagged, tinny beckoning. With her cloak wrapped tightly around her and the book lodged safely under it, Aine crept out into the cold air. This might be only night she had before Daithi tracked her down, her only chance to use the cover of the night, so she dared not hesitate. She had to deposit the book somewhere, temporarily, of course. As soon as she was able, she would bring the book safely to her mother's people, Aine's people, relations she had yet to meet. But since her mother had come from them, Aine was certain life would be better for her there.

Although she had never been to the village of her birth, Cillian had talked of it when she was growing up. He'd said that her mother had raised her in the vicinity of their people, but they had not been allowed too close after she married Aine's father. They despised him, as of course they would. He was an evil man, like most husbands.

"They're a desperate lot," Cillian had said, speaking of his own clan. "Living up there in those mountains with no more than a sheep or two. My sister was wise to get away, though not wise enough to choose a decent man to marry."

Daithi's tribe had many cattle, strong and healthy, reproducing much each season. The book had brought them good fortune, and now Aine would bring it to her people.

Aine knew this because, after she mischievously took the book from the clan's library, Nessa, the cattleman's wife, plunged the book into the animals' drinking trough. She could still picture the old scribe's face—she didn't know his name. He came barreling out of the scriptorium, calling out that someone had stolen a sacred book. How was Aine to know the woman would do such a thing? Aine had supposed she would stow it in the dresser in her wee cottage. But instead, she had thrown it to the cattle.

"What are you doing, Nessa?" Aine had said at the time. "You'll ruin it."

The old woman shook a finger at her. Aine could still see the mud under her fingernails, evidence of a life of labor. "A bit of water will not harm it. It will dry. But enough of its magic will swim into the water where my animals will drink it. Fertile, they'll be, don't you know. Just wait and see."

About that time the scribe arrived, nearly tumbling down the hill toward the pasture. He had obviously spotted the book under the clear water because he started gasping for air and holding his chest with one hand while trying to steady himself, waving his free arm in the air.

Nessa indeed was correct about the book's power. The following spring, Nessa's cows bore twice as many young as anyone else's. And did she ever tell about it. There was scarcely anyone in the land who did not hear the legend of the book. A lucky charm, of sorts. Aine later learned that the book also possessed the capacity to warm, vibrate, and shiver—whatever was needed to indicate its will. She did not fear it. She knew in her heart the book was not evil, just incredibly powerful like Brigid.

What she was about to do, take prosperity from one clan and give it to another, did give Aine cause to ponder. Guilt flowed like a muddy gusher. She told herself she would borrow the book's magic for a wee while. She must. For her mother. She would not let Daithi and his people starve, if taking the book came to that. She could return the book to them in due time, after it had brought wealth to her mother's clan. But when—and if—she did return, she would not become Daithi's wife.

The well-tended path encircled the monastery buildings with no stones to trip her up. She had no torch but she was growing accustomed to strolling about in the dark. A woman on the run had no other choice.

11

Holding her cowl tight to her neck, she considered the possibility that Brigid's magic might transform her and conceal her identity. What would it be like to be a hawk or even a wolf? Druids and druidesses had the ability to change shapes, some said. Brigid probably did too. She could teach Aine. Then Aine could hide herself away whenever she pleased. Uncle Cillian snubbed his nose at such beliefs, but being a man, what did he know about womanly powers?

The path suddenly narrowed and ended at a hedge of dense, dark bushes. A soft murmuring came from behind them. Wee splinters of light fingered through the shrubs.

Aine crouched low, straining to see between the branches. A fire crackled somewhere nearby. She wedged herself into the bush to get a better look. Peering into the night, she saw a small fire burning within a ring of stones. A woman fed the flames with twigs, chanting all the while.

A bell tolled again in the direction of Brigid's church. Why were the abbey's residents not here tending this fire? Only one was here to celebrate, and from the ordinary appearance of her clothing, she was not a member of Cill Dara's community.

Aine's foot snagged on a branch and the resulting snap echoed louder than the fire's crackling, causing the keeper of the flames to turn in her direction. She had been found out, but the celebrant did not appear menacing. Aine slipped through the hedge and faced the fire. The lass stared at her while circling the flames, chanting, "Come, Exalted One, and bless us."

A pile of oak branches lay on the far side of the fire. Aine grabbed a twig, tossed it into the fire, and followed the path of the woman, tentatively at first, but then with vigor as she found the woman accepting of her presence. After many rotations around the fire, another joined them. Soon, the first young woman darted off into the snug woods. Aine sat down on a log while the second woman took up the ritual. Staring at the yellow and orange glow, Aine murmured, "Protect us, myself and the book." It wasn't that she wasn't strong—Cillian was always saying she was as bullheaded a lass he'd ever the chance to meet—but she needed a champion by her side. Someone who actually had the power to defend her must hear her plea.

Aine rubbed her fingers over her face. She must have been too distraught, too self-absorbed to realize it before, but this was no festival fire. While Aine had come toward the direction of the great fair to find Brigid, it was not the season for it. So what did it mean? There were no musicians, no jugglers, no merchants. This was no new undertaking, judging by the charred appearance of the fire ring. It seemed one person at a time cared for the blaze rather than a convergence of fair-goers. There was no indication that this might be a cooking fire, either. The center lacked the three stones most fires held to support cooking pots. The flames danced free and clear up to the inky sky. The only explanation was that she sat before a ceremonial fire, an offering of some type. Maybe the god for whom the fire had been built would show favor on her.

Aine sprung to her feet and joined in the sacred dance once again, the treasured book still tied firmly at her waist.

Later, when the fire keeper rested, Aine crept away from the flame, thankful that the woman had not asked her why she was there. She was tired and weary, and the lambswool-clad cot in the guesthouse beckoned her to return to it. But she could not. Not yet. Under the cover of darkness, she must hide the book. But where?

She pushed her way through the bushes encircling the fire. Then she turned back and looked at the hedge. The sisters never came there. Hardly anyone did, she guessed, because the ground was not packed down from many feet. Those who had come had done so only for the purpose of worship. Quiet. Unmolested. She rubbed her chin. This patch of ground must be a special place, exceptional enough for the book.

She dropped to her knees and began to hollow out a space between two of the bushes. The ground was pliable, and with the help of a stick, she soon had a hole big enough to hold the book. She wrestled it from her belt and dropped it in. Its presence would surely please the god of the fire. All would be safe at last. She smacked her hands together when she turned to leave. *Safe at last!*

At dawn, Aine joined the community for morning prayers and to break her fast. She wouldn't be staying long, but she'd placate the abbess by participating for now. The seating arrangement in the church and afterward in the refectory told her who the abbess's closest advisors were. Besides Brigid's blind mother, there was a tower-tall woman who took orders directly from the abbess and a petite, blonde woman named Fianna who had seen to Aine's needs when she first arrived at the guesthouse. Fianna and the tall one had their heads together a moment before conferring with Brigid, who immediately cast her attention on Aine.

They were talking about her. Had one of them seen her bury the book? They had all been engrossed in their prayers at the time.

When Brigid stopped staring, Aine slid from bench to bench, hiding behind taller girls until she was close enough to overhear.

Brigid's voice carried the lilt of a scolding granny. "Fianna, if you knew our guest had left her bed during prayers, then you were not where you should have been. You will mind your duties and not concern yourself with anything but our guests' needs."

Aine's heart pounded. She'd been so careful not to be seen.

Fianna tilted her head in compliance and disappeared into the cloud of brown-robed faithful. Those around Aine left too, leaving her exposed. She put an elbow on the table board to shield her face with her forearm.

Brigid inclined her head toward the tall nun. "Sometimes I feel as though all I do here is dole out discipline. Surely God has more for me here than that."

The spindly one raised one brow. "You have another visitor. This one a man."

Brigid seemed surprised. "Oh?"

"The Poet has returned."

Brigid clapped her hands. "I haven't seen him in years. Where is he?"

"He told Fianna he would wait at the church for you. Said he didn't want to disturb your routine."

The abbess nearly sprung from her bench. Aine watched as she waded past the other women who had crowded near the door. They turned to glare at Aine after the abbess had gone.

Brigid's tall assistant paused in front of Aine on her way out. "Whatever you are up to, you mind yourself. Brigid might not throw you out, but I will, if need be."

Aine put on her best smile, the one that usually worked with Daithi, and carried her bowl to the washers waiting in the yard. It was difficult to appear unmoved. She wanted them to like her, or at least to tolerate her presence. She sucked in a breath as she made her way back to the stone path that encircled the community of buildings.

She spotted something white near the yew grove. The tip of Brigid's hood rose and fell among the branches. She was walking there and perhaps talking to her visitor. Aine desperately needed to know if anyone had seen her bury the book. When the path led her directly in front of the yews, she paused, pretending to be searching her pocket for a lost item.

Brigid sounded irritated. "I'm on my way to see our visitor, Etain. What could be so important?"

Aine recognized the voice. The rude, lanky one had rushed on ahead to intercept Brigid.

"Forgive me, but Fianna just told me where Aine was last night. I think you should know."

"Tell me if 'tis important."

"She's been dancing with the pagans."

Aine put a hand over her mouth, fearful that the nun was about to tell Brigid that Aine had buried something near that fire. She strained to hear. Did she need to retrieve the book now and leave?

"And why was Sister Fianna not in her bed or at prayers?"

There was a pause. The tall nun had evidently not expected that response.

"Really," Brigid said, "you must get control of your tongue."

Etain's voice softened, and she apologized. Aine feared Brigid was about to return to the path, so she ducked behind one of the thickest branches where she had an even better view of the two women while still remaining concealed.

Etain raised her straw-like eyebrows. "Your maither. She's fond of that poet, aye?"

"Of course. What of it?"

"I hear you are quite fond of him too."

Brigid grabbed the woman's arm. "Etain, you will not start rumors that could disrupt this community. I will not allow it. I'd sooner turn you out."

Sure, and Brigid didn't need a man. Aine could have told Etain so.

The sister's voice softened. "I would never hurt you with malicious talk, friend Brigid. You must know that."

"Even so, you must be careful what you repeat."

"But others are saying it, and I thought you should know."

"Etain, just what are they saying?" Brigid clicked her tongue. "Tell me only if it pertains to the well-being of Cill Dara."

Furrows lifted from Etain's forehead. "'Tis no harm in our bishop taking a husband. Everyone thinks that's why the Poet's come. That's why he spends so much time speaking to your maither."

Brigid sighed. "We are longtime friends, the Poet and I. That is the truth, and 'tis all anyone need know."

Etain nodded. "And what of the lass? Whether Fianna should have been near the pagan fire or not, she did see your young friend there."

"I will speak to Fianna again. And as for Aine, she is not a resident here. She has taken no vows. She may very well be in trouble, but we do well to remember she is a guest at Cill Dara. We do not hold her to the same level of accountability."

Aine smiled to herself. Brigid was still her defender.

Three

"Stoop as you walk the path of life and
you'll not be struck by the branch of
pride."

Irish proverb

N innidh paced on the path in front of the men's
guesthouse. Too much time had passed since he last
saw his old friend. He'd had many places to go, many people
to entertain and educate. As the only high royal poet he
knew of who was also a Christian, he'd been quite occupied
the last few years.

He fingered the fringe of his forest green tunic, a mark
of his status in society. He used his position of influence for

Jesu, but sometimes he longed to wear an anonymous dirt-colored cloak to blend in with the common people.

Today, he planned to tell Brigid his true name. He'd felt spiritually convicted for withholding it. Previously, he'd reasoned that if no one knew his name, he would never become revered by the people. He wanted the attention to be on the message rather than the messenger. But it had not worked out that way. A poet was respected more than a king.

He sighed, glad for fresh revelation. God, of course, knew how the people viewed poets. God was the one who had given Ninnidh the gift of song, after all. Trying to remain anonymous had been Ninnidh's attempt at taking control, at deciding what was best. He had been wrong. Now that he no longer desired to keep his name secret, his old friend should know.

He perched on a stone outside the guesthouse, strumming his harp. How many years had it been since he'd seen Brigid? Six at least.

He turned when he heard footsteps. "Maither Brigid! That's what they call you now. You are as beautiful as ever."

Her cheeks blushed as she reached to embrace him. "God be with you, friend. There is welcome here for you."

He gently kissed her cheeks and then stepped back. "'Tis a wonderful establishment you have here. God has richly blessed you."

"So that I may bless others. Come to the refectory and eat. The men's door is on the west side. When you have satisfied your belly, we will talk."

He held tightly to her hand. "I am satisfied just seeing you again."

He willed himself not to have special feelings for his old friend, but he was losing the battle. He had been with her when she was horribly disfigured. He had been there when Bishop Mel had read the vows of bishop over her head. And with God's help, he had saved her mother Brocca from calamity by pretending to be an evil druid's cohort. They had a history as rich as though they had grown up together as foster children.

Brigid's tepid green eyes smiled. "Very well. Let's go to the church, then."

The sanctuary was empty and cold, but rays of morning sun pouring in from the east wall's transoms cast the place in a friendly light. Brigid seated herself on a low bench a few paces away from the altar, and he joined her. "You have been traveling?" she asked.

"Aye. Always traveling. You should be pleased to know, Maither Brigid, that word of what God is doing through you is spreading over the whole island."

"I shall have to visit some of those people."

"And you should. I will be happy to escort you."

A sunbeam kissed her shoulder, sending glimmering light through her golden hair.

"I would like that."

He moved his harp to his back, having no desire to play it while he spoke to her. "So, I have heard that many of those in your life since last we met have passed on."

"That is true. Even my earthly father, God bless him, is buried in this church's graveyard. In fact, he was the first one buried there."

"And you didn't even know 'twas him when you laid him in his grave."

"King Dunlaing told you?"

"Ah, Leinster has a Christian king, thanks to you. He did tell me about it. I've been singing the story about the cross you wove. You'll not be minding it, will you?"

Brigid gazed straight ahead as though envisioning her father's grave beyond the building's walls. "I do not mind at all if it brings others to Jesu. That wee cross 'twas just something to keep my hands busy while I spoke to a dying man. I have woven them many times since, telling of Jesu's sacrifice."

"Aye. And the telling of the story with the cross seems to help folks understand. You should see those I sing to, reaching for rushes to weave a cross while I make rhyme about it."

Brigid shrugged her shoulders. "God uses even the most ordinary things."

"Like me."

"Ordinary? A royal poet like you? I do not think so."

"Ninnidh. My name's Ninnidh."

Brigid held a hand to her heart. "I am pleased to know your name."

He winked at her. "Ah, well, 'twas foolish pride kept me from sharing it. There's many who will know it now, especially at Loch Erne."

"Loch Erne? Wasn't that where you were headed when we first met? Up north?"

"Indeed. I am directing my father's Christian learning center there when I'm not traveling."

"Oh, praise God. What a wonderful example you must be to the young people."

He shrugged.

"Are you still making music, then?" She pointed to his harp.

"Of course. Teaching takes many forms."

The sunbeam had moved to her back, casting an impressive glow. "What brings you to Cill Dara?"

"You mean besides your smiling face?" His words caused her to blush again, just as he'd hoped. "Truth is, I've run out of manuscripts to copy. I'd been thinking about traveling to Rome or maybe Tours, but 'tis such an arduous journey, that. I heard about your illustrious school here and thought I would visit."

"I am delighted you did. Our scribes are quite gifted. They are working on a magnificent book for celebratory mass."

He smiled. "Ah, books. There are those requiring deep contemplation and study, and those created as a supreme act of worship. Those illuminated codices are such a wonder. Worship for the scribe and worship for the beholder."

"Indeed." She tilted her blond head to the side. "I suspect, though, you have come today seeking volumes for scholarship." She seemed to be reaching for his hand when the church door thumped open.

"Brigid?"

"Aye, Maither?" Brigid turned toward the door where Brocca stood, wringing her hands.

"I heard the Poet has returned."

Ninnidh leapt to his feet and hurried to Brocca, taking her into a hug while his harp bounced on the rope strewn over his back.

Brigid's mother laughed. "The rumors were true, then. What are you two doing alone in here? Come celebrate with us in the refectory."

They linked arms and left to join the community.

Later, after much visiting and honey mead and song, Ninnidh stood with the abbess at the central well.

Brigid worried her lip. "I have to deal with internal problems at Cill Dara. You understand. I am saddened that I'll not be enjoying your company, friend, though I wish to very much."

"I understand." He held a hand to his chest, hoping he could still the pounding disappointment in his chest. "I will return at another time."

"Stop at Cillian's place. Sister Etain will direct you there. You can return some manuscripts I've borrowed and ask if he might lend some to you. I don't believe we have anything you haven't already seen."

"You are very thoughtful." He kicked the toe of his boot at the root of a clump of grass.

"'Tis not that I don't want your company. I do." She extended her hand and he tried not to meet her gaze. "I must put the sisters first."

He put on his most pleasant tone of voice. "I do indeed understand, Brigid." He focused his gaze on the dipping sun in the west. "Will you come visit later then? We have so much to catch up on, and"—he kicked again at the ground and then studied her watery eyes—"well, I would just like to talk with you further. I miss your company."

"Sometimes I wish I could toss all my responsibilities aside, board a chariot, and ride off into the quiet countryside. But God wants me here, Ninnidh."

"Of course."

"I will take a pilgrimage, when I'm able. God willing. And then of course I will come see you and your father."

He would be content with that promise. For now.

four

"The lie often goes further than the truth."

Irish proverb

T he whole monastery buzzed with talk about Aine and the pagan fire. Aine cringed at the attention. Fortunately, no one had mentioned the book, and that was her main concern. She kept reminding herself that whatever they said about her did not matter. These people would soon be gone from her life anyway. Her mother's people, Aine's birth clan—they'd accept her.

She brushed the moisture away from her cheeks.

The guesthouse hostess called to her from near the window. "We've company."

The guests have guests? "What do you mean?"

"I mean the abbess is on her way over here."

She no more than spoke when a rapping sound came from the front door. The hostess flung the door wide and let the woman wearing the pearl-white cloak in.

"Where's Fianna?" the abbess asked.

The sister shrugged her shoulders. "She asked me to take her chores for the evening. Didn't say why, and I didn't ask."

"Very well."

The sister led Brigid to the cot near the central fire where Aine sat rubbing her arms.

Brigid frowned at the nun. "She's cold."

The sister hurriedly fetched a blanket and laid it in Aine's lap.

Aine looked up at Brigid. "I am so happy to see you."

Brigid sat close. "I am happy to have you here. I apologize that I did not come to speak with you before now."

Aine waved an arm and raised her voice. "Well, this is a big place. And you are in charge of it. Everyone wants to speak with you. I understand. Thank you for coming to see me."

"Well, not everyone wants to see me, but you are most welcome, Aine."

Aine's spirit was lifted. "And why would they not? You can do miraculous things. I'm the perfect example. Look at my face." She turned her head from side to side. "Not a scar. You would never know how marked I once was by looking at me now. I may have been only a child, but I do remember how folks used to recoil from my ugliness."

Brigid held a finger under Aine's chin. "People fail to see the true beauty of the heart that God sees, but what you say is true. Your complexion now is pure like mountain snow. God is good."

"You are good." Aine reached out and squeezed Brigid's hand.

"He does great things through me. I am his willing servant." Brigid's smooth hand patted hers. "What can I do for you, Aine?"

She knew she would ask sooner or later. She searched her mind for an answer that might keep Brigid from prying too deeply. Brigid was the only person since Aine's mother died who was kind to her. "I want to stay here." She opened her fingers and let Brigid's hand fall away.

"Stay as long as you like. Is there anything else?"

"That is all."

"I must tell you, Aine. If you stay more than a few days, you will be expected to work and to attend prayers faithfully."

Aine relaxed, hoping this was all the abbess came to discuss. "I don't know how to do very many things."

Brigid smoothed her tunic as if to give her hands something to do. "Well, perhaps if you tell me a bit about where you came from, what you did there, we could find you a suitable occupation."

Aine tried not to think about where she'd come from. She crossed her arms against her chest. "I'll do whatever you ask, Maither Brigid, but I have one request."

"Oh? What is that?"

"There are men at the monastery?"

"There are. We have brothers and sisters at Cill Dara." Brigid cocked her head to one side, seemingly trying to understand.

"I must say…well…please know that I'll not be a slave to a man."

Brigid sat up straight. "We have no slaves here." She brought a hand to her lips. "You are bound, then? How could Cillian let that happen? If you've escaped a rightful owner, I'll be required to return you, child."

Aine held up a finger. "Nay, not like that. Not that kind of slave. A married woman kind of slave."

"I have no intention of…wait a moment. Are you married, Aine?" Brigid sounded surprised.

"Not yet. I'm promised to someone, but I will not have him treat me ill as though I were a slave."

"That is why you're here."

"It is." Aine knew that to stay at Cill Dara she had to let Brigid know about Daithi, but she did not have to tell her about the book.

"A betrothed has no right to mistreat his promised bride. You can do something about it. I know the law, child. If he's beat you or not, you have the right to a detachment, should you want it."

Daithi had not hit her. He got angry sometimes, but he had never lifted a fist toward her. His restraint was probably what caused his face to turn blood red so often. Still, she needed Brigid on her side because she truly cared and was not honor-bound to pretend to care for her. "And what can a woman do to get this detachment?"

"I've seen abused women before and I know how blind they can be to what is happening. 'Tis not your fault, any of it. I understand that you likely feel a kind of loyalty to your man."

Aine leaned a cheek to her shoulder, trying to block memories. Being with Brigid ignited many childhood recollections, and she didn't want to go back to that time. Her father married her mother and created a household that no child should have to live in. She did not want that kind of life.

Brigid continued. "You can void the promise, should you want to, and if he hits you, you should. I've no tolerance for a man who mistreats women. How much longer is the engagement?"

"As much as two years, but he considers me his now."

Brigid reached for the girl's hand again. "Has he...violated you, child?"

"I don't mean that." She was still pure and wanted that known. "He tries to control my every movement. He wants to make my decisions. I have no free will."

Brigid relaxed her shoulders. "In the eyes of the law, we still have time to deal with the situation."

Aine turned to the glowing peat fire in the center of the room, contemplating what Brigid had said.

Brigid patted the girl's knee. "No need to decide anything now. You are safe with us. There is something else I need to discuss with you, if you're agreeable."

"What is it?"

"The sisters have been telling me about a pagan fire that burns near our walls, just on the other side of a hedge of bushes. Have you seen it?"

Aine wove her fingers together and tried not to look at the abbess. "If I have, am I in trouble?'"

31

"Oh, nay, child. I just want to know. I was thinking of inviting those who tend this fire to come visit with us. There is nothing better than a crowd to talk, eat, drink, and sing with."

"I have seen it—while out walking. But I do not know those who tend it."

"I will find out then. Would you like to go with me?"

"I would." What would the nuns have to whisper about if she went there with the abbess?

"Fine, then. We will go at dusk tomorrow."

The next evening, as the sun dipped below the vast arms of the oak tree, Aine joined Brigid to hurry toward the edge of Cill Dara. Brigid would miss compline, but confessed to Aine that when duty calls, it must be answered.

They were silent as they walked. Aine wondered what horrible things Brigid imagined had been done to her. She should explain, but she didn't want to say something that would anger the abbess. She hadn't actually been harmed—not yet, anyway. Aine's mission was to prevent ill things from occurring, and she still needed to complete it. Brigid, no doubt, wondered how Aine came to be betrothed. She might even assume Cillian had forced her out of his monastery. As much as she didn't want to malign her uncle, Aine needed her story to be believable. Leaving out a few details in order to accomplish her mission was justified. A whole tribe depended on her even though they did not yet know it.

As they approached, the wide hedge seemed to glimmer with flames burning behind the branches. The oranges and yellows cast an almost otherworldly glow. The murmur of a female voice floated toward them. Aine turned to the abbess, whose fine white clothing kept her from fading into the darkness. "What is she saying? I heard it before, but I wasn't sure."

They paused to listen in the still night air. "I believe she is saying, 'Come, Exalted One, and bless us.' It always troubles me when I hear the voices of the broken-hearted, the lonely, the hungry, crying out to a god or a goddess who can never help them."

"Never?"

"Nay, never. You know so, Aine. The One True God said to the spiritual seekers of His day, 'I am the bread of life. He who comes to me will never go hungry, and he who believes in me will never be thirsty.' He alone provides what they seek."

"Is that what you'll tell them when we arrive?"

"Perhaps, or something similar. But first I will feed them, share our home, give them warm clothing. Come. We will speak with the lass now."

Aine followed the abbess through the nettlesome hedge. Once on the other side, they paused to observe the fire keeper, who lifted thin arms toward the sky, mimicking the smoke rising from the flames. She spun around three times and then threw a branch into the fire. "Come, O Exalted One. Bless us!" Her voice rose up, surprisingly vigorous from such a stick-thin dancer.

"Look at the poor thing," Brigid whispered. "She looks as though she hasn't eaten for days. She is pleading for help."

Aine had seen the dance differently. She thought it was worship, a beautiful display of emotion. She had not considered that the women here were really desperate.

Brigid's eyes filled with tears. "Oh, bless you, child." The abbess held out her arms toward the lass.

The startled woman halted her prancing.

Brigid lowered her arms and held a hand to her chin. "I mean God—"

Before Brigid could say more, a team of emaciated women sprung from the dark border around the fire. They flung themselves at Brigid's feet and rubbed their hands down her white robe. Their pleading reminded Aine of the day long ago when she and Brigid had been surprised on the road. That day, Aine had received her healing. Hungry masses had pursued them along the route to Cillian's place, frightening them both. Brigid had dropped to her knees and pulled Aine, who was then only a wee lass, up under her chin. Brigid had uttered words Aine now could not remember, and miraculously, the leprosy had vanished.

This time, Brigid did not hide. "Please, rise. All of you must come to Cill Dara and have something to eat."

In the refectory, as the women supped, Aine overheard Brocca speaking to Brigid. "'Tis a fine thing, Daughter, that you brought them here. Their voices are weary and crackling, like those who haven't had a satisfying meal since before harvest began."

"You could be right, Maither. But one refused to come. I'm afraid we will have to deliver her meal."

"Where?"

"To the fire. She would not leave it. Aine believes one of them tends the fire at all times."

"Then I will tend it for her so she will come."

"You will do no such thing, Maither. What will the sisters, let alone the brothers, think about you tending a pagan fire?"

Aine stayed quiet although they had to have known she was listening.

Brocca rubbed her chin. "But if you, the Abbess of Cill Dara, tended it, what could they say about it? A bishop in God's church would surely bless the fire, aye?"

Brigid gripped both of her mother's hands in hers. "Brilliant, Maither. That way the fire will be sacred, dedicated to God, and the woman left behind will not have to stay there. She will get a warm bed tonight. I will do it."

"I'll come with you." No one objected to Aine's offer, so she grabbed her cloak from the pegs near the door and waited outside for the abbess.

In a few moments, Brigid joined her. "You don't have to accompany me, Aine."

"I want to. I'm fascinated by what they are doing."

"Nothing to be in awe of, child."

"Still, I want to come."

"As you wish."

Brigid retrieved one of the torches from a wall pocket inside the refectory. She tugged her cowl over her head and stepped into the night.

Aine followed, pulling on her own cloak. An adventure was more intriguing than sitting inside her dreary room, and if more blessings came to the book buried nearby, then she wanted to witness it. A chill wind whipped her cloak around her legs and sent shivers up her back, almost convincing her to turn back. They pressed on, face forward into the gale. If Brigid went near the place Aine buried the book, Aine needed to know in order to steer the abbess away, to keep her from discovering it. The gods knew it was there. That was enough.

She drew the frosty air into her lungs. One never knew with the book. Magical things could happen, and it might make its presence known. With one as powerful as Brigid nearby, Aine would need to keep watch. On the way there, Aine would try to learn more about the things Cillian would never tell her, things that might help her on her journey. Her uncle and the abbess had been good friends when Aine was a child, and she'd heard from the guesthouse hostess that they still were. Cillian was the only one who could direct Aine to her homeland, her mother's people. The place where the book belonged.

When they reached the fire, they found the attendant seated on a log, arms wrapped tightly about her. If it weren't for the warmth of the flames, she would surely be frozen by now. "Can you find the way to the refectory while we tend your fire?" Brigid asked.

The woman bent her head low. "I will do as you wish, O Exalted One." When she tried to edge past Brigid, the abbess halted her, holding firmly to her bony arm.

"God is the Exalted One, child."

The woman bowed and crept off.

"There is a bed there for you," Brigid called after her. "We will keep the night watch."

When the woods no longer echoed the woman's footsteps, Brigid made the sign of the cross across her chest, something Aine had seen the folks at Cill Dara do many times. Then the abbess circled the fire three times, declaring out loud: once for the Father, once for the Son, once for the Holy Spirit, three in one. She blessed the fire and asked God to keep it burning for the safety of the poor ones.

Brigid paused, looked at Aine a moment, and then added, "Jesu, please keep all the women who come to the fire safe and keep out those men who seek to hurt them."

Aine leaned against the trunk of an elm, content that Brigid's god would do exactly that. She eventually dozed, the sound of Brigid's prayers lulling her.

"Won't you rest?" Aine asked when she awoke to see the abbess holding her palms up to the sky.

"Patrick prayed a hundred times a night while keeping watch over the herds belonging to his Irish master."

Aine knew from Cillian that Patrick was the one who brought the teaching from across the sea.

"Jesu be praised!" Brigid shouted. "May this fire burn forever with the love of the Maker."

A rustling noise emerged from one corner of the hedge. The sound came from large human feet because no nighttime creature trudged about in such a clumsy manner. Aine glimpsed a streak of brown robe as someone scampered away, and Brigid seemed to notice it as well.

The abbess folded her arms across her chest. "That Fianna! What can be done with such a meddlesome lass?"

The next morning, Brigid's mother sat with Aine as the other sisters got the newcomers settled in. Aine wasn't sure she was happy with all this company. And this woman, Brocca? She was so unlike her daughter. She had not stopped asking questions since they got to the guesthouse.

"Does he beat you, your husband-to-be?"

Aine was glad the woman could not see her roll her eyes. "I do not wish to talk about him, if you do not mind."

"But dear…" Brocca patted her arm. "How can we help you if you don't tell us what's happening? That's what we're here for. We're to help everyone, aren't we, Etain?"

The lanky sister paused from spreading a linen sheet on a straw cot. "Indeed, Brocca."

Almost everyone had gone to the refectory, and Aine wished she had gone as well. She drew in a deep breath. "There are things folks don't know. 'Tis complicated."

"Ah, life is that." The sightless woman tilted her head to one side as though contemplating the thought. "I am not one to complain about my lot in life, but perhaps it would help you to understand that others have gone through trials."

No one could understand the value of the book she hid. Without it, Daithi's tribe might struggle a bit. They would not know why their opulence had faltered, but they would manage. The strong always do. The weak, the unfortunate? They needed help. With this book, her birth tribe might avoid starvation and perhaps total annihilation.

"I know you have experienced loss, child. Your own mother, God rest her soul."

"What?" Aine sprung to her feet. "How do you know this?"

38

Brocca sighed heavily. "Please forgive me. I did not mean to upset you. Cillian sent word last week. He thought Brigid would want to know."

And he'd sent word to Aine as well. Did not come to tell her himself.

Aine sat down, willing her grief not to bring tears. "I did not know her well, only a few faded memories."

Brocca patted her arm. "Still, a loss. I am so sorry."

Aine had hopes, unfounded hopes, of a reunion. The fact that they had not known each other well was the true tragedy. Her mother had died, mostly likely from poverty, but Aine could still do something. Truly needy people, like her mother, should have such things as a magical book. "I don't mean to be selfish, Sister Brocca. I know that others have been through trials. I don't say mine is worse."

"Nay, child. Let yourself mourn. There is a time for everything."

Aine nodded, then realized the woman could not see her. "Thank you, Brocca. My lot? 'Tis hard to explain. Maybe I'll try later. I'm tired now."

"Of course, dear. You lie back, and I'll pray for you."

The woman put a cool hand to Aine's forehead. She didn't have the touch that Brigid did. As she mumbled a blessing over her, Aine was aware of Etain's staring. Fianna was probably there too. They didn't like her for some reason. She closed her eyes and concentrated on more important matters--the book lying in a dark hole near the fire. Had it been blessed by the gods yet? Had she?

Later that night, while all the guests snored in a staggering rhythm, Aine rose from her bed. Something seemed to call to her, urging her toward that fire. She slipped on her cloak and squeezed out the door without making a sound. A torch on a high pole stood outside the guesthouse like a sentry in the night, placed there, she knew, to guide those who had to take care of necessities in the middle of the night. It cast an accusing shadow on Aine, proclaiming that the unwanted visitor was wandering around again in the dark. She had heard the rumors. The sisters thought she was up to something evil. How little they knew that she was up to good.

She stepped forward, away from the light. Just as she reached the path that encircled the monastery, she detected movement near the sisters' cluster of cells. She hid herself beside a stack of peat and waited. A few moments later, a dark figure crept like a fox from cell to cell, running, then stopping, then running again. As Aine's eyes adjusted to the dark, she realized the scampering figure was one of the sisters. They all wore the same long, brown cloaks with ample cowls. Aine calculated that the next call to prayer was several hours hence. There was no reason she could think for someone to creep about like that.

The figure disappeared inside one of the stone cells. Aine waited a moment, but the person did not come back out. Finally, when all seemed clear, she continued on toward the fire.

Aine hesitated in the shadows. Maybe she should tell the abbess about the book. She contemplated a moment, remembering the image of Brigid from last night with her arms outstretched toward the fire, then visualized the dark hole covered with leaves where the precious codex rested. Nay, she could not reveal the treasure. Not yet anyway. Daithi was sure to turn up soon, and she had to be sure that she and the book were safe at Cill Dara. Brigid, even with her miraculous powers, was no match for Daithi if he had the book in his possession again.

Aine moved closer to the fire. Brigid never asked more questions than a breath could hold, unlike that Brocca. Aine and Brigid had stood by the fire silently the night before. After a time, Brigid had sung a tune Aine remembered from her childhood. Had Brigid sung it to her long ago? Or perhaps Aine's mother? Pity that what she wanted to recall was just beyond her grasp, and what she wanted to forget haunted her like a banshee.

She squeezed her eyes tight and let the melody of Brigid's song fill her mind and chase away all other thoughts. The tune the abbess had sung the night they watched the fire together had spoken of angels watching. Brigid's voice soothed as they stood arm in arm, moving in rhythm. Aine asked Brigid where she had learned the song.

"I learned it from the Poet."

"What does it mean?" Aine had wondered if a special blessing had been spoken by the gods through this wonderful woman. After all, the book was buried nearby.

He shall give his angel watch over you.

Aine straightened her neck now as she remembered. A curse? Daithi's face, his accusing stare, flashed in her mind. Angels are like fairies—good ones, she supposed. But who

41

was this 'He?' She surely didn't need a man watching over her. She knew Cillian's monks worshiped a god called Jesu, but she'd never heard of these angels. She had been a female child in a male monastery, so they'd not taught her anything. She'd seen their fearful looks, heard their pitiful cries for mercy from this Jesu, and hadn't cared in the least that she had not been part of it.

She didn't remember if she had asked the question in her head the night of the fire, but Brigid had responded. "Ah, 'tis the Good Lord Jesu, child. The One True God." Aine had backed up a step. Brigid embraced the same god Cillian did. She had heard it mentioned before, but she hadn't realized Brigid put her faith in only one god. That seemed too risky.

Tonight's fire keeper barely gave Aine a glance. Aine threw a stick into the flames just as a loud crack came from the area near where her secret possession was hidden. She jumped to her feet and ran toward the sound. It was dark apart from the fire, and her eyes had already gotten used to the brightness. She stumbled, wondering how Brocca functioned in her sightless world. But she soon found the place. Flinging herself to the ground, she brushed leaves and sticks aside. She ran her fingers over the smooth dirt. It was still there, undisturbed. She dumped dirt and debris back over the spot.

Aine should return to her bed. Fianna, or someone as nosey as she was, might take to following her, and she couldn't risk anyone discovering the book. She almost willed Daithi to come soon. Once he was turned away, she could leave Cill Dara because he'd think she was there and wouldn't try to stop her.

Voices coming from the darkened church met her ears as she passed by. Fianna's voice, booming like a man with too much ale in his belly, rang out.

"I am not spying on anyone, Maither Brigid."

There was some mumbling then. Brigid's voice was not nearly as strong as the Sister's, so Aine resorted to what she had gotten good at, eavesdropping. She crept closer, crouching near the door.

"What I mean to ask is, are you attending to your study? Lectio Divina? Are you taking time to listen, child? Your devotion should not be rushed. I would like you to consider the Psalm, *"Rescue me, O LORD, from evil men; protect me from men of violence, who devise evil plans in their hearts and stir up war every day. They make their tongues as sharp as a serpent's; the poison of vipers is on their lips."*

Aine was amused. The woman was skilled at getting her point across. She'd reprimanded her follower to good effect. These words also spoke a warning to Aine's heart. *Protect me from men of violence.*

The voice of the sister. "I shall practice it as soon as I leave you, Maither Brigid."

"Then I am correct in believing you have not recited the Psalm enough, not listened for God's direction through the words, child?"

"I have not, Maither. Forgive me."

"Of course. One hundred times after you break fast and one hundred times after vespers, then."

"It shall be done."

A clatter of footsteps on the church's stone floor sent Aine darting to the shadows just as the door creaked open. She scurried through the grasses surrounding the graves and rushed back to the guesthouse before her absence could be detected.

As she lay under a linen sheet watching the moon sail past an open window, Aine remembered how the fire keeper had addressed the abbess. A twitter ran up her neck. The pagans called Brigid the Exalted One, and she had visibly recoiled at the term. But she did have powers, a gift from the gods few others possessed. Aine wanted to be like her. With the book, she thought she could be. *Come soon, Daithi, so I can be on my way.*

At morning prayers, Aine noticed that the abbess blended in with the others. Gone was the fine white clothing, and in its place Brigid wore a plain brown tunic and a cloak the color of dampened soil. Everyone here still knew she was the abbess, of course, and afforded her the respect her authority deserved. They listened without interrupting when she spoke. They bowed their heads when she passed by, just as before. But any visitor to Cill Dara would not be able to immediately identify the abbess dressed as she now was. As Aine watched the woman move about, she wondered if Brigid might have been so offended by the honor the pagan women paid her that now she sought the ways of the ordinary? Either way, her powers could not be hidden.

Some of the others also gawked, but no one commented. Aine could not imagine why Brigid was trying to appear less "exalted."

five

"face the sun, but turn your back on the storm."

Irish proverb

I t was nearly nightfall when Ninnidh reached Cillian's settlement. He had just dismounted when the balding man bolted from his shelter.

"I've received word of your coming, Poet."

"From whom?"

"That blue-eyed sister from Cill Dara. She's gone now, but not only did she tell me you were coming for fresh manuscripts, she told me Brigid was on her way to the Brehon."

Ninnidh scratched his head. "I don't understand."

"Back on your horse, man. No time to waste. Meet me at the barn." He nodded toward a crumbling stone shed opposite the shelter and then scrambled that direction.

Ninnidh remounted and turned his horse around. Once Cillian was perched atop a spotted mare, they rode out, ducking under brambles until they met a path.

The monk slowed when the trail widened, allowing Ninnidh to pull up beside him. "Not far now. This way will lead us there."

"Brigid needs assistance?"

"Fianna said had it to do with Aine. That lass, always causing trouble, don't ye know. I trusted she was settled in with the Uí Naír, but I suppose she caused a ruckus among them."

"Aine?"

"My niece. She showed up at Cill Dara recently."

"I…uh…still don't know why we're needed. Is Brigid in trouble?"

"Doubtful." He pulled ahead.

Ninnidh shouted at his back. "If she was in need, she knew she could count on me. Why didn't she ask? I might have been able to help without summoning the Brehon."

"It came up all sudden-like, friend. If you do not want to come with me, please yourself. Turn around to find the road out."

"I'll come."

Ninnidh was confused, and not only by the fact that Brigid had gone to the Brehon instead of consulting him. How had the abbess gotten word to Cillian in advance of Ninnidh's arrival? How was that possible? He shook his head. No matter. If Brigid needed his help, he was happy to provide it.

A hound announced their arrival outside a wee cottage. They remained mounted as the door creaked open. A man stepped out, his neatly combed and parted beard flowing in the wind like castle flags. "You are welcome here, weary travelers."

Cillian spoke up. "We have come to aid Maither Brigid. Is she with you?"

The man moved away from the cottage entrance and Brigid stepped outside. She raised her hands in welcome. "What a surprise. I do not need assistance, but 'tis wonderful you've come."

They dismounted and allowed the man to take their horses to his barn. Stepping inside the house, Ninnidh inhaled the aromas of roasted meat and hot buttered bread.

A woman wearing an apron welcomed them. "You may wash at the bin outside the door, but then please join us." Two pairs of emerald green eyes gazed at them from straw mats near the fire—children.

"You are very kind," Ninnidh said. When he was prepared, he entered and invited the children to examine his harp.

When the woman's husband joined them, Cillian wasted no time. "Are you the Brehon?"

"'Tis me himself."

The Brehon waited until his wife placed a jar of hot tea into each of their hands. "I had not yet had the opportunity to learn what business this woman has for her visit, so I will ask her now." He turned to her. "What brings you to the house of the Brehon?"

"A woman has come to Cill Dara seeking help."

The man's lined faced erupted into a sunny smile. "Forgive me, Maither Brigid. I did not recognize you."

"There is nothing to forgive, but I am surprised you know my name."

"Everyone in the kingdom of Leinster has heard of your great deeds, Maither. Whatever you need from me, it shall be done."

Amused, Ninnidh tipped his head toward Cillian. Brigid hadn't needed their presence after all.

The man's wife placed a wooden platter in the center of the table board. Roasted pig, plenty of brown bread smothered in butter, and a portion of cheese as big as his fist. He was famished.

Cillian gave thanks for the food.

Brigid nodded at the children. "I wish them to eat first. Bring them here. We will have what is left."

Abbess or no, this woman had not changed since Ninnidh had last known her.

"As you wish." The man waved to his wife, and she brought the children, a boy and a girl, to the table. The wee lass snuggled onto Brigid's lap and the other child sat shyly by.

Soon, they were all feasting as though they were at a king's table. The wife filled more platters, and they sat laughing and eating and telling stories of old.

The hour grew late. Brigid had not spoken of the urgent business at Cill Dara. Ninnidh didn't mind, but he wondered how Brigid could spare the time for such leisure after she had essentially shooed him away, saying she was much too busy for gaiety.

The Brehon's wife took the children to bed while her husband invited the guests to recline in chairs near the hearth. His expression turned stony as he addressed the abbess. "Now then, what kind of trouble is your visitor about?"

She motioned to Ninnidh and Cillian. "My friends are concerned about me traveling alone, and that's why they've come. But the problem doesn't involve them."

The abbess's dismissal stung. She was independent indeed, but didn't everyone need help at times? She had brushed him aside so much that he probably should have given up long ago. Cillian was there, of course, out of concern for his niece, but Brigid had made it clear she didn't need him either.

"You understand this is a private matter?" she asked.

Ninnidh and the monk moved to the table board.

Brigid spoke in a low voice as the man tilted his stool to lean against one wall of the house. He stroked his long beard as she continued. When she finished, he took a prolonged swig from his mug of mead. At long last, he spoke, loud enough for them all to hear. "If the lass is truthful and she came with bruises to prove so, there will be no debate."

Ninnidh had only seen Aine briefly, but he'd noticed no bruises. In fact, she had a youthful, healthy glow. He glanced at Cillian, whose eyes were as wide as soup caldrons. Evidently, he didn't believe the story either.

Brigid sat up straight. "And if there is no physical evidence? What then?"

The Brehon pointed a finger at her. "Then, it can be done, but there must be much investigation, Maither Brigid. We will not punish an innocent man."

Brigid cupped her palms over her knees and tapped her fingers. "But a guilty man could go unpunished."

"Perhaps. But consider this: the law requires that a false accusation be punished in the same manner. Did she leave her clan without permission? If so, she's an *elúdach*, a fugitive without rights. If a case is brought to us, and the woman is considered an *elúdach*, we have no choice but to return her and order a fine."

Brigid pressed her hands together in her lap. "And if she cannot pay, she'll become a slave."

"That's the truth of it."

Cillian could stay silent no longer. "Absurd! And if, after consideration, she does not bring a case before you? What then?"

The Brehon brought all the legs of his stool to the ground and swiveled to face the monk. "Ah, well. I will suppose all parties will have worked it out. We don't get involved unless we are summoned. Are you confident this woman is telling the truth, Maither Brigid?"

Brigid clicked her tongue. "Certainly. Why else would someone come to Cill Dara in the dark and seek sanctuary? People only do that to escape harm."

The Brehon blinked. "Do they, then?"

Cillian appeared to want to say something. His cheeks puffed as he restrained himself.

Brigid rose. "I thank you for your hospitality." She turned to his wife. "I thank you, dear woman."

Ninnidh and Cillian expressed gratitude as well and followed Brigid out into the night air.

Cillian took the abbess's arm. "What a surprise. Even after your messenger fetched me, I didn't believe you had actually left Cill Dara until I saw you for myself."

"What messenger? I didn't send anyone." She turned to Ninnidh. "Did you send Cillian after me?"

"I didn't know myself that you were coming here," Ninnidh said. "He told me he'd been summoned and bade me to join him."

Brigid put a hand on the large monk's shoulder. "Did you see this messenger?"

"I did not. Philib informed me. It sounded quite urgent, so I did not waste time asking him questions. Seemed there was trouble about, and when Ninnidh came to my door, I asked him to come with me."

Brigid wagged her head. "I apologize for the inconvenience. I have meddling sisters at Cill Dara, I'm afraid."

"They care about their abbess." Ninnidh's suggestion did not seem to lessen Brigid's annoyance.

They found their horses and set out on the road.

"There is much to talk about," Cillian declared as he took the lead. "'Tis late for sure. I shall put you both up for the night."

With Brigid gone, Aine would need to tend the midnight fire. The women had settled into a routine that required the abbess to watch the fire every twentieth time. The sisters would not openly allow the visitors to do it. Aine was sure that this was because they thought demons lurked near the fire late at night. Of course, she knew otherwise. Brigid had not feared such a thing, and neither would she. What no one knew was that the book was near, protecting them all.

Aine shuddered in the frigid air as she approached the fire. The keeper was happy to take her leave, and Aine was glad she didn't stay to chat. She needed time to think. There was much to arrange. As she threw branches on the fire, she thought about Daithi. Her first inclination was to run before he found her, but she had to resist. If he understood that she was at Cill Dara and therefore beyond his reach, she could then sneak out and deliver the book to her clan without him following her. She would wait on him to arrive.

Aine began to dance around the fire, the imaginary tunes of flutes and horns echoing in her mind. The gods would be pleased with her. All was well. She floated on the wind, and magically, her garments became as wisps of smoke and flurries of fragrant flowers—offerings to the gods. The images did not seem to be just in her mind. They felt genuine. The power of the book was hers. She couldn't keep it to herself for long, but for now, this night, she embraced the mystical dance with her entire being.

A rumbling in the bushes made her pause, the lovely magic ending abruptly. "Listen, you nosy badger," she cried out. "Stop watching me or I'll…"

"You'll what?" A small figure approached her. All Aine could see of the person were eyes blazing with hate deep within a thick cloak that hid the rest entirely.

"What do you want?"

"To rid this monastery of evil people like you!"

"Who are you? What right do you have to say such a thing?"

The woman lowered her hood. "I am Fianna, sister of Cill Dara. Maither Brigid will learn about what you are doing here. I knew I was right. She should have listened to me."

Aine dropped her hands to her side, stunned. "Why are you following me? I'm a guest at Cill Dara. Brigid will not be pleased to hear how you've spoken to me."

The woman laughed and pulled her hood back over her head. She turned to leave and then paused, turning back. "She'll not be pleased to hear about your pagan worship, young one. She'll kick you out."

"Fianna!" a voice called from just beyond the bushes. "What are you doing out here?" Etain joined them, clicking her tongue.

"Did you see this?" Fianna said, pointing at Aine.

"What I saw or didn't see does not excuse your actions. Didn't the abbess tell you to stop your nighttime wandering, child?"

The smaller sister's face grew pale even in the light of the fire. "She did not say that exactly, sister."

"Did she not give you penance?"

"She did."

"'Twas not for nothing, then, was it? Hurry inside now."

Fianna rushed off, leaving Aine alone with the woman who was in charge when Brigid was away. "Whatever you think you're doing out here," Etain said, hands on hips, "you will not involve the sisters. You hear me?"

Aine nodded, and seemingly satisfied, the woman left. Hopefully, Etain would not ask Aine to leave, at least not before Daithi visited and went away. She thought about what Etain said. Aine surely did not wish to involve the sisters in anything she was doing. What an odd thing to say.

She was dozing much later when her relief came. The next fire tender, silver jewelry dripping from her hair and neck, dismissed Aine cheerfully. "The gods are smiling on you," she said as Aine walked away.

Aine wasn't sure they were. She would have to act soon. Without Brigid to protect her, the sisters at Cill Dara were likely to turn her out to the wolves. She shuddered again, feeling the lack of warmth from the fire as she returned to the guesthouse.

The next day, he came, yelling at the top of his lungs from somewhere near the monastery gate. Aine made herself as invisible as she could within the deepest branches of the oak.

"Aine, are you there? I love you, darlin'. Come home."

It mattered little what he said. The way he was hollering told everyone he was trying to control her. They would send him away, certainly.

He continued to shout. Aine didn't feel safe in her hiding place. She left the oak to join the crowd forming near one of the high crosses, blending in adequately in a cloak the sisters had lent her. Some of the faithful made the sign of the cross across their chests and bowed their heads, some wrung their hands, and many wished aloud that their abbess was in residence to deal with the obnoxious man still standing on the opposite side of the gate.

A bevy of men shuffled in mass toward the stranger. One of the brothers from the front of the crowd, a priest distinguishable only by the crosier he carried, stood on an upturned milk bucket and raised his trembling hands into the air. He was old and decrepit and had to be steadied by the others. He was no match for Daithi, although Daithi would never hurt him. He had no reason to because it was Aine he was after and her alone.

"What is it you want, young man?" The elderly man's words creaked like an old wagon wheel.

"My promised one. Is she here?"

"Who our guests are is not a matter for discussion. What can we do for *you*?"

"You can send her out."

"If you are in need of a meal or a prayer, we will accommodate you without hesitation. But we will not turn over anyone who has come here seeking sanctuary."

Oh, may the gods forbid it! What was the old senile man saying? Let Daithi in here for a meal? Did they not understand he would still search for her? Aine felt a hand on her shoulder.

Brocca's voice whispered in her ear. "You must come to my cell at once." She turned and looked into the woman's clear, unseeing eyes. How had she found Aine in this crowd?

Gladly, Aine took Brocca's hand and allowed her to lead the way toward a cluster of cells. Beside the larger one belonging to Brigid was a cell nearly identical to it. They ducked inside, and Brocca closed the oak door. Aine plopped down on a sheepskin and put her fists to her cheeks. Maybe she should get the book and run. Aine lifted her head to look at the woman.

Brocca was dipping a clay pot into a reservoir of water. "A nice spot of tea will calm your nerves, child. Do not worry. The brothers will feed him and send him on his way. He won't hurt you. You are safe."

"Thank you."

She watched the woman work. Having memorized the location of all her belongings in the cell, she moved deftly about. She crumbled dried herbs into a pot over the fire. "In the name of the Father," Brocca said as she dropped one pinch into the pot. She gathered a bit more from a sack and sprinkled that in. "And the name of the Son." One last pinch. "And the name of the Holy Spirit."

Brocca was obviously asking the gods to help Aine. The book had power, but it was a distance from where she now found herself, and with the abbess away, she appreciated the beseeching Brocca was doing on her behalf. She would eagerly drink of this potion and hope that Daithi would be told she was there but not succeed in finding her. He would have to honor the sanctuary she had found at Cill Dara. Soon, she could be on her way.

She sighed, a little too loudly because Brocca turned to her.

"The waiting is the difficult part. Patience, child."

Indeed.

Aine sipped her tea in weary silence. Her nighttime fire watch had pilfered her sleep. Brocca invited her to rest. She would lie down only a moment.

Aine awoke in darkness to hear Brocca whispering toward the open door, cold breezes streaming in. "I don't care if she is a pagan, and neither would Brigid. Send the man on his way. You should never have engaged him on this matter."

She couldn't hear the other end of the conversation, but through Brocca's words, Aine discerned that Daithi must soon leave, escorted out by Etain and some of the men. Drifting back to Brocca's sleeping board, Aine released a breath as quietly as she could and plotted her next move in her mind. How could she find her way to her people in the mountains?

She rolled to one side as Brocca climbed in next to her. She must think. Where in the mountains? There was a road through the flatlands, she knew. The trail led a bit southward and then east to the mountains. She'd seen a map of it in the scriptorium back in Daithi's village when the caretaker hadn't known she was snooping. She tried to recreate it in her mind. If she went the wrong way, she would end up in the bog lands and would have to turn back—if she could even get out without falling in. If she went astray, could she find her way back, especially in a rush? Why had she not stolen the map as well?

Curses! There was no choice but to speak to Cillian and pray that he would not turn her in to her betrothed.

Early the next morning, after Brocca assured her Daithi had been turned away and the watchman had witnessed his going, Aine headed toward the workhouse near the weavers where she always began her day mending. Thankfully, she had been allowed to skip the prayers in the middle of the night and again at daylight because of the trauma of Daithi's visit. Brocca had been sweet and accommodating. And now it was time for Aine to slip away for good, not an easy undertaking with all the women scurrying about the looms.

She could not just walk out. They would know she had not been truthful and tell Brigid. She needed Brigid's good energy. The book must be her secret. Etain or some other hostile resident might steal the book from her. Worse yet, they might tell Daithi. If they believed she feared for her life, they would be more likely not to tell him she'd left. Walking out in clear view of everyone would say otherwise.

She had to pass the smiths on the way. One standing near a fire called out to her, rubbing his hands on his smudged apron, black soot dotting his cheeks. "Lassie, would you be heading to the kitchen?"

"I was…" She paused. If she were to run an errand, her departure would be easier to accomplish. "I am happy to help." She took a leather *pait* from his hand. "Water or ale?"

He winked at her, a kindly gesture. "I'm feeling a bit like an old horse today. And I've so much work to do. I thank ye for some spring water to get me through the hours."

"Quite wise, so." She skipped off, swinging the vessel from a rope over her arm. She left the *pait* at Etain's feet when she got to the kitchen well. "The smith is feeling puny this morn. I must hurry back to my work. Is there someone else who can take him some water?"

"Ill, is he?" The woman's face paled. Aine had forgotten the smith was Etain's brother. "I will take it to him, child. Thank you for telling me."

When Aine departed, she turned left instead of right, unnoticed by the kitchen maids who busied themselves pitying the poor smith who had to labor long over the hot furnace. He would get his water quickly. Once she was behind the kitchen, she rushed toward the path to the sacred fire. With no one working on that side of the abbey, she would not be seen. Scrambling to the spot where she'd hidden the book, Aine dropped to her knees and dug at the earth with her hands. Once she had cleared away most of the forest debris, she searched for a stone to use to dig further, bemoaning the fact that she had pounded down the dirt so completely with her feet. Finally, the leather cover peeked through. She dug faster. A mouse scampered past her, but she did not stop despite its insistent chatter. At last, the book came free. She tugged at her belt until it loosened enough for her to tuck it in. Once she had everything adjusted and the book secured, Aine shook loose the dirt clinging to her skirt and made for Cillian's scriptorium.

Morning light filtered through the east window, alerting Ninnidh to the fact that he'd slept through prayers. Even when he was at his father's school he had difficulty getting used to the routine. His inclination was to follow nature's rhythm. Pray whenever he saw evidence of Jesu, which was nearly every waking moment. He was alerted to the work of the Creator when the birds welcomed the dawn. He acknowledged his mortal state when his stomach told him he needed to eat, and was humbled by how dearly he relied on his Lord. He felt the Almighty's power whenever he heard the gurgle of a pulsing water stream or the crash of the ocean tides. Such observations, he knew, had been devised by an all-powerful God, piled up and overflowing. Yet each thought worked upon one another to build up a lifetime of moments. These moments told Ninnidh it was time to pray. He needed no tolling bells or sundials to remind him.

Ninnidh groaned and rubbed his eyes. Cillian had been on the cot next to him, but he'd already risen and departed. Splashing water on his face, Ninnidh decided to stop by the women's guesthouse, even though Brigid was not likely to be there. The discipline of the religious order answered the call to spiritual contemplation whether they felt like it or not. Ninnidh could never be a monk. He liked to take his time and discover whatever may come his way, not plod along behind others and do as they did. Brigid, though she'd taken a vow in the tradition of Patrick, was unlike anyone he had ever met. He knew her spirit allowed for a bit of adventure.

That was why he'd invited her to travel with him. Perhaps one day she would accept his overture. His thoughts of her prompted him to call at the guesthouse, just in case she hadn't joined the others in the abbey.

As he tied on his shoes, he wondered if there had actually been a call to prayer. He had not heard one. Cillian's monastery seemed less orthodox than others he'd visited. He'd heard that these monks lived in fear of the druid named Ardan. Ninnidh knew better than most that the man was evil, having witnessed his acts several years ago. Thankfully, the Christians' tormentor was now long gone, kidnapped by marauders right after his foolhardy plan to kidnap Brigid's mother and force Brigid to follow his ways had failed. Ninnidh had never learned the identity of those who had taken Ardan, but rumor had it, the druid landed on a whaling ship headed north to the island where the Picts lived.

Ninnidh shuddered at the thought. Picts were savages, and he'd heard more tales about their brutality than he cared to remember. Thankfully, a wee band of Christian men had begun Jesu's work in that country, a light to the dark isle. There was no reason for Cillian's monastery to continue to fear a druid who was so far away. There must be another reason for lack of tolling bells.

As he approached the other wee guesthouse, he noticed a woman seated near a well. She had probably come to trade for the monks' wool or honey, as folks often did at monasteries. He started to turn away and then stopped. These monks were so secretive that they were not likely to be trading with anyone, at least not so close to their dwellings. He turned back to the woman. There was something familiar about her.

The lass lifted her head. *Aine!*

Six

"The eyes of the LORD are everywhere,
keeping watch on the wicked and the
good."

Proverbs 15:3 NIV

Ninnidh approached Aine. "You came from Cill Dara?"

"Oh, I…uh, you see, I needed to speak to the abbesses." She tilted her head to one side. "Have we met?"

"I knew you as a wee lass."

"You are Brigid's poet friend, aren't you?"

"I am. She is here, the one you seek."

The girl sighed. "Would you take me to her?"

"You could have waited for her to return. She is not staying here long."

"I…uh. Please forgive me. I cannot explain. She is the only one who will help me."

Ninnidh brought the girl to the church in time to find Brigid about to depart. "A foolish thing to do, Aine," she scolded, "coming here without escort."

When the initial annoyance wore off, Ninnidh, Brigid, and Aine sat under a hazel tree, an ancient symbol of wisdom that Ninnidh hoped would inspire them. Just what do you do when someone you are trying to help makes it so difficult?

"What's this?" Cillian approached, worry wrinkled on his brow.

"I've decided to return to Daithi." Aine's stare never left the ground.

"Good lass," the monk said, nodding.

Brigid patted the girl's hand. "And why, child? Were you not seeking sanctuary at Cill Dara?"

"I was, but I've changed my mind."

Brigid let out a long, slow breath. "As you wish, Aine, but first you will tell me something."

Aine's eyes widened as she lifted them to look at the abbess. "What is it, Maither Brigid?"

"Tell me what is hidden under your belt. I noticed it when you first came."

"What?" Cillian's face reddened.

Brigid held up a hand, and the monk restrained himself.

There did indeed seem to be something rigid and rectangular shaped under the lass's clothing. He had not noticed it before. He reached for his harp and strummed in the uncomfortable silence that followed Brigid's question.

At long last, Aine pulled away from Brigid and tapped the lump at her waist. "'Tis my own property and nothing for you to worry about, Maither Brigid. I did not steal from you, if that's what you think."

Brigid reached for the lass, but Aine scooted away.

"I do not accuse you. I know you had whatever 'tis when you first arrived. But perhaps this object is a matter of contention. I must ask for the safety of my house. I do not wish to be unprepared should an angry party arrive at my gate."

"I told you I was going back." Aine glanced at her uncle, but Cillian did not speak.

Aine lowered her voice. "'Tis a book with magical powers, Maither. I only mean it for good."

"Is it, now? Whose book? Did you take it from Cillian?"

Cillian glared at her, as if he himself didn't know if he was missing anything.

"I did not." She turned to her uncle. "I have never stolen from you, ever."

Brigid tugged on her arm. "Whose then?"

"Daithi's clan, the Uí Náir."

"And you are now returning it?"

Aine's face wrinkled in an attempt, Ninnidh believed, to hide the truth. "I will return it. I need directions from Cillian. That is why I've come."

Brigid shook her head. "Child, we at Cill Dara would have taken you there. You should have asked."

Aine straightened her shoulders. "There is no need to trouble you. My uncle will give me a map. Won't you, Uncle?"

Cillian grunted. "Did you not come to Cill Dara from the Uí Náir? Do you not remember the way?"

"I…uh…I did. But it was dark, and strangers on the road directed me. It took some time…"

Brigid held out her hand. "Give it to me. I want to see it."

Aine pulled the object out from underneath her mantle, a wee leather-bound book. She handed it to Brigid.

Brigid examined it while Ninnidh gazed over her shoulder. *Lebor na Uí Náir* was written inside—Book of the Uí Náir. And just below it, in a script obviously written by a different hand, *Leathanaigh hÉireann*. Pages of Ireland. There were lots of stories pertaining to the Irish people, many tales from their heritage. He knew them all. The Uí Náir claimed this book, that much was certain. Brigid was right to be concerned. Wars had been fought over stolen manuscripts. He wanted to get a closer look but decided to allow the abbess time to handle matters with the lass who had come to her for help.

Brigid tapped her fingers on the front page. "Obviously you have come here to seek your uncle's counsel. The Poet and I will leave you two alone." She placed the book down gently on the forest carpet.

Ninnidh and Brigid moved toward a stand of oak trees. The abbess stooped and collected acorns from the forest floor, cradling them in her cupped hands as Ninnidh admired her patience. "Do you think she'll go back, then?"

Brigid let out a breath. "She had better. She left without permission. You heard the Brehon."

He could not pretend he hadn't. "Do you think she had good reason to leave?"

"I am not sure."

Ninnidh began to help in the collecting. Rubbing a wee nut's rough cap between his fingers, he began to think of all the poems he'd recited having to do with the growth of a tree. How patient the Creator is. "Cillian seems to think his

68

niece is capable of causing some trouble. He supposes she is in a bit of a mess herself. That's why he rushed to find you at the Brehon's cottage." The acorn cap popped off in his palm, causing him to consider how the cap's usefulness diminished after the nut fell from the tree. Tossing the piece to the side, he studied Brigid's face as waited for her response.

"I don't know if she will cause trouble for us. I only know she is distressed. It will be up to her to ask for help."

Aine had what she wanted, an audience with her uncle. But she hadn't expected to feel so trapped. She didn't think they had all followed her. She'd been careful. Perhaps they had come to copy manuscripts in Cillian's library. Religious communities did that all the time. It was just a stroke of bad luck that they'd all arrived at the same time. And then consorted against her. She placed her hand on top of the book. She had possession. It belonged to her.

"Tell me, lass, what caused you to leave Daithi's protection?"

Aine could think of no answer he would accept.

"Has he hurt you?" Cillian reached for the dirk kept at his ankle.

"Always rash, you are. Leave it be."

Cillian shrugged. "'Tis prudent to be prepared."

"I know why you carry that, and it's not because you think Daithi will come looking for you."

"You don't know." He stood. "Come, let us walk."

She rose and hurried to match his pace. "Oh, I do. You are afraid that druid will come back. Here you are, hiding still all these seasons, and he's no threat to you anymore. Don't you know he was taken away? All of Ireland sings that tale. Do as you wish, Uncle, and I will as well."

"'Tis my duty—"

"Duty, is it?" Her voice escalated against her will. She supposed he hadn't wanted to take her in as a child, but she'd hoped never to hear him say it.

He huffed. "I only want the best for you, lass. It is not Ardan we fear at Aghade. Sure, he's been taken away. Don't be forgetting there are others who wish to harm, steal, and destroy. We must always be prepared. You'd be well advised to remember that." He paused to remove the weapon from its sheath. "Do you fear Daithi, Aine?"

She took his free hand and caught his gaze. "I am not wary for myself. Look. Not a mark on me. And you know I have never feared anyone. You always said so."

"'Twas not a compliment. Foolishness is the downfall of youth, lass." He drew back from her as he stowed his weapon.

"'Tis the book he'll harm." She'd said it. The truth.

Cillian drew his shoulders forward in surprise. "Why would he harm the tribe's precious book?"

She had gotten his attention. Cillian loved books. "I don't know, Uncle. He's mad, I suppose."

"Daithi? Certainly not. He's the finest man in the tribe, and you, a monk's orphaned niece, should be happy he accepted you."

"As you say." This had been a mistake. She only needed information. She had hoped that, by lying about where she was going, they would send her off with a map or at least allow a look at what the scriptorium held. Clearly, she had not puzzled this out far enough. If Cillian's scriptorium had not been locked up so tightly, she would have taken a map without him ever knowing she'd been there. "Uncle, if I return on my own, with no escort, the tribe will believe I'm contrite. I do not wish to be accompanied as though I'm a criminal. Allow me the dignity to depart on my own, straightaway."

He motioned to her to keep walking. "Where are we going?"

"What you say makes some sense. Philib will direct you."

That had not been difficult at all. "But before I go, would you please tell me about some things I've pondered since I was a young girl? I don't know when I will see you again, me a married woman within such a large clan. Surely you understand that my status will require me to turn away from what little family I have left." Even though he'd been a strict guardian, he would understand this request. He would want to give her this parting gift of knowledge, the story of their ancestors. And, if she was sly enough, also their location.

Cillian glanced back toward the place they'd left Brigid and the Poet. "Aine, have I not told you seventy times seven that you are better off forgetting your birth family?" He kicked a stone off the path. "Most young people, when they are fostered out, are content to belong to a new family."

She'd guessed wrong. "But mine was not a fosterage. My mother, you always told me, loved me. She didn't want to give me up. She had to. I want to know more about her, about *your* people, Cillian. Once my curiosity is satisfied, you have my word that I will never ask you about it again."

He mumbled under his breath. "The good Lord knew it was not in my nature to be a father. I am not even called abbot. May he have mercy on me for all my failures." He quickened his steps as they passed the monks' dwellings. "I'll tell you whatever you wish to know. Let us hasten and find Philib at the scriptorium before he scurries off to other chores."

Questions surged forward, but she bit them back. How should she ask where her mother had lived without letting him know that was where she wanted to go? She'd need to be careful. "Uh, was my mother's name Maire?"

"It was. You didn't know?"

"I was not sure I remembered. I am right that she wanted me?"

"Of course she did. She had to get you away from your father. I thought you understood that."

"I do. Thank you. 'Tis just that things look different to adults than they do to children." She would lead him slowly to what she needed to know.

"Indeed they do." He patted the precious book that was now tied to his waist. Earlier he had described it as the clan's genealogy. He'd licked a finger and shuffled through a few pages, squinting as he examined the writing. He spoke now as he kept a hand on the book. "Besides the clan's story, it bears a tale or two, the lineage of priests, the granting of land for a monastery, Gospels in Latin at the back. 'Tis quite nice, but tell me, Aine, why would you want such a manuscript? Why take this?"

She knew all she needed to know about its pages. She'd read them, but the words did not matter. The power it held was most important. Why the book did not glow when Cillian or Brigid touched it was baffling. She rubbed her neck. For some reason, they lacked the insight to understand its power. Nonetheless, the codex brought prosperity to its owner, she knew. Perhaps the magic she had witnessed before had been meant only for her, because the book wanted her to courier it. It wished to be free of the Uí Náir and to have the name expunged from its pages.

May the gods deem hers more worthy.

"I have wondered about my own genealogy, Uncle."

"I've told you about your people. What else do you want to know?" Before she could answer, he tapped a thick finger to his bare forehead. "Wait a moment. You don't need the book, but Daithi's clan does. Is that not why you absconded with it? Because your betrothed's clan values it?" He raised an eyebrow, as thoughts seemed to align in his head. "The book gives you power, an object with which to bargain. What is it you want from them, child?" Cillian's brows rose to the crinkles in his forehead.

He did not comprehend that the book brought so much more than bartering wealth. He might with time, however, if the community realized the prosperity it could bring and tried to take it.

A shiver pulsed up her spine. Cillian might even enjoy the power of the book and refuse to give it up. He never trusted her. She had to make haste.

He lifted her chin with a cupped hand. "I asked you a question, child. Why?"

She wiggled free. Tears came as the old familiar feeling of standing on the edge of an ocean cliff came back to her. Alone. With no safety net.

Her uncle softened his tone as they entered the building. "I cannot tell you how to make yourself as valuable to them as this book probably is."

She could barely look at him and instead studied the walls lined with satchels that were stuffed with parchments. "You love all your stored manuscripts more than anything else, don't you, Uncle? Of course you'd think these pages mean more to them than I do. They mean more to you, after all."

"Nonsense. It is clear you are no scholar, child." He guided her to a bench along one wall where they sat side by side. "Listen to me. What is valuable is the knowledge books deliver, not the physical pages themselves. That is why the brothers memorize all the scripture they can—to take that knowledge and wisdom with them and not leave it here in the scriptorium. It begins with the books, quite right. Without the written word we'd be left to our own faulty and inadequate understanding of life, but the books themselves have no worth beyond that."

He didn't understand the worth of this particular book. With his head in his studies here in the deep woods, Cillian could not possibly know the challenges she faced.

He put a hand on her shoulder. "I can't say what the tribe values above all else, but I believed Daithi to be a good man. What I should have said is that perhaps the man you are to marry saw that you treasured this leather-bound script more than him." He laid it on a desk. "Indeed, people are more precious than books, Aine."

"I know that. But as you said, without this book's pages, people lack something."

"If the Lord's words are contained within, that's true."

"So I am right to want this book, to make sure no harm comes to it."

"Within reason. I am sure the clan would protect it."

"I told you they wanted to destroy it."

"Ah, I see. They contrived an illustration to teach you, Aine."

"No, they would really do it." He was making her angry, just as he had done when she was a child. He never listened to her.

He clucked his tongue. "A man wants to believe his woman adores him, but if you begin to appreciate objects more than a husband? Well, think on that now. I will put this book to bed here, Aine."

"No! Wait."

"It will be safe, I assure you. 'Tis a wee bit grimy. The brothers will tidy it up tomorrow."

"I want—"

He rose, nearly hitting his head on a shelf. She swallowed her amusement. The book's revenge.

He marched away quickly. "Come along. Philib is not here."

A map! She had wanted to ask for a map. She glanced around but had no idea where to look. Cillian either did not realize she had more to say or didn't care. A predictable response from a man whose sole ambition in life was to stay hidden. She didn't need him. The book would lead her. She would get it back and trust its power.

Later that night as her companions slept, Aine calculated the time between the moon's rising and the call to prayer in order to know when best to slip away unnoticed. At the darkest hour, she rose, gathered her cloak, and crept out of the guesthouse. A stiff wind blew from the direction of the river. Cloud cover concealed the stars. She must depart now, even without a map from her uncle.

Cillian had left the book with his other treasured manuscripts. Just for safekeeping, he'd said, as though she hadn't kept it safe thus far.

Now that Cillian had returned to Aghade, the lock had not been put back on the scriptorium's door. Scrambling to the side to gaze in the window, she determined that Philib was not inside working. Exhaling her relief, she rushed back to the front. She found the scriptorium door just as heavy as ever. Once, when she was a child, she had imagined that the door would be easier to open once she grew up. But she hadn't grown much. She hadn't achieved her father's size or even Cillian's. She remembered her mother as a diminutive woman with thin arms, and it seemed that Aine took after her.

She lifted the latch, and with all her might, shoved the door with her hip until it cracked open just enough to allow her to enter. With the door ajar, she hoped that the night sky would lend enough light to help her find the book, but fortune did not smile on her this night. A cloak of darkness covered the scriptorium. No torches burned as they did at night at Cill Dara. She shouldn't have been surprised. The monks extinguished every candle and fire, shunning anything that might cast them into daylight and lead pilgrims to their door. She stretched both arms out in front of her, stepping from one transcription table to another until she came to the front where Cillian's desk was.

Pushing aside some loose velum pages scattered across the desk like fallen leaves—the man always had been a bit muddled—her hands finally reached the small book she came for. Her uncle was careless to leave it there. He probably had not imagined she would leave her warm bed to retrieve it. Or, more likely, the book had made itself known to Aine, no matter how Cillian might have tried to conceal it. Tucking it inside her belt, she turned back to the door. A dark figure shadowed the entry. Aine's heart beat an unsteady rhythm as she ducked under the desk, hoping the person hadn't seen her. It was terribly dark, after all.

A tiny light glowed beside the figure—a flame inside a wee clay lantern pot. Before long, Brigid held it over Aine's head.

Seven

"Autumn days come quickly like the
running of
a hound on the moor."

Irish saying.

A ine was marched from the scriptorium and forced into
a late night meeting with her uncle and the woman
with the great powers. Laying in front of them on the
refectory table was the powerful charm that Daithi had
threatened to destroy if Aine did not stop revering it so.
"'Tis druid magic you believe in," he had said to her, holding
the book aloft in the library when he'd discovered her there
late one night. Now it seemed she was living the scene again,
but with different folks.

"You are afraid of a druid who can no longer desecrate our land," Brigid said to Cillian, taking up the argument Aine had started hours ago. The usually reserved woman seemed indignant. "And you have convinced this child to be fearful as well. When trepidation is allowed to fester, false beliefs take root. She thinks this book is some kind of talisman."

Aine opened her mouth to argue that it was, whether anyone else believed it or not, but Cillian spoke first. "You are talking about things you don't understand, Maither Brigid, just as you always have."

Brigid paused a moment, as though gathering strength. "Then explain it to me, Cillian. Why are you still fearful?"

He gritted his teeth, spit to the side, and then answered. "One druid alone is not the guardian of all evil, Brigid."

"Of course not, but things are peaceful. No one has taken up his cause in his absence."

"Can you be sure, now?"

The abbess turned her attention to Aine. "You must tell me the truth, child. Is the man you flee abusive? Has he harmed you in any way?"

Aine chose her words carefully. "He was about to cause harm. He was going to burn this book or plunge it into the bog."

Brigid eyes grew wide. As a lover of books, she had to find that alarming. "Tell me more, Aine. 'Tis obvious you left your clan without permission. Are there others in the clan like Daithi? Those who do not believe this book's supposed influence?"

"You mean do they think the book powerless? Certainly not. They know it brings health to the cattle and fertility to the fields. Daithi and my foster father were both willing to destroy it to gain my loyalty. They only want to control me,

Maither. I will not tolerate it. Just because I find wonder in that book does not mean they have to destroy it."

She'd heard that the king of Daithi's province would sacrifice his champion warrior for the book, although one could not always believe what folks said. Only if he'd seen the power of the book could that be true. Daithi had not seen it. No one had witnessed it at Cill Dara or Aghade. But Aine had, in Nessa's field, and then later, in the dark hours of the night when she was alone in the library. It glowed for her alone in Brigid's guesthouse. No one but Daithi was coming for the book, and he came only because she wanted it.

Cillian spoke up, snapping Aine from her thoughts. "'Tis not unusual, Brigid, for the people to believe in a talisman."

Brigid turned in his direction. "And if they believe in it, will they not go to war to get it back?"

Cillian sat up straight. "I'm afraid so. And therefore I must demand that Aine return it. We cannot have it here." He emphasized the word "here" as though his place, his monks, his possessions were all more important than anyone else's. Clearly he did not care where the book was, so long as it was not with him. And that was good fortune.

Brigid reached to touch Cillian's arm gently. "Aine has said she will return to Daithi, but I'm not sure she knows what's good for her." Aine nearly bolted out of her shoes, but the abbess kept talking. "Cillian, would you have the book returned and allow this misguided belief to continue?"

"What choice do we have, lass? I certainly will not put the faithful of Aghade at risk because of it. Can you harbor the book and at the same time protect the residents of Cill

Dara? You've a much more secure and populated community."

Brigid looked beyond him as if gathering her thoughts. "I don't know. You heard the Brehon. Aine has no other proof of harm. In fact, they will hold her liable for leaving the clan without cause and order her returned."

She didn't have proof, but could she wait around to see what Daithi might do? "I didn't mean it." Aine's words caused them both to turn toward her, mouths open. "I won't go back to Daithi. I just told you that to appease you, Maither Brigid. Please forgive me. I am telling you the truth now." Aine snatched the book off the table and clutched it to her chest. "I will take this book to my mother's clan. They need it. They need fertile cattle and bountiful fields."

Cillian put his arm around her. "Your mother's clan? Whatever gave you that idea, child?"

"You did!" She rocked back and forth as she clutched the leather binding to her chest. "You said they had nothing. They need help. Daithi doesn't want the good fortune this book can bring, so why not deliver it to the people who truly need it, who will treasure it for its great power? I must do this, Cillian, even if you don't tell me how to find them."

He squeezed her tight to her chest. "Oh, child. Don't you realize that the Uí Náir will hunt you down before you can get there?"

She had only been thinking of Daithi, not the lot of them. "I do not think the rest of them believe in what the book can do."

"Whether or not they do, child, it is their possession."

"But didn't you tell me the value of a book was not in its physical state?"

He sighed heavily. "I did, but that doesn't mean King Donal will see it that way."

Aine had come to a safe place. "Maither Brigid will protect me like she did before. She has the power to protect us all."

Brigid closed her eyes. "Only God can protect you, Aine. You came to Cill Dara for sanctuary, and if you return, you will have it. They cannot harm you there. However, justice must be served. You cannot decide these things yourself, steal away under the cover of darkness, and expect there will be no repercussions."

"But what about what you said before, Maither Brigid? You don't really think I'll be safe, do you?"

"You will be shielded at Cill Dara, Aine. I promise you that. You can depend on fair treatment. As for the book, we will put it safely into the hands of the church where its fate will be decided. If 'tis only a genealogy the king needs, perhaps he will accept a copy. Then there will be no destruction of the book."

Cillian huffed. "You believe the church will convince the king there is no worth in the codex as a talisman?"

"'Tis the truth."

"The island has not yet accepted the church as an authority, Brigid."

"God is our authority. I will ride up to Armagh. Cillian, will you see her safely back to Cill Dara?"

"I will do that. The sooner the better." He released Aine and locked his arms across his chest as if the matter had been settled.

No book? No Brigid? How would she ever be able to help her mother's people without something or someone to protect her and bring fortune? Still clutching the book, she glared at them both. "I wish to be heard."

Brigid held out her hand. "Of course, Aine. Go on."

"Perhaps I can postpone finding my mother's family. For now."

"That is wise," Cillian agreed. "Wait until this matter of a stolen book has been resolved. Then go, if you must."

Aine raised her palm in front of her. "I will go with Cillian back to Cill Dara, but the book comes with me. You do not have to have it to speak to the church about this matter, Maither Brigid. Ask if they think there's a need to intervene. If they do, let them come to Cill Dara to retrieve it. If the clan is as dangerous as you think, the book will be safer at Cill Dara than with you traveling about in the open with it."

Cillian laid both of his large arms on the table. "What she says makes sense, Brigid. 'Tis not the safety of the book that concerns me but yours. If you are out in the open with it, you'll be a target as sure as if you waved a flag over your head."

Brigid tilted her chin toward the rafters. "You change your mind too much to convince me of your sincerity." She began to drum her fingers on the table. Finally, she spoke again. "You two are impossible. You fear things that may not even occur. How can you live without the confidence that God will protect the righteous?"

Cillian motioned toward the abbess. "Now, Brigid. Don't be letting your impatience cloud your good sense. 'Tis a war-loving clan out there. They'd just as soon have your head than spit, righteous believer of God or not. Heathens, they are."

"Heathens?" Aine gave him a puzzled look. He'd sent her to that clan.

"Well, Daithi's a good man, to be sure. But that king? I do not trust him when it comes to things like this. He's a hard man when he believes he's been betrayed."

Aine wasn't sure what he meant, but at least he seemed to be on her side in this. She would go to Cill Dara with Cillian, but they could not make her stay there. She would never go back to Daithi. She would not become a wife, ever. She'd seen what that was like for her mother. Somehow, she'd have to convince Cillian to take her to her people sooner rather than later.

Brigid stood, marched to the opposite side of the table where Cillian and Aine sat, and leaned in close to Cillian, her long gleaming tresses spilling onto his shoulder. "You promise me that you will hand that book over to Etain just as soon as you arrive at Cill Dara."

"Indeed, I will."

"No matter what Aine says?"

"No matter."

"Your word is your sacred vow," she warned him.

"I have never lied to you before."

With the decision made, Aine excused herself to take a walk, reluctantly leaving the book. Cillian's tight shelters made her long to feel the breezes on her shoulders while she tried to determine her options. She nearly bumped into the Poet with his head drooping downward. His harp hung silently over his shoulder. No one had told him what the plan was. He was Brigid's closest friend. Aine couldn't guess why he'd been left out, but maybe he could assist Aine in getting what she wanted.

"Have you ever visited the people at the base of the mountain *Log na Coille*?" she asked him.

The man turned his focus to her. "I never have."

Her disappointment must have shown, because he placed a gentle hand on her shoulder. "Whatever the trouble is, running away won't solve it."

She nodded and moved on down the path.

Aine pretended to be asleep when Brigid came back from saying her prayers. Sounds of the abbess tucking her belongings into her leather traveling bag drifted to Aine's ears. The abbess said something over Aine's head and then left.

Throwing her covers off, she padded over to the window and cracked open the shutter. The torchlights Cillian kept burning all night near the path—for safety he'd said—gave off just enough illumination for Aine to see what was happening. Her uncle stood beside Brigid's horse. No sign of the Poet. Aine had thought he might go with Brigid, but the abbess, being a strong woman, had probably rejected him.

"All ready for you." Cillian handed the horse's lead to Brigid. "Watered, fed, and there's a bag of food tied up for you as well."

Brigid accepted his help as she mounted. "I thank you, Cillian." She paused. "I know I've spoken harshly—"

He raised his hand to interrupt her. "We have had our differences, Brigid, but God has called us both to do his work. The love of Christ binds us."

Those two trusted one god instead of many. Why anyone would not avail themselves of all the spiritual help they possibly could was something she would never understand.

Aine turned from the window, tossed her belongings into her bag, and began to dress. By the time she got outside, the Poet had joined Cillian, but Brigid was gone. He clasped arms with Cillian in a farewell gesture. "I thank you for your hospitality, friend."

They nodded to acknowledge her, but then continued their conversation.

Cillian nudged the man with his elbow. "I kidnapped you, didn't I? You are quite patient and a great friend to the abbess."

The Poet gazed down the path. "Who didn't even say goodbye."

Cillian wagged his large head. "Has a lot on her mind, that one. Will you join Aine and me on our trip back to Cill Dara?"

Aine noticed the bag the Poet clutched in his right hand. He was ready to go depart now.

"I plan to travel to Armagh. Am I right she plans to speak to the bishops there?"

"You are right."

"She might need my help. She has not been there in some time."

"Agreed." Cillian gave the Poet a good-natured slap. "Why were you coming to see me, man? We never discussed it."

"I had been seeking manuscripts to borrow, but I will come back. No time for transcription now anyway."

"I am happy to share whenever you're ready."

Aine kicked at the dirt, eager to begin the journey. She despised delays once a decision to depart had been made. Clutching her own bag, she looked up at the Poet as he spoke to her uncle and began to wonder if one so gentle and kind might somehow morph into a monster once he'd married. She'd seen it happen but now had trouble imagining the Poet behaving that way.

The man continued to talk about manuscripts. "I left the pages Brigid borrowed in your scriptorium this morning. A monk there told me he'd take charge of storing them."

"Aye. Thank you. You have been a good friend to Brigid and to her mother. Now you are my friend, too." Cillian gave the Poet a hug that would crush a bear.

Aine bid goodbye to the man and then told herself she should gather food for her journey. Instead, she continued to compare Daithi to the Poet. She leaned against the rough bark of a tree and pondered. Could he and the gentle Poet be in any way similar? Her very first glimpse of Daithi had come at the fair. He was sitting atop a horse just as the Poet was a moment ago. Daithi's coal black hair had trailed down his back, much like the Poet's. That day, she had wanted nothing more than to marry the handsome man, but she had let her attraction to him cloud her good sense. His touch sent a warm tingle down her back. Aine blinked her eyes, willing herself to resist such thoughts. She could have nothing to do with him, although she was certain he'd never understand. She had led him to believe differently. He thought she was fond of him. Perhaps she was. Whenever he came close, she longed to touch his face and lean against his neck, but she had to fight off her longings—for her own good. Perhaps it was the same for Brigid and her poet friend.

Cillian's voice slapped her back to the present. "She is hard-headed."

Aine stepped back from the tree, surprised to discover the Poet had not left. The two men continued their chat, thinking Aine had gone away. She slipped back among the leafy branches and listened, just on the other side of the horses where they could not see her.

"Aine? What do you mean?"

"Oh, she seems to be a quiet one, but ever since she reached the age of accountability—thirteen summers or so—she exerted her will at the exact moment everyone thought she was content. A riddle, to be sure. You think she's happy, and she appears to be. Then out of a thunder cloud she comes."

The horse stomped his hooves and the Poet whispered to soothe him. "How could you know, then, that she really was happy when you sent her to marry into that tribe? You are far away here in this cavernous wood."

Cillian grunted. "I would know because I traveled weekly to the clan to counsel and pray with Daithi. He is the only Christian left there, save for Aine's foster family, I suppose, and he asked me to come. I agreed because that way I could check up on Aine. Everything seemed agreeable to me. No cause for alarm."

Aine placed a palm to her cheek. She had never noticed her uncle's visits. Daithi had not mentioned their meetings. What did they think they were doing talking about her temperament without even addressing her, then and now?

The Poet's voice was easier to hear now that his horse had calmed. "Are you saying you did not know the faith of the family you placed her with?"

"I know as well as can be known, lad. Daithi shares what he believes with me. Not everyone is so inclined. But they are good people all the same. My sister entrusted her daughter to me. I would not betray that trust. I made sure she would be cared for."

Aine rushed back toward the guesthouse, despising her uncle and Daithi for manipulating her.

Eight

"Do not be far from me, for trouble is
near,
and there is no one to help."

Psalm 22:11 NIV

Ninnidh caught up with Brigid at a stream. She had
plunged her feet into the cool, rushing water. "Not
used to that much traveling, aye?"

She saw him approaching but did not get up. "Forgive
me if I don't rise to meet you."

"Forgiven."

"You always seem to find me when I need you."

"I would have accompanied you if you had asked."

Brigid shifted on the flat rock she sat on. "I did not wish to burden you. You have places to go."

"I came to see you, remember?"

She brushed a hand across her forehead. "I have not shown you proper hospitality. Again, I must ask to be forgiven. 'Tis just that the gossiping and disobedience at Cill Dara has required all my attention. And now this."

He sat next to her and unlaced his shoes. "So, you decided to leave your sisters for a time after all." He plopped his bare feet into the water just as a minnow swam by. Soaking one's feet helped to lessen traveling pains. He was sure he'd told her this in the past.

"You were right."

"About the stream?"

"Aye, but also you told me I needed a journey."

He stood. "You wanted to be alone."

She muffled a laugh with her small fingers. "I am going to the busiest ecclesiastical center on the island. I doubt I'll be alone."

He bobbed his head.

"I'm delighted you've come." She reached for his hand, gave it a squeeze, and then released it.

He'd come because he missed her. She had work to do. So did he. He should leave her be despite his inclination. "Do you have your direction from here?"

"Etain told me to look for a hostel just beyond the stream. Please God we'll make it there before dusk."

He dried his feet in the moss. The ground was cooler than it had been just a few weeks ago. Winter crept forward, the usual end time of his respite. The school would need his services. "Although I wish it weren't so, I should be on my way home."

Her smile left. "You changed your mind about coming with me?"

"You don't really need me. In fact, you've gotten along quite well alone since we last parted. I meant what I said. Everyone knows of the good works you are doing at Cill Dara."

"I'm not trying to be popular."

He didn't mean to offend her. "Of course not. I just meant that you're doing a good job. I do not want to get in the way."

She stood, shaking droplets from her toes. "I shouldn't have sent you away when you first arrived at Cill Dara. 'Twas not my intention to have you think you were in the way."

"I am sure not, but 'tis true you are a busy woman."

She gripped his hand again. "Did you get the manuscripts you came for?"

"Not this time."

"Well, then, come to Armagh. Your students will benefit from what you can borrow there."

He felt his hand tremble inside hers and he pulled away. "I suppose I could. I'll head home right after, if you do not mind."

"Not at all. You are most welcome. I would enjoy your company, friend."

After riding alongside the brook for a time, they came upon a large wooden house. Smoky tallow candlelight glowed from the windows, and song from within burst into the night. They tied their horses to a tree and went inside, Brigid a bit wobbly from the travel.

"You are not as accustomed to riding as I am."

"I am fine." She bent to rub her knee before they went inside.

"Peace to all here," Ninnidh uttered, though not loudly.

A dozen men and a few women huddled around a bard who prattled on, waving about a jar of ale as he spoke. A pretty girl with auburn hair tied back with a ribbon left the group to greet them.

"Many welcomes to you, travelers. Are you here for the night?"

Ninnidh removed his hood. "We are, thank you. But we are just friends. We will need separate accommodations." He knew Brigid would want that known.

"That makes it easier." She pointed to a ladder to the left of the entry. "Lads up there and lassies down on the main floor." She inclined her head toward the merrymakers. "Don't be worrying. They're here for the bard. Most of 'em will be leaving when they've had enough ale and food." She raised her eyebrows. "Are you two hungry, then?"

"Indeed," Brigid answered.

They followed the lass to a table board where they were handed bowls of steaming pork stew and chunks of brown bread. Brigid blessed the food as the lass smiled at her. After a moment, the hostess ducked away and joined the others.

When the crowd dispersed much later, Brigid was given a mat and Ninnidh headed to the ladder leading to the second floor. Stopping at the first rung, he noticed Brigid placing her blanket into the arms of proprietor.

"My gift," she said. "I must leave tomorrow before daylight."

The girl ran her hands over the wool. "I have never seen such fine fleece. Wherever did you get it?"

"At Cill Dara, we have the finest sheep in all of Ireland."

The girl's bright eyes widened. "You are Maither Brigid of Cill Dara?"

"I am. There was so much music when I came that I did not introduce myself. I apologize."

"There is welcome here, no matter." The girl reached for Brigid's hand. "No need to introduce yourself. I accept all travelers, even those who wish to be anonymous. I am Kyna, proprietor."

Ninnidh climbed up to his bed, shaking his head at the generosity of that woman. She would give away her last crumb of bread to a beggar.

As Brigid had promised, they left early.

"If we can manage it," she told him as they led their horses to the road, "we should find one more hostel and then arrive in Armagh the day after. Wouldn't you agree?"

"I would normally say so, but 'tis a hard pace when you're not used to it."

"I can do it." She turned to coo to the horse she called Geall. She caught him staring at her. "He's been with me many years. A faithful servant. Do not doubt him, Ninnidh."

The horse appeared strong and sturdy, though a bit gray. But could the abbess's legs bear so many long days of riding? She was determined, but if she grew weary, Ninnidh knew of a few dwellings along the road where they could rest. The way to Armagh was a frequent quest for many, a well-traveled path since Patrick passed on.

Late in the day alongside the dusty road, they encountered a band of travelers who told them there was shelter just ahead.

When the others had passed by, Ninnidh leaned toward Brigid's mount to whisper to her. "I remember the place. 'Tis rough there."

"Is there another?"

"Not for some way."

"I am sure we can endure it." Her eyes drooped and her fingers trembled from grasping the rein. She needed rest. The night was damp and windy. If he could guard her long enough for her strength to return, the stop might be worth it. He knew taking a young, beautiful woman to that public house might not be wise, but neither was riding to exhaustion. The great band of lodgers they had just met had recently vacated the place. If another had not yet taken their place, Ninnidh and Brigid might stay there in peace. It would be worth a look.

Before long, a wattle and wicker structure came into view. The sinking sun cast a gray shadow over the hut, and not so much as a ribbon of smoke rose from the roof. The owners were stingy. They would not find a warm meal and soft bed tonight, but at least they'd rest under a roof.

Ninnidh tied the horses to a hazel, hoping the small stub of a trunk would be adequate. He didn't want the animals too far from the house, and there was no barn. He glanced around. No chariots, wagons, or donkeys. He let out a breath. "Wait while I inquire." He sensed her close behind him as he knocked on the door. The woman would not listen.

A man wearing a dirty linen scarf on his head opened the door but gave no greeting.

"Got room?" Ninnidh asked. He cringed at the volume of chatter. They would not be alone as he had hoped.

"How many?"

"Two, but one's a woman and not my wife."

The man cocked his head to the side to get a glimpse at Brigid. "Up to you to watch over her. Don't want no trouble, but I'll not evict anyone either."

"Agreed."

Brigid whispered to him. "They do not know here that you are a great poet?"

"They have little respect for anyone, and I'll not be trying to force it upon them."

"Of course not. You among all your brethren are the most humble—a servant. The man should be glad you are not the kind to threaten him with satire and curses."

Ninnidh had never done that, and while the laws required the people to show poets hospitality and for kings to bestow gifts, he didn't like a show of stature. One reason why he did not share his name. But he would do it for Brigid. If he had to.

They stepped inside the cave-like structure. Unfortunately, the place was packed, brimming with folks who smelled like rotting fish and sweat. They all must have

97

arrived on foot. He would need to keep a close eye on the horses. Ninnidh tugged on the man's arm. "The special."

The man leaned his head back like a proud rooster and held out a hand. Ninnidh fished around in his pack and produced a golden chain. His father's smith was one of the most talented craftsmen in all Ireland, and Ninnidh had been saving this piece in case he ran into trouble. The man snatched it from his hand. "Over here." He waved at Brigid, who gave Ninnidh a surprised look.

"Go on. He'll show you to your bed."

She followed the man to an interior door. He flung it open. A startled young couple bolted when the man ordered them out. "They didn't pay sufficiently, you understand. I only let them rest there until I had another renter."

She started to protest, but he shouted over her. "There's a mattress and a washing bin, and a bell here by the door if you need anything." He closed the door behind her and turned to Ninnidh. "Did you want to go in there with her, lad?"

"Nay, but lock her in."

The man bolted the door securely and Ninnidh leaned against it. He tugged his blanket from his bag to make a bed on the floor, though he would not close his eyes.

A man with stringy yellow hair and a face that had probably never seen soap approached. "Was that Maither Brigid?" His head was absent a tooth or two.

"Why do you want to know?"

"She helped me once. My cow was stolen. She replaced it. I owe her my life. Would have starved without her help."

Ninnidh cradled his harp against his stomach as he shifted to get comfortable. "She helps lots of folks just as Jesu would."

98

The man looked as though his legs wouldn't hold him. Too much ale. Ninnidh didn't wish to engage anyone in conversation. Some places weren't right for that kind of thing, and this was one of them. If they hadn't been so desperate for sleep, he would have never stopped.

The fellow kept staring down at him. "She should not be here. I know she's a kind woman, but she should not be here."

"Agreed."

"You do not understand."

"Look, man. I'm tired. Got a long journey tomorrow. What are you blabbering about?"

He glanced around as though wishing not to be heard. He crouched low and cupped his hands near Ninnidh's ear. "He's in Armagh. She should not be here." His voice began to quiver. "I'll help you get out. There's another road less taken. We can go now." His head bobbed up and down as though this movement would convince Ninnidh.

"What has you so scared, man? Who is in Armagh?"

"That evil druid, that's who. Ardan."

Nine

"Three strongest forces: the force of fire, the force of water, and the force of hatred."

Irish Triad

Ardan paced the length of the church, silently cursing the annoyance of having to wear a Christian priest's robes. He hated Christians. Before he'd been captured, he was simply amused by them. But now...now, he would have revenge.

The church door swung open, and a stout man in a long satin robe the color of apple flesh entered. "Your excellency," Ardan greeted him, and kneeled down on his left knee to kiss his hand—a detestable but necessary concession. "Here you are, our visitor. My helpers have been looking everywhere for you, and I have found you myself." The man's voice squawked like a hungry crow.

Ardan forced a smile. "I can usually be found in my Father's house."

"Indeed, so. When you are finished here, come to the meeting room so we may discuss your plans, will you?"

The man was a Briton, condescending, and totally out of place in Ireland, even more so than that pitiful bishop Ardan had disposed of many years ago while tracking Brigid—an accident, of course. When the time was right, Ardan would rip this man's throat out. He no longer felt bound to the druids' code of honor. But right now, he needed the pompous idiot. "I am finished here," Ardan said, expertly crossing himself and saying amen. "Please forgive me for keeping you waiting."

The two men emerged onto the green path leading from the church to the main meeting hall. Armagh was teeming with Christians who either worked for the church or had arrived on what they called a pilgrimage. Imbeciles! They would not find what they were looking for in this place. How he longed to show them the powers of the gods, the majesty that only a high druid could conjure. *Not yet. Patience.*

Inside the meeting room, the bishop waddled along on his ancient, decrepit knees toward an elevated table in the center of the room. Two aides helped him slide onto an ornately scrolled backed chair that reached several arm lengths above the man's capped head. The chair reminded Ardan of those the Brehons sat on when announcing legal decisions. Ardan was shown to a smaller chair beside the bishop.

They bowed their heads to pray, a futile practice. When the bishop announced the end of his prayer, Ardan lifted his gaze. This man was not the only bishop in residence. There were many men in shiny robes populating the room. How many there were or what they were doing there, he did not know. Christians believed this place to be most…what had they said? Ah, holy. Like an ancient oak grove, yet constructed by man. The gods had bestowed blessings and curses from Erin's soil for many generations. But this? Why these fools thought Armagh, with its cathedral and high crosses and houses filled with traveling monks, constituted a most worthy place of Christian worship was beyond his understanding. On the outskirts, of course, lay Emain Macha, the ancient druid seat of kings. This Christian enclave in Armagh was much too close, and that irritated him to no end.

Ardan turned toward the light pouring in through an arched window in the direction of Cill Dara. He'd been told Brigid had claimed that sacred site under the grand oak tree for her own Christian monastery, and he could not allow that. He would reclaim Cill Dara for the gods and especially for the goddess who dwelt there. How perfect that his quest for revenge had led him right back to that vexatious lass.

The bishop cleared his throat and turned to look at Ardan. "We will drink and talk, and you will tell me what we can do for you. You are welcome to stay here as long as you like, but we want to be prepared to aid you and your efforts when you leave. For that reason, might you share your plans with me, Ardan?" He wrinkled his nose as he examined Ardan's costume. "Come now, where did you say you received the blessing of your consecration?"

Ardan was cornered, and how he hated that. But he was smart, much more clever than this simpleton. "I wear humble clothing because of my travels, Your Excellency."

"Hmm." The man nodded.

"I was under the teaching of Finian, but that was long ago. A man called Brendan and I have been...ministering to the Picts. I have just returned." This was, for the most part, a lie, but at least he had turned the talk back to the land he knew something about, should he be questioned. He had no knowledge of Rome, Tours, Ephesus, or even Egypt—places he'd heard Christians went for training. If he tried to construe a story of how it had been done, he would trip up and be exposed.

The bishop drew his lip into a snarl.

A thought came to him. "But long before that I was under the guidance of Patrick."

The bishop's face brightened. That had been the right thing to say in this place. No matter that Ardan was too young to have met that long dead Christian. To these fools, it did not matter. They probably considered this—ah, what would they say? Aye, a divine miracle.

"God rest the great man's soul. This explains why the flock has brought you to me. What a blessing our Saint Patrick must have been to you, son."

"Of course." He had bribed his way into this cathedral. How little this man knew about his "flock."

The bishop continued. "The land of the Picts? Ach, that is a wild, distasteful place. How good of you to sacrifice your comfort for those poor lost souls, Ardan."

"Indeed."

The bishop clasped his hands together. "I have been told you have important work to do raising gold and silver for your mission, but I do hope you will honor us by joining us at the feast of Saint Matthew."

"I am the one honored." Ardan kissed the bishop's hand again and then was led away to dress for the occasion.

He did not know the protocol, but how hard could it be? When the attendants opened the door to the guest chamber, Ardan asked to dress alone. "To pray and prepare myself," he said. He was not questioned.

He paced the wee room, his hand clutched behind his back. It had not been difficult to escape Brendan, once he convinced the man he had embraced his religion. Ardan had the gift of persuasion, and although his effort had taken years, he'd done it and convinced the man it was best he go off alone to acquire new recruits for the tiny monastery on the lonely speck of an island off Ireland's northern coast. Little did Brendan know Ardan was finished with the repetitive prayers offered to the Christian god at regular intervals day and night. No longer would he be forced into the self-mortification ritual to purge his supposed sins. Ardan knew the importance of sacrificing to the gods, but the Christians insisted on a humility that Ardan could never embrace. Power was within his grasp, and he had always had the upper hand—that is, until he'd been kidnapped and taken to a far land. That was behind him now. He only needed to keep up the pretense a bit longer.

Ardan tugged at the wooden cross around his neck until it snapped from its leather cord. He tossed the charm onto his sleeping board. He admired the silk robe laid out for him and a thick, golden amulet in the shape of a cross. These garments would serve him well. It amused him, how easy it had been.

He glanced to the plain wooden cross that he'd worn ever since his kidnapping. It meant something to the Christians. Something about surrender. No god would ever take away his power. Gods were to be appeased, not surrendered to. Weak, these Christians were, but not him. Oh, no. Not him. He would become the druid priest of Cill Dara. He knew how to make it happen—just find their leader and make her do the surrendering—to him.

After a lengthy mass, Ardan joined the merrymakers out in a flat field surrounded by a stone rampart. A massive fire burned in the middle, much like the pagan fires he'd once built himself. Perhaps these folks had not given up the old ways after all. He approached a meat vendor who was bartering with patrons over his roasted birds on a stick. "Ah, Father." The man held out a juice-dripping bird. "Take it, please. No charge. Enjoy. Say a prayer for me."

"Bless you, my son." Ardan accepted the gift and turned away. No prayer would be said for that fool. He ate as he wandered among the people, listening for bits of gossip that might aide in his quest to overtake Cill Dara.

He studied the crowd, herds of scrawny men in priestly robes surrounded by common people who sought blessings. Others wandered the merchant tents, but where were the women? Clusters of women huddled together like roosting fowl always provided the best morsels of information.

Ardan made his way to a well to clean his hands. There he found what he'd been looking for. He turned his back to group of women as he splashed cold water on his hands from a wooden bucket beside a well.

A woman with a high pitched voice addressed the others. "The Uí Náir clan lost their chronicle."

"Lost it?" someone asked. "Had it stolen, I'd say."

"Don't you know?" a third chimed in. "That was one of those talismans, I hear. 'Twas a book of such power that those who possess it acquire great wealth."

A young woman's voice floated above the others, bearing the tone of one more confident. Ardan's interest was piqued. He casually turned to look. A fair and freckled lass held both arms out to the group. "That's why it was pilfered, I suppose. Does anyone know where it is? God forbid that my Declan goes off to war to reclaim it. Always doing such things, he is. Who's got it, Cliona?"

Ardan turned slightly and cast his eyes on the fair redhead who stood in the middle of the group. She turned dramatically to look each listener in the eye, just like an old *seanchaí*. But somehow Ardan trusted what she was about to say. They were in the middle of a Christian festival, after all. If she lied, wouldn't Saint Matthew hear and invoke some kind of revenge? Ardan's gods would have, he knew.

The woman, looking to be about twenty summers, no more, stood still again. "The book, as I hear, is in safekeeping at Cill Dara."

Cill Dara? Could it be so? Ardan marched toward the group. "Tell me, young woman, do you speak the truth?"

Her face turned the shade of oyster shells. "I do not lie, Father. That is what I heard. The book has sanctuary there, though none can tell if the Uí Náirs will honor that or if

107

they will attack." She stammered. "I…I was just there, you see. My father trades with that tribe. I heard it with my own ears."

He joined their circle and sat on a rock. "I have been away a long time. Perhaps you will tell me, is this a powerful tribe?"

The women became deaf and dumb, their mouths drooping. He tried to redeem himself. "Of course, they are, or they were when last I was on this island. But I've been in the Land of the Picts for many years. Does this tribe still have the authority to wage war?"

"Oh, they do," the storyteller answered. "Very much so, Father. We must pray for the safety of Cill Dara."

"Aye, we must." He stood and walked away, leaving the women to pray on their own. He would leave immediately to find the Uí Náir leaders. This was just the thing he'd hoped for. The gods be praised!

Ten

"There are two tellings to every story."
Irish proverb

The great high crosses shadowed Aine and her uncle as they passed by. Crowds of people milled about. "Where did all these people come from?"

"They come and go," Cillian answered. "They've work to do. You probably did not see so many before because most of them have just returned from working in the fields. Harvest has almost ended."

"I suppose 'tis so. The guesthouse lies in a far corner."

With all the people milling about in the daytime, she would have to steal away at night again. If they had stayed at Cillian's monastery with no more than a handful of hard-of-hearing monks, sneaking out would have been easier. She would have gone from there if her uncle hadn't guarded the book. It didn't seem as though she was going to get much information out of him anyway. "Uncle, tell me about our people."

"There isn't much to tell, Aine."

She clutched his hand the way she had when she was a child. He obviously still thought of her as one. "Oh, please. A wee story or two?"

"We must speak to the sister in charge. Let us take care of business first, lass."

That was what she had been trying to do.

Brocca shuffled toward them from the refectory. "I was told you had come. Welcome, welcome, Abbot Cillian."

Ah, here was one person who called him abbot.

He grasped her shoulders and planted a kiss on each of her cheeks.

The blind woman blushed. "Brigid has gone to Armagh to seek council, but I expect she will return within the week."

Cillian nodded to the monk who came to take charge of his cart.

Brocca turned toward the refectory again, clutching Cillian's arm. "Is someone with you?"

"'Tis me, Aine."

"I was concerned, child. I'm pleased you are in your uncle's care."

"I...uh—I am sorry to have cause you to worry."

"Come. Have something to eat."

Aine hurried to keep up with them.

Brocca's small feet made a shuffling noise as she took two steps for every one Cillian took. "My daughter visited you, I assume."

110

"She did."

"I am glad for this news. A mother always worries, you know."

A mother worries. Perhaps Aine's mother's family had wanted to correspond with her all these years but didn't know how. Or they were all in ill health. Soon, very soon, Aine would know for sure.

They paused at an outdoor well to refresh themselves and to scrub the dust from their hands and faces. A few oblates joined them and did the same as they prepared for their cooking duties.

Inside the large building, a delightful aroma met them. The only good meals Aine had enjoyed since leaving Daithi's tribe had been at Cill Dara. Cillian's brothers were not very good cooks. They desired to deny themselves, so they said. Perhaps they just lacked adequate cooking skills and settled for flat breads and dried berries because it was easier. Cillian and his monks always seemed to choose what was easiest.

"Sit." Brocca showed Cillian to a table, but he remained standing until Aine sat.

"I'm sure you both are weary from the journey."

The cold way Brocca treated her disturbed Aine. Sure, she had sneaked away, but Brocca had shown her kindness before. The others didn't like Aine, she knew, because of her tending that ceremonial fire. But the abbess hadn't prohibited it. Brigid had gone there herself. Why would Brigid's mother denounce Aine for such a thing?

After the woman left them, Aine asked again. "Please, Uncle, I wish to know more about our clan."

Cillian rubbed his broad hands over his face. "You tire me, child. What is it you wish to know?"

"Where do they live?"

111

"I have told you that before."

"Aye, but I'm wondering, how did you get from there to…where you live today? Was it a difficult journey when you made it?"

He placed a knuckle under his chin. "You will not get me to tell you the way there. You are safe at Cill Dara, and at Cill Dara you should stay for now, until we work things out."

At least she had tried again before she trusted her navigation to the book alone. She sighed.

He stretched his long legs under the table. "Why do you want to go to our homeland? There is nothing there for you and everything here. You will have a husband with high standing in his tribe. You desired that once. Remember?"

"I had not seen my mother in a long time before she died."

"'Tis good, that."

"Why?"

He flexed his fingers as though carrying his staff for the length of the journey had caused his joints to stiffen. "That, you do have a right to know. Your mother was a woman of God and long suffering. Credit is due her for that."

"I know my father did not want me. I know my leprosy caused me to be an outcast."

His mountainous shoulders rose and fell. "I would have had your mother come with me when I left home, but I only have men in my community, you understand. Doubt she would have come anyway, and besides, if she would have joined me, you would not have been born."

"'Twas not your fault."

"It was not, although I wish things had happened differently."

"Was my father cruel to her?" The words stuck in her throat and burned like coals. She knew the answer, but still she wanted it confirmed, to know that her childhood memories had been reliable.

"I know 'tis a hard bit to hear, Aine."

Her eyes began to blur, and a vision of a dark room and loud voices emerged.

Huddled.

Blackness.

Crash. Thump. A cry sliced through.

Aine put her hands over her ears. *Please stop. Oh, stop. Hurry, stop!*

"I will offer a safe place for travelers when I can," her mother's voice bellowed. "I do not care what you do to me."

It was a taunt. *No, Maither. Don't say it.*

"We cannot feed the mouths we have."

A thump. A slap. A groan.

Then silence.

Aine moved her fingers to her temples as the images left her. "Why didn't she run from him, Uncle? Why didn't she come away with me?"

Cillian looked up as Brocca brought them mugs of steaming tea. "I wish I knew, child. I sent a messenger to tell her to come to Brigid's Cill Dara, but I heard nothing."

"What?" Aine nearly burned herself on the hot beverage and returned her mug to the table board. "Why didn't you go and see for yourself? Didn't you want to know if she was well?"

"'Twas not for me to do. I did what I could. I prayed for her twice every day."

"A lot of good that did." She heard Brocca gasp but ignored her. "You must tell me how to get there, Uncle. I'll go myself. It might be too late for my mother, but we've cousins, there must be children—"

"Oh, you cannot, child," Brocca said. "I am afraid we cannot allow a young girl to travel off on her own. 'Tis unsafe."

Brigid was afraid they'd be attacked. Aine should have run away from her uncle when she had the chance, stealing the book when he wasn't looking, but she hadn't because, well, she felt like a child around him. He could convince her to listen to him with a look. She was angry with herself. The codex would be safe only if no one knew where it was. Saying so would get her nowhere, however. Aine bowed her head respectfully while Cillian blessed their food.

The book would provide all the good fortune she needed. She had to go. She would shed all the shackles these folks had clamped on her.

Brocca tapped a hand on the table in front of Aine. "The book?" Brocca stretched out her hand. "I have summoned Etain, and she is on her way to take possession of it."

Cillian removed it from his traveling pack. "Of course you may have it. We have no need of it, do we, Aine?"

"We do not, even if those less fortunate do." She bit back tears. Patting her knees, she focused on the page of the book that rested secretly inside her clothing. Fortunately, along the journey when Cillian left her to relieve himself, she had torn the first page loose, rolled it tight, and hidden it between her undergarment and her bare skin. She had it tied to her waist with a tangled harp string the Poet had casted away. This page, now separated from the binding, would call out and guide her to the rest. The stories of old spoke of the scrolls of the Jewish people. The pages called to each other in order to be collected and read together. There would be no problem in handing most of the manuscript over now. She could get it back later.

Aine pretended to sleep. She had been told to report to the refectory after morning prayers but before the sun rose. She was to receive instruction on her new duties. The sisters supposed she would be living with them for some time and would need assignment. She would not. But she retired early to give the impression that she wanted to be ready.

The parchment seemed to burn against her skin. She longed to pull it out, but she would not—not until she was far away from the guesthouse.

At long last, the other guests were still. Aine pulled the fleece off her body. A light glowed from her middle. She gathered her cloak as quickly as she could, wrapping it snugly against her to defuse the light. She collected her bag and slipped out the door unnoticed.

Which way? She shed her cloak as soon as she was behind the smith's house and tugged until she freed the scroll. It was as dark as the sky. She held it out in front of her. "I will return you. Just show me the way." She heard footsteps on the path in front of the house and plunged the scroll back under her garment.

Voices murmured low as two monks passed by on their way to the lookout. She peered around the corner, keeping close to the shadows, and watched the two hooded figures move away. A hand grabbed her shoulder, and she jumped, her heart throbbing in her throat.

"What are you doing out here?"

"Fianna!"

"I heard you were back and I suspected you'd be wandering about after dark. I've been watching."

"What do you want?" Aine wrapped her arms around her as if she were cold.

"To keep you inside. To keep all…pagan influences away."

"I don't need you to take care of me." The page burned against her belly once again.

Fianna tugged on Aine's arm. "Let's go. Back to bed with you."

Aine resisted and struggled against the woman. The page fell at her feet.

"What's this?" Fianna picked it up and it began to glow orange in her hand. She dropped it. "Magic! I knew you were a druidess."

Aine snatched up the page. "I don't care what you call me." She echoed her memory of her mother's words. "I don't care what you do to me."

Fianna's cheeks were as white as dove feathers.

Aine pushed the parchment in Fianna's face. "Leave me be!"

The woman squealed like a pig and rushed away. Aine chuckled and held the page out again to lead her on her way.

The scriptorium was dimly lit with just three straw torches positioned in far corners. Someone would come tend them soon because they burned low. The page had stopped glowing, so Aine knew she must be close. The smell of ink and musty parchments made her sneeze.

"Who's there?" came a voice from somewhere in the massive hall.

Aine ducked beneath a transcription table. Why was someone awake at this hour? She was having such terrible luck hiding lately. Hadn't she come all the way from the Uí Náir to Cill Dara without being detected? Someone, perhaps Fianna, had given her away.

The sound of shuffling feet stopped near her head. "I know you're under there. Come out, child."

Cillian!

"Come on, now. You'll not get that book back. I've hidden it well."

There was nowhere he could hide it that its page would not uncover. She kept still, hoping the page under her cloak would stay calm.

"Aine, come out right now!"

Cillian's booming made her shiver. Men could cause rocks to tumble from mountains with just their voices. She rose to her knees and when she peeked around the table she found herself nose to nose with him.

"I…I…wasn't looking for…"

"Oh, and sure you weren't, now." He lifted her to her feet. "Suppose you explain why you said the book doesn't matter to you now and here you are, looking for it anyway."

She sucked her lower lip, aware that, as long as he hung on to her like that, she couldn't get a grip on the rolled parchment page under her cloak.

"Never mind. You just get along to bed." He pushed her toward the door.

"Won't you give me a map, Uncle? To get to my homeland. Won't you do that?"

"Not at this hour. We will speak of this later, when the matter of the book has been decided."

He left her alone to scurry back to the guesthouse, tossing her out like yesterday's porridge. The night air was frigid. The dark half of the year approached. She could not afford to wait weeks. Traveling would become more bone-chilling with each passing night. She might not have gotten the book this time, but she would get it. The parchment crinkled as she squeezed it tightly against her. Once she was freed from Cill Dara, bullies like Cillian and Daithi would not be able to order her around anymore.

Eleven

"I am in hope, in its proper time,
That the great and gracious God
Will not put out for me the light of grace
Even as thou dost leave me this night."

Carmina Gadelica

You did not need to lock me in."

Ninnidh knew that he'd have some explaining to do when the innkeeper freed Brigid from her private room in the morning. He'd been trying for the last hour, unsuccessfully, to convince her that it had been necessary for her safekeeping. "I believe I did have to lock you in." He yawned. The odd man who'd said that Ardan was about had kept him up half the night as Ninnidh tried to convince him that he'd had too much ale and was imagining things. The rest of the time he spent checking on the horses. Praise God no one had stolen them.

The talk of Ardan was bothersome, however. The druid had been exiled, certainly. Pray God he was right about that.

"Believe what you may, but here. Take this." She handed him a gold chain.

It was heavy and ornate, not identical to the one he'd given away, but surely equal in value. "Where did you get this?"

"God provides." She kept her eyes on the road before her.

"If you were anyone but Maither Brigid, I'd ask if you'd stolen it."

She laughed. "As I said, God provides. No one is lacking back there. Not the publican, not any of the poor souls in the house. This, my friend, is something God has given us to sustain us on our journey."

Blessed with the gift of miracles, she was. He had sung tunes about this woman, witnessed some of the unexplainable events she was becoming famous for, but never before had he seen this—wealth restored. He pivoted on his horse's back until he could look at her. "I did not need to get what I spent back."

"One never knows what the future will hold. The innkeeper has his payment."

He dropped the gold chain into his saddlebag and meandered down a road that was growing ever wider and ever more populated.

Some time later they reached a knoll that overlooked the center of Armagh. They paused to take in the beauty. A high cross rose above the treetops and rich, rolling green hills spilled out toward a massive church building. "A city of kings that Patrick transformed into the city of God," he observed.

She turned her green eyes on him, and a smile softened her face. She was no longer angry with him for trying to protect her. As she turned away, the afternoon sun bathed her face in light. She stared straight ahead as she spoke. "I suppose this place has been in your songs."

"It has. Patrick asked the local king, a man named Daire, for land for his church. The king granted the lower field instead of the hill that Patrick wanted. Then, to make it worse, mind you, the king sent one of his men to the field to let his horse graze. God would avenge this affront, however, and the story's one of my favorites."

She nodded to him and pointed at his harp.

He strummed it until he found the right chord. "'Who sends this beast to defile the Lord's territory?' the holy man decried. 'King Daire sent me down here,' the timid man replied."

They stared in silence. After awhile, Ninnidh said, "'Tis a thin place where one can feel the touch of God, aye?"

"'Tis. Go on with your song, please."

Ninnidh's emerald robe flapped against his ankles as he stood next to her, gazing down at the lush, green pasture where Patrick had once dwelled not long after he returned to Ireland to convert her people. Nearly a century had passed since then—no one knew for sure just how long, and no one he knew really cared. Storytellers extolled the story, not the mundane details. He drew in his breath and continued to sing the story about how the fellow found his horse dead not long after Patrick had voiced his displeasure. The man returned to report to the king, who promptly called for Patrick's death in exchange.

"A death sleep came over the king as soon as he had said it. 'The Christian caused it,' said his wife, 'and he's the one to lift it.'"

Patrick had responded by giving the king's man some holy water to cure the horse so he could take the animal back with him. The holy water healed the king as well, and so Daire gave Patrick the land he had first desired, the very hill that Ninnidh and Brigid now stood on.

Brigid looked at him as he was storing his instrument. "'Tis a beautiful tale of how God provides."

"And a beautiful landscape. 'Tis good to see these thin places and to feel them. All the better is the song then when you tell it to others. Having seen it for yourself, how much more completely will you describe the wonder to your followers?"

"You are right. I needed a bit of time away from Cill Dara. The vision of this place will be mine from now on." A frown replaced her contented expression. "I'm not pleased that we've arrived during the fest of Saint Matthew, though. I should have calculated better. Do you think the bishop will hear me?"

"We'll make sure he does."

When they reached the outmost buildings of the settlement, a young man greeted them and helped Brigid from her horse after she told him who she was. "We are pleased for you to visit. The deeds and works of Maither Brigid of Cill Dara are known all over the land."

"I am much humbled." She offered the lad a silver broach for his troubles, but he declined. "I am happy to show you to the guesthouse." He turned to Ninnidh. "I'm afraid the male guesthouse is full."

Ninnidh patted the pack strapped to his horse. "I can make my bed anywhere."

The lad turned back to the abbess. "No one is at the guesthouse at the moment. All are feasting in the meadow. Perhaps you would like to join them. I can take your belongings to the house."

"God bless you. You are very kind." She turned to Ninnidh, who had just scrambled down from his own horse. "I would like to be among the people."

As the young man retrieved Ninnidh's horse, Brigid discreetly slipped the broach she held into his pocket and put a finger to her lips. Then they turned toward the meadow.

Celebrants mingled among tall grasses and wilting late autumn wildflowers. Brigid scurried up to them and took an infant into her arms. "May God send his angels to watch you sleep." She kissed the wee one's forehead and handed him back to his mother. Then she moved on toward a crippled man. Ninnidh did not hear what she said, but the man smiled at her touch. She continued, making the sign of the cross over several heads.

"Will you bless the cattle, Maither?" A trio of young boys led them to a fenced area where four beasts grazed.

When she finished, there she removed wee gifts from her pockets—seashells, combs, even chunks of cheese wrapped in tight linen balls.

"Thank you, kind Brigid. God be with you," they called at her. Her supply seemed unending. Ninnidh could sing and weave tales, but this woman's gift of miracles was a wonder to see.

Finally, she sat, and he joined her. She began weaving crosses from meadow grass and handed them to the children. One of the listeners, a young woman with auburn braids, approached her. "Maither Brigid, I have asked a priest to pray for your monastery."

Brigid handed a finished cross to a towheaded toddler and urged him toward his mother. Then she turned to the newcomer. "I thank you for your prayers."

The woman sat at Brigid's feet and laid her head on Brigid's lap. Her braids fell across Brigid's knees.

Ninnidh marveled at how people were drawn to his friend. She brought them comfort in a manner that he had never witnessed before.

The woman lifted her head. "Have you come to Armagh to pray, Maither?"

"I commune with my Lord wherever I am, child. What bothers you?"

Sorrow swam in her eyes. "I fear war will come to Cill Dara. Don't you, Maither?"

Brigid smoothed down stray strands of the woman's hair with the palm of her hand. "Some trust in chariots, and some in horses. But we, dear one, will call upon the name of the Lord our God."

The woman blue eyes flashed. "Has it started then? Have you fled Cill Dara and sought refuge here?"

Ninnidh wondered how Brigid would respond. There hadn't been a war, not yet so far as he knew, but surely Brigid thought there would be trouble.

Brigid continued stroking the woman's head, as if trying to console her. "Oh, child. Do not start rumors. Cill Dara is safe. I have come to seek wise counsel."

"About the book?"

Brigid pulled back. "What do you know about this?"

A crowd started to encircle them. Ninnidh stood protectively.

"I don't know anything, Maither. Just that the Uí Náir book is at Cill Dara and they want it back."

Ninnidh glanced around at the faces. The woman's proclamation could endanger all of Cill Dara. He grabbed the gossip's arm. "To whom have you spoken of this?"

The woman tried to back away, but he held firm. "You're hurting me."

Brigid clutched the woman's free arm. "Answer, child."

The crowd had closed in so tightly that there would be no escape should they decide to protest violently. They released the woman, and she rubbed her arms.

"I have spoken only to those right here." She nodded to the others. "And that priest. The one I asked to pray for you. He wanted to know more, and I told him what I'd heard. People are concerned."

Ninnidh towered over the woman. "What did that priest look like?"

The woman's face tensed. "Like any other. Long brown robe, tonsure. He didn't wear the cross, though. Now that I think about it, that is odd, isn't it? He paced around me as he asked questions. Never seen a priest act quite that way. He held a walking staff, but not the kind that bishops use."

"If you thought him suspicious looking, woman, why tell him anything?" A panic rose from Ninnidh's throat to his cheeks. Ardan liked to stride about in such a manner, as though the motion helped him gather thoughts. Ardan carried a druid staff, something someone who spent their whole life in Armagh might not be familiar with.

Brigid put a hand on Ninnidh's chest to urge him to step back. "I am sure she is just now remembering this. We do not blame her. Go along now, child. But don't speak of this to anyone." She pointed her finger at the sea of faces that had not moved a smidgen. "That goes for all of you as well. The safety of Cill Dara depends on your silent tongues until this matter is resolved."

A hush fell on the community. Brigid smiled. "Do not worry. Resolved, it shall be."

The gathering broke up. Ninnidh was sure that, despite Brigid's warning, there would be no silent tongues in that crowd.

Even as that crowd dispersed, another took its place. Hordes of people holding cups, begging for alms. Brigid blessed them as she was able, but even the saints with wondrous spiritual gifts are human and can only do so much. Ninnidh guided Brigid away from the meadow and back toward the church.

Brigid released a frustrated groan. "Why did I convince myself to come here? Word travels faster than wildfire. I should have brought that book with me, as I had wanted to before Cillian convinced me otherwise. I could have left it here and Cill Dara would not be a target. Word travels faster than a raven flies."

The time had come for him to tell her what he knew. "The book may not be the only mark." As calmly as he could, he related what the man in the hostel had said.

"Ardan? Is it possible the fellow you met was referring to someone else with the same name?"

"He meant the message specifically for you. He wanted to alert you. Why would someone want to warn you about a man named Ardan if it wasn't the same man?"

126

She stopped short of the stables and planted her hands on her hips. "Why did you not tell me this sooner?"

Why, indeed? Ninnidh felt an overwhelming need to protect Brigid, but he could not do it alone. Armagh's walls offered a better defense than returning to her monastery would. He wanted her here before she changed her mind. "You were determined to come here. 'Twas your undertaking. I am looking out for you. I…I did not know if the man was correct, but after hearing that woman's description…I just told you now, did I not?"

"I don't need you to look after me. God will do that." She hid trembling hands behind her back. "So you think that inquiring priest, the one the lass in the meadow spoke of, is Ardan in disguise?"

"There is no time to waste. You must seek your audience with the bishop. I will retrieve the horses." He turned away.

She scrambled up behind him. "Wait. Answer me. Ardan?"

"I hope not, but it could be." He let his arms fall to his side. "You said you didn't need me, and truly, as soon as I escort you to the church, you won't." He settled up with the stable boy and, after he returned with Brigid's traveling bag, Ninnidh helped the abbess mount her horse. Stubborn woman. He lunged onto his horse's back, no longer weary from lack of sleep. Anger had a way of making up for it all.

Brigid seemed vulnerable atop the large animal. Her stare bore into him. "Why would he be here, Ninnidh, pretending to be a Christian priest?"

Ninnidh studied the clumps of people lining the path to the church. Clusters of brown hooded priests were everywhere. Armagh had more clerics than an anthill has ants. "Pull your hood up."

"What?"

He nodded toward the crowd of people. "Do it."

She lifted the bulky material to cover her blonde hair. "Why would he come back?" she hissed. "Why would he care about Cill Dara? I wasn't the one who sent him away."

He smirked at her, hoping she'd get the hint that her questions were unanswerable. How could anyone understand the mind of a twisted, evil man?

They rode as tightly together as they could manage. As soon as they were safely out of eavesdropping distance, Ninnidh formed an answer. "We know he was cruel. We know he could hold a grudge. If he somehow escaped his captors, he might come looking for you. And where else to hear news of Maither Brigid but at the ecclesiastical center of the island?"

She sighed heavily. "We need to warn Cillian. His monks are vulnerable. They have no effective defense, and Ardan harbors a grudge with them as well, however unjustified."

"You might need to evict Aine and her book from Cill Dara."

"What do you mean?"

"That lass is leading the man to your door. Such a talisman will draw Ardan's keen interest, and who on all the island will not know of the theft of the Uí Náir book by week's end?"

Brigid turned Geall around. "You speak the truth, Ninnidh. It might be too late. Never mind my meeting with the bishop."

He followed. "It might indeed be too late," he called after her.

She stopped and turned toward him. "I was a fool to think Cillian a coward all this time. The druid is dangerous. If you are correct and Ardan has returned, I will have to admit that Cillian was wise to realize that the fight was not over. Pray God we arrive in time to warn him."

They paused at the top of the hill where they had earlier admired the scenery. Ninnidh patted his horse with an outstretched arm. "We won't make it back before sunset, and I'd rather not stop at the public house again."

"I'm afraid you're right. We are tired. The horses are weary. If we start early in the morning, we'll get past that place. I'll go back and pay a messenger."

"A good idea, but I'll find the messenger. You wait here."

"I'll go too."

"Be sensible, Brigid. Everyone knows who you are. They crowd around you like starving ducklings. Remain here, please. I won't be long, and then we'll inquire about lodging."

She lowered her hood and allowed her loose hair to flow freely in the wind. "I might as well speak to the bishop before I leave."

"I said 'tis not safe to go down to the meadow during the fest."

She wrinkled her button nose at him. "And I told you God will keep me safe."

"He doesn't want you to be foolish."

"Seeking counsel is not foolish, Poet."

He groaned. "All right, but keep your hood up and speak to no one. I'll do the talking."

"But first, the messenger."

"Aye. Back to the stables."

He found the stable boy and pressed two silver bracelets into his palm, currency Brigid had given him from Cill Dara's silversmith. Not as convincing as the gold chain, but definitely adequate for a lad. "We've an urgent message to get to Cill Dara. Do not refuse us." He gripped the lad's wrist as tightly as he could. "And tell no one of your mission."

The boy nearly bolted out of his shoes with excitement. "I'm the fastest rider. My brother will tend the stables. I will tell no one. For the abbess of Cill Dara, I will do this. You can depend on me."

Ninnidh squeezed tighter. "God will be watching, son." He released him and watched the lad mount a black mare and race toward the road.

Bishop Duach was a wee man with glassy eyes. He gripped Brigid's hands, but probably could not even see her face. "A pleasure to have you here," he said.

Brigid lowered her head in respect. "I am honored that you greet me, Your Excellency. I thought the fest might consume your attentions this day."

"Nonsense. When the abbess of Cill Dara pays a visit, I am the one honored."

Ninnidh carefully surveyed the inner chamber of the church where they sat. He had been told the meeting would be secret, per the abbess's wishes, but Ardan could be lurking anywhere. *Hurry and finish, Brigid.*

Brigid explained her concerns about Aine and the book.

The old bishop rubbed his pink lips together as he listened and then raised a finger. "A very grave matter indeed. You will do as you see fit, of course."

"You have no advice?" Brigid's pale face flushed.

"You are more than abbess. Isn't that so?"

"The vow of bishop was read over my head, but that doesn't not mean I do not seek the counsel of my elders. The people…they would listen to you. Just your presence would be enough."

The man smacked his lips, and a lad brought him a chalice of spring water. Brigid waved him away when he offered her a drink, and Ninnidh did the same.

They should not have come. Ninnidh should have brought the book here. Alone. He was always giving in to Brigid. He must resist in the future when it came to her safety. To everyone's safety.

The bishop wiped his chin on the sleeve of his robe. "Then you shall have it."

Brigid sat taller. "Your counsel?"

"Indeed. The book does not belong here at Armagh. It has no value to the church. I must be in residence here, of course. But you wanted counsel. Here it is: Do as you see fit."

Brigid was clearly disappointed as they made their way back to the stables. "A waste of time, that was."

"Perhaps. But not all was lost. It was worth hearing that compliment, I'd say."

"Is it, now? Please, be telling me." She forced her words through clenched teeth.

"If he rode in to Cill Dara and took charge of the situation, that would mean he did not trust your authority."

"I suppose you're right."

Of course he was. Now, however, all Ninnidh could think about was how they must get away from Armagh. A dark cloud seemed to hover over what before seemed like such a sacred place. What once seemed to have God's blessing, now appeared cursed. Or was it a warning from God? An inner prompting told him to get the abbess away as soon as possible. As weary as he felt from the travel, she must feel worse. She was not used to taking arduous journeys. He'd have to hire a chariot driver and pray that their horses had been adequately rested.

When they approached a different stable, one where merchants hired out wagons and other means of transporting their goods, Brigid dropped to the ground and emptied the contents of her traveling bag. She had one spare tunic, a bone comb, a Psalter, a linen bag stained purple from the berries it held, and extra leather strips for shoe repair. "I gave away my last trinket to the church attendant. I've nothing left of value." She plunged her fingers back into the bag and came out empty. No silver or gold miraculously appeared. She turned sad eyes to him. "I've nothing to give the driver."

She did not say it—she would never—but Ninnidh supposed she felt as though God had forgotten them.

He retrieved the long gold chain from his bag. It was heavy and worth more than a year's worth of wages. "You may not need me, but God does."

The words sounded sharper than he meant, but she smiled just the same. "God provides."

The chain allowed Ninnidh to purchase rather than rent the chariot, and soon, they were on their way.

Twelve

"What is nearest the heart is usually
nearest the lips."

Irish proverb

A clanging bell woke Aine in the still night. She would
not rise for Cill Dara's nighttime prayers. They could
not force her. She rolled to her side and pulled a fleece cover
over her head. She had been dreaming about springtime and
the birth of new sheep and calves. She wanted to go back to
that springtime place, not stay in the cold, dark reality of the
guesthouse, a place she would nonetheless be leaving soon.

She must have dozed off again because someone began
shaking her.

"Get up, wee one. A visitor has come for you."

More shaking.

"Get up, I say. Either you will see him or you will run from him."

"What?" She sat up and pushed her tangled hair from her eyes.

Brocca sat on the edge of her cot. "Your betrothed has come again."

"Daithi? Tell him I won't see him."

"I'm afraid I can't do that."

Aine stood and flung a tunic over her undergarment.

"Why can't you do that, Sister Brocca? Maither Brigid knows he's not been good to me."

Brocca crossed her arms and turned vacant eyes in her direction. "I can't do what you wish because Maither Brigid has insisted that you either speak to him or you depart Cill Dara in secret, never to return again."

Aine ran a comb through her hair, wanting more than anything to appear self-assured. Surely that was not exactly what the abbess had said. "She's back, then? I mean…I was leaving anyway, but never to return? Tell me she did not truly say that."

"She gave me instructions before she left, in case he should come around. I have not been informed that Brigid has returned yet."

"I see." She noted the empty beds and realized that the other visitors were off breaking their fasts. "I need just a moment to…uh, gather things. Please?"

Brocca stood. "Don't tarry long, lass. Etain and I will be in the church."

Aine held the door for Brocca and then shut it firmly behind her. She hurried to the parchment page hidden under her cloak and dug in the soft ground under her cot with her bone comb. After sliding the page into the hole, she covered it with rushes and then scrubbed the dirt from under her fingernails with the water in the washing basin.

As she hurried toward the church, she rehearsed the speech she prepared for Brigid, but would now have to give to Etain.

Daithi had shown himself to be oppressive.

He had to be sent away immediately.

Her life with him would be so much less than it had been with Cillian.

Cillian had allowed her to read books. Daithi wanted to take that pleasure away, beginning with the tribe's coveted book. That much was true.

She hoped no one would be astute enough to ask why Aine had not simply informed the tribe of Daithi's intent to destroy the book. True, there were men who could protect it and discipline Daithi for his behavior if she wanted that. What they would do to him and her foster father, however, she had no way of knowing. She did not wish to see them harmed. Her own clan needed this book. She could not have handed it over to the king's men. The tribe would blame her alone for taking the book because she and Daithi had not yet married. Had she done it after their wedding, she would have disgraced him more. Hopefully he would one day understand that that she had actually spared him.

There was no time for putting the tail on the cat, for making sure all matters were in order. She held her head low as she entered the building. Marrying Daithi would rob her of her freedom. That was all the women at Cill Dara needed to know.

"Aine."

137

The shock of hearing a male voice caused her to take a step back. They had brought him here and hadn't even allowed her the chance to convince them he should leave. Stunned by seeing him, she barely noticed Etain and Brocca standing nearby.

"Oh, Daithi."

He stared back at her, his expression soft and tender. Not at all how he'd appeared during their last discussion regarding the book.

She pursed her lips and whispered his name again. "Daithi, why are you here?" The gods only knew what had they discussed before Aine got to the church.

Etain escorted Aine to the front bench facing the altar. "We will talk together, Aine. Daithi knows you have sanctuary here. He will not be permitted to take you from Cill Dara without your consent."

He sat very close to Aine on the bench. "I never meant to send you away, *a ghrá mo chroí*—love of my heart."

She turned from him, but she could not escape those tender words, the closeness of his body, the music of his voice. It had been so much easier to be separated when she could not see his forlorn face.

"Come home, Aine."

She held a hand to her chest, afraid that she would not be able to draw another breath. A single tear dripped to her chin. She fanned her fingers across her cheek. She could not give in to his charms. All would be lost if she did. Still covering her face, she said, "Sister Etain, I do not wish to be here. Call for me when he is gone, please." She rose, and he did too, drawing her into his chest.

"Aine, my sweet. Please listen to me. The book is secure here at Cill Dara. We have nothing to fight over. Come home."

More tears came, frustrating her. "Leave me alone, Daithi." A pain rose in her chest as she spoke the words she hoped she would not regret. *This is for the best. For everyone.*

"We must go," she heard Brocca say. "You have heard Aine's request."

Daithi stepped back, and Brocca moved between them. "She does not wish you to be here."

Etain's squeaky voice intervened. "Brocca, take our visitor to the refectory and give him something to eat. I will meet with him there in a moment."

A knock erupted, and a man cracked open the door. "Message from Maither Brigid."

Etain touched Brocca's elbow. "Attend to it on your way out." Etain urged Aine to sit back down.

Once they were alone, Aine expected Etain to launch into a barrage of questions. Instead, they sat side-by-side, staring up at the large bronze cross that Aine had thought was wood when she first visited the church. She had never been this close to the front. An aura of peace blanketed the building. The altar was special to Brigid, the place where she conducted the spiritual business of the abbey. Aine sensed the sacredness, similar to the fire outside the border of the monastery, but strangely warmer and with unfathomable depth.

They sat quietly, and the solitude seemed to ruffle Aine's resolve. Had that been the nun's intent? The stillness reminded Aine of the night she had come there when Brigid had not asked her a lot of questions. Etain, in charge during the abbess's absence, appeared just as patient, surprising since Aine had not witnessed that behavior previously. She supposed there was much about the operation of a monastery that she did not understand.

As Aine continued to stare at the cross, she wondered if stealing the book might have been a terrible idea after all. Like this cross, the book was a magical possession treasured by many.

She closed her eyes, not wishing to second-guess her actions. Where had those thoughts come from? No one was pressing her to change her mind. All they were doing was sitting silently in the church.

Drawing in a deep breath, she focused on her plan. She must convince the sister to send Daithi away and then make her escape. Her quest had not changed. So long as everyone stood by and permitted men to govern their wives as they might vassals…well, nothing would change if she did not act. She knew that as well as she knew her own name. She tapped her fingers together. "Shall we see what Brigid has to say when she returns?"

"I have received instruction."

"Perhaps that message said something about me."

This seemed to amuse the woman. "Very well. I will not force you to go until the abbess has returned. I do not think she will stay away from Cill Dara long. She never does."

"Oh, I will go, truly. I had just not planned to go so soon. I need…more time."

"You will not be taking that book with you, lass."

"I did not mean that." But she did.

Another long silence.

Moments later, Etain took Aine's face in her hands. "Child, I do not think this man has abused you. You have deceived us."

Aine wanted to shove her away and run out, but she knew rudeness would not help her cause. "Oh, no, Sister, I have not. 'Tis true that he is a man of hot temper. You did not see it just then, but he is indeed."

"Has he harmed you physically?"

"Well, no, but—"

"Threatened to? Not the book, but you?"

"No. But that does not matter. You do not understand."

"I understand some things. There is a closeness between you. I saw it. Even sightless Brocca could sense it. Aine, you are in love with this man, and for some reason, you resist it."

Thirteen

"A friend's eye is a good mirror."

Irish proverb

Brigid and Ninnidh arrived at Cill Dara quickly by
taking turns to nap while the other drove. They made
infrequent stops, rode all through the night, and arrived just
a few hours after the messenger. Ninnidh saw that their
horses surviving the pace was yet another miracle. When
they arrived, they found that the faithful had begun to secure
the monastery as best they could. What was the proper way
for a religious community to prepare for an invading army?

Brigid disappeared to see to her duties while Ninnidh
helped the men hide the church's bronze and gold
communion chalice and platen and some of the more

valuable manuscripts. One book in particular he found most marvelous: a red-, blue-, yellow-, and purple-inked, illuminated treasure. He had not heard its title, but soon all of Ireland would be talking about this masterpiece book of Cill Dara. Where the Uí Náir book was that had led to all the trouble, he didn't know.

The waiting began. A lookout party had been dispatched to bring news of the approaching army, but Ninnidh knew that the threat could come from just one man, Ardan. He approached the lookout. "See here, man. Watch for a stranger traveling alone, won't you? Not only an entire tribe."

The fellow called back from his high post. "Been one here already, Poet. Before the messenger came."

Ninnidh cringed. "Tell me." He scrambled up the ladder.

The lookout conversed without taking his eyes off the landscape. "The guest, Aine? A man came to see her. The one she sought sanctuary from. But do not worry. The lass is safe, and the man has been sent away."

Ninnidh let out a breath. "He seeks the book. I do hope no one told him it was here."

The man shrugged and continued to stare into the surrounding woodland.

"A druid…uh, likely dressed as a Christian priest, might approach. Let no one in, no matter how innocent he might appear."

"I understand, Poet."

Ninnidh climbed back down and, after a time, returned to the guesthouse. Entering, he rested his shoulder against the wall. The house was vacant and secluded. No songs came to him. He'd prayed, eaten, and taken a long walk along Cill

Dara's rampart since returning. He'd carefully avoided the pagan fire pit, however. No men were welcome there. He knew this place well, had visited even before Brigid chose the spot for her community. Cill Dara's site was choice, well-nourished for centuries by the Creator, something the people knew instinctively even before they knew His name. There was no question it was a sacred spot and had been probably since the creation of the world. God would protect the faithful here. Still, he felt restless, like a storm was coming.

He collected his cloak from a peg rack and stepped outside. The key-like leaves of the ash had mostly fallen, and soon the other trees would follow, shedding more foliage. A stiff breeze stirred the fringe of his tunic. He turned his face to the sky. *What can I do, Lord?*

Hearing no response, no stirring in his soul of certainty, he wandered toward the large central church. A few men hurried past him. He rarely felt the urge to rush—the jaunt from Armagh had been a jarring exception. He preferred a slower pace as he listened for the Spirit's leading, even during times like this.

He paused near a well, focusing on the church in the distance. Suddenly, one of the large oak doors pushed open and Aine burst out, her honey-colored hair whipping into her face.

Her voice carried to him on the wind. "I will not listen to you or to him."

Brigid came out next, holding both arms out toward the lass. The girl ran off and Brigid put a hand over her eyes. Ninnidh went to her.

She glanced up. "Oh, Ninnidh. I fear I have broken my own rule and invaded Aine's privacy. She will never trust me again."

145

He urged her back into the church and out of the wind. Closing the door behind them, he reached for her hand. She didn't pull away, as he had expected she might after earlier insisting she did not need his help. "Let's speak about this, Brigid. That is why I'm here."

She sighed, staring at the stone floor.

"Won't you allow me to listen? Did I not hear you once say that the absence of an *anamcara* is like a body without a head?"

She laughed. "Ah, a soul friend. I did say that. The sisters here, I try to be their *anamcara*, but me? I confess I am nonetheless the body without a head."

"I will try to stand in, Brigid. Just this once, if you'll allow me to be your confidant. Come." He led the abbess to a bench in a corner of the large room. "Your church has grown since I was here last."

"I suppose it has." Her brow wrinkled. "Oh, Ninnidh, I fear I am losing Him."

"Who?"

"God. I fear He'll leave me."

"God will never leave you. You know that."

"He left me once, due to my own selfishness. I wanted my mother so badly. My father kept her from me. You know what happened once I found her. Ardan kidnapped her."

"I do know."

"And we are ever grateful that you rescued her, Ninnidh."

"God rescued her. He was there all the time." He lifted her chin with one finger. "That has nothing to do with what is happening now. Brigid, I know you fear Ardan, and now perhaps the whole Uí Náir clan will break down your walls.

But no matter what happens, God is in control because he is already here. You know that."

"Ardan, the king's army? They are the least of my worries. I've told you what I fear."

"I don't understand."

She swallowed hard and wove her fingers together. "I should not have spoken so freely."

"You should have." He bent his head low to make her look at him. "I am here to listen, and I hope you will do the same for me when I need it."

"'Tis not good for the community to know their abbess has doubts."

He shook his head. "You cannot pretend or be untruthful, but the community is not here with you now. 'Tis just the two of us. Tell me what troubles you."

She clutched his wrist, digging her nails into his skin. "Ninnidh, what if God has abandoned us? What if he tires of our selfishness and has left us to fend for ourselves?"

He glanced around to be sure they were still alone. She was right not to want to be overheard. The others would not understand. He understood. He spent many hours alone with only God's voice as company. And sometimes the Creator did not speak. The silence could make even the most faithful doubt. "You are tired. There is no immediate threat. You should rest."

Her eyes darkened to the color of the deep sea. "I am speaking quite earnestly. God forsook me once, took away my gift of miracles."

"He has not taken that away. I've seen it myself."

"For a time, He did. How am I to know it won't happen again? How can I protect these people?"

"If God takes away a gift, there is a reason for it. 'Tis nothing to fear. He knows what He's doing. Brigid, remember the One who loves you the most. He is with you, even now. Can't you sense Him?"

They held hands and listened to the sounds of people scampering about outside. Slowly, as Ninnidh pushed the human noise out of his mind, he heeded the wind, the birds, the humming he often heard during times of meditation. A sound he believed came from Erin, the earth itself, which God created.

She squeezed his hand, and he opened his eyes to find her staring at him. "Please do pray for me."

He put a hand on her cheek.

She pulled his hand away and held it in hers for a moment before leaning away from him. "I must visit Aine."

He stood with her. "Is that not what you needed to talk about when we came in here?"

"'Twas, aye, but now I know what I need to do." Her expression brightened. "Thank you." She turned her back to him.

"For what?"

"For coming."

He stood there listening as she walked away. Her garments, plain, not the robes of a priest or bishop, made a shuffling sound as she walked toward the door. He would know her movements even if his eyes became as unseeing as Brocca's. "Come back after you speak to her," he said. "I will wait for you."

Aine, her bag packed, stood at the end of her cot in the guesthouse just as Brigid entered.

"I'm leaving Cill Dara, Maither. I must. I am sorry for the trouble I've caused."

"Nonsense. You have sanctuary at Cill Dara."

"I have been told otherwise. I sent Daithi away. Etain told me I must go if I refuse to speak to him."

"I spoke out of turn, causing some misunderstanding. There are still things to be worked out. Besides, I afterward sent a messenger."

Aine read despair in the woman's face.

"Aine, it is not safe. We believe a battle could ensue over that book if we do not give it back."

"Oh, no. Daithi wanted to destroy it. He won't fight you for it."

"He is not the only one to be concerned about."

"I do not think the king cares enough, I mean, he has great wealth without the book. 'Tis the others who prospered. Daithi's given up and gone home, though. No, Maither Brigid, I do not think there is cause for alarm. You do not need to send the book back, if that's what you're thinking."

"It is."

Aine felt her shoulders droop. "I won't bother you further then."

Brigid's trepidation still showed in her expression. "Stay until the danger has passed. Please."

"There is no danger. You are beginning to sound like my uncle."

Fianna entered the guesthouse and began to refresh the rush floor with a small wooden rake. Exasperated by being ignored by everyone, Aine's temper flared. She pointed at the guesthouse worker. "She follows me day and night."

Fianna looked up.

"And besides that, the others mock me for tending the fire when you yourself have done it."

Fianna's eyes went wide, as though this was news to her.

"I apologize if anyone here has caused you discomfort, Aine." Brigid glared at Fianna and then pointed to the door. The woman hurried out.

"'Tis not just that." Aine flung herself to her cot. "I long to see my mother's people, and Cillian will not tell me where they are."

Brigid pulled her into an embrace. "Oh, Aine. No one understands that better than I do. You are grasping for the wrong things."

"You found your mother. You brought her to live with you."

"Aine, listen to me. Looking for happiness will not bring it about. Not until the seeker returns to her own house. Fulfillment cannot be had in a distant land." Brigid rubbed her temples, drew in a breath, and then screwed up her face the way she might when lecturing a room full of novices. "If you have trouble when you leave, you won't outrun it. It follows you wherever you go. True pleasure and contentment must be found in your own heart, in the face of the trials of life, Aine." Brigid fingered the cross around her neck, her eyes sparkling with tears. "From the Giver of life comes joy. Please consider that, whether or not you return to your betrothed, your home is in this land with the people who love you."

"My uncle?"

"And me."

"I am grateful. Truly I am. But I know my mother's people are poor and desperately hungry, and I want to help them."

"And Cillian forbids you to do so because he fears you will be treated as you were when you were a young, afflicted child?"

"He does."

"I can understand his concern for you." She stared a moment at the rafters. "We cannot let these people go hungry. 'Twould not be right."

"You'll help me?"

"We will do whatever we can. Let me look into the matter, won't you? I do not like to hear of a people with no food." She brushed Aine's hair from her eyes.

"You really are the kind Brigid that everyone says you are, the same as you were when I was a wee lass."

She wrapped her arms around Brigid's neck, causing her to lose her balance and kick something on the floor as she steadied herself. Reaching down with one hand, she retrieved from within the rushes the sheet of vellum Aine had tried to hide. "What's this?"

Aine snatched it from her hand. Fianna's sweeping had dug it up. "'Tis my private writing."

"Ah, 'tis good that you are still writing. May I see?"

Aine held tightly to it. "Private. You understand." She willed her face to relax. "'Tis my feelings I've penned. The things I cannot tell Daithi." She sucked in a breath. It was never good to weave a lie you might not later be able to escape.

"And would you care to be telling me why you cannot allow him to know what's on your heart?" Brigid bit her lip. She obviously realized that her earlier probing had almost caused Aine to flee from her.

Aine backed away, squeezing the parchment in both hands. It turned coal hot and she dropped it.

Brigid retrieved the piece, seemingly undisturbed by its burning. "This doesn't look like your writing, Aine. 'Tis a much older script." She unrolled it. "A genealogy." She fingered the rough edges. "You tore this from the book, didn't you?" The infliction in her voice rose.

Aine stared wordless, like a child caught with stolen cakes. Whenever she tried to lie, it never worked. She was a terrible thief as well.

Brigid stood. "I will find out, sure enough. I'll take it to Cillian."

"Nay!" Aine fell to the ground like an obstinate child.

Brigid was unmoved. "You stay here. I will not renege on my promise to help your mother's people. Trust me." She embraced Aine, then stepped back. "I will return." She opened the guesthouse door and nearly tripped over Fianna, who had apparently been listening with an ear to the door.

Aine picked up her bag and pushed through the door on her way to the scriptorium. When she got there, she bemoaned her lack of a plan. Brigid would give the page to Cillian and tell him he'd been right about her. He had always said Aine would do what she could to get whatever she wanted. They would conspire against her, but it was not Brigid's fault. Men had a way of maneuvering women toward their point of view. Aine headed to the pagan fire. The gods who dwelt there had surely sensed the power of the book. She would petition their help. She didn't know how—no one had taught her the ways of the country people—but she had to try.

Fourteen

"The horse with the most scars kicks the highest."

Irish proverb

Druim Craig, the Ridge of Clay, was Ardan's ultimate destination. He preferred to call the region by its ancient name, rather than Cill Dara, the name Brigid had given it. His arrival would need to be well timed. He would first visit the Uí Náir clan to find out about this book of theirs.

He had driven his own chariot out of Armagh, a gift from the bishop that had been blessed and entrusted to the doing of God's work. The horse? Well, the lame-minded man had forgotten to give him one, but Ardan had taken the bishop's best. "I'm to give him a good run," he'd told the stable boy. "The bishop trusts his best horse only to a holy man." The statement must have convinced him because the lad readily handed the beast over. Christians! They were so easily fooled there was almost no pleasure in it. Almost.

There was no doubt when Ardan arrived in Uí Náir territory. The fields were more lush and greener than others he had driven past. The grazing land was fertile, and therefore so must the cattle be. There was great wealth here. He liked that.

Ardan slowed his rig. Barley fields and pastures stretched as far as his eye could see. Here and there, herds of brown cows meandered. Black bulls bolted about in another pasture. The road he traveled on was well-worn, so surely it led to the castle. He continued on, coveting the prosperity all around him. How much he could take from them, only the gods knew, but he was confident the spirits would reward him.

Two farmers trekked toward him on the road, picking their way with long staffs. When Ardan was close enough, he greeted them. "Blessings on you, my sons."

They lifted their caps. The older one spoke. "Welcome, Father. On your way to see the king?"

"I am. Might you know if he's in residence?"

The elder farmer tipped his chin. "He is, indeed. I saw his colors flying just this morn. Got business with him, do you?"

"God's business." Ardan carefully crossed his chest with his fingers.

"Nothing but," the younger one put in. "All about us is Jesu's business."

More Christians! What had happened to Ireland since Ardan left? This new religion had to be slowed if he was going to be successful. Yet, here he was dressed as a priest and appearing to promote their Jesu wherever he went. He would revert back to his true identity as a high druid before speaking to the king. He was tired of the farce.

"Blessings on your day." He steered past the men.

"Thank you, Father," they called after him.

Curses was more like it. Curses on their day!

As he ascended a small rise, a stone castle within a hill fort came into view. Two parallel earthen ramparts encircled the fortress. He would ride through them within the hour.

Doubts began to shadow his thoughts. Just how many Christians were there in this tribe? If there were very many, the talisman might not be as treasured as he had thought. Jesu's followers revered only specific books, usually written in Latin. He drew a hand to his forehead, surprised that he had not thought of it before. Perhaps the book *was* Christian in nature. They called them Bibles. Monks created them with stylus and ink in buildings called scriptoriums. He'd learned that from his exile among them. He shook his head, flinging his gray locks free from his ecclesiastical cap. Even if the object did contain a mere genealogy, the king would pay dearly to have it back, Christian or not. Kings need to prove entitlement to their castles and grazing land. Once Ardan had the book in hand, he could ask for Brigid and her entire community in exchange. Such a wee concession should not prove to be problematic for such a wealthy ruler. The deal would be simple to achieve, not even requiring a powerful druid's influence. Easy.

Ardan tilted his head back and cackled toward the sky. What a delight to hatch such a perfect plan. Certainly, there

157

would be a war on a small scale, and Brigid would be taken prisoner. Then he would exile *her*, perhaps to a place like the Skellig rocks or to one of the frozen islands in the northern sea. Once she was gone, he would lead her followers in the old ways. Return Ireland to its ancient purpose. A flawless plan.

Ardan traded his robes for his druid cloak before he reached the outskirts of the royal residence. Even this he'd had to steal because he had nothing left of his old things. He wished for a torque, but the druid he took the robe from was of a lower order and had no gold. There was a time when Ardan would never have done such a thing—not by his own hand. Now, slashing another man's throat came easily to him. One thing he'd learned during his captivity was that a man had to do whatever was needed for survival. There were no rules in the Land of the Picts, no one to hold him to a brotherhood's code. Each man to his own. He was glad to be away from a place where he could not anticipate others' actions. He longed to regain his standing in Ireland where he knew how he must conduct himself. And there was no dubiety for him when it came to doing what was necessary.

How well he remembered his exploits in the Land of the Picts, though he wished not to.

"Have you no mercy?" one victim had wailed at him during one of his rampages.

"None," he had replied.

"But I've done nothing to you," the man had countered.

"I must be one degree more brutal than anyone else," Ardan had said. "I cannot gain the upper hand if I am not. And if I am two or three degrees more cruel, there will be no one in this land who will dare try to stop me."

158

He shivered now beneath the white robe. He had feared the Picts, but thank the gods, he had not encountered the most barbaric of them during his escape. Such savagery no one here had seen. It hardened a man.

He studied his hands a moment, wondering if the blood of those he'd slain would stain them. He quickly pulled his arms behind his waist. Nonsense. Now that he was back in his homeland where his gods resided, he could call on them to change him into whatever shape he wished and flee from any danger he encountered. He pulled his hands out again and studied them, turning them over and back. His palms were white, and yet shadows of blood seemed to hover over them, echoes of what he'd done.

He stashed his horse and chariot behind a grove of holly and then approached the castle.

"Who goes there?" a sentry called from somewhere on the castle wall.

"Ardan, druid of the highest order."

"What's your business?"

Come down here and ask me. Ardan glared at the man until the soldier lost his balance and began to wobble. Another man attempted to come to his aide, but the sentry tumbled and fell before help could reach him. After much scurrying around, a soldier wearing a leather helmet met him. "We can arrest you for provoking that injury," he barked.

"Arrest me?" Ardan stood close enough to smell the soldier's sour breath. "That never would have happened if your king still had possession of his book."

The watchman grabbed Ardan's arm and twisted it painfully behind his back.

"I alone, a great druid, can see that this book is returned to this kingdom. Tell your king, if you value your life." Ardan silently pleaded to the gods to change his shape. A pulling sensation burned at his chest. His arms sprouted black feathers and then they disappeared, leaving his arms white. He resisted the soldier's grip as best he could, but he could neither free himself nor change his shape.

He realized that it might be the will of the gods that he go with this solider to see the king. He ceased struggling.

Ardan was taken swiftly for an audience with King Donal. The king sat on an elevated chair, his silk robes dripping from his shoulders like a jeweled waterfall. Ardan had never seen such splendor. Even the curtains were woven from the finest purple cloth. The king held out a ruby-topped scepter and Ardan touched it respectfully.

"Are you the druid who caused my sentry injury?"

"I assure you, Your Majesty, I was a great distance from the man when he fell."

"Distance has not prevented druids from inflicting injury before. Why did you do this?"

"'Twas a matter of disrespect."

"But you did not wish him dead."

The man was still alive. Ardan would have to state that the man's survival had been his intention. "Respect can be learned, King Donal. He deserves a second chance."

The king bobbed his bejeweled head and smoothed his long, yellow beard with one hand. "I hear you have business with me, something to do with a book."

"Not just any book, King Donal. I am here to assist you in retrieving your talisman."

The man's eyes went wide. The delight on his face told Ardan that he wanted nothing more. Ardan paced the stone-tiled floor in front of the king. "Of course, I'll need more

160

information since I have never seen this book. What does it contain?"

King Donal waved golden-clad fingers in front of his face. "Matters not the words inside," he said. "The book has the power of wealth. Without it, what you see today in my kingdom will wither away. My own druids have not been able to retrieve it. I have already ordered my army to prepare for war. What can you do for me that my army cannot?"

Ardan twirled his own beard between his fingers. "I have intimate knowledge that will help you. No one knows the abbess who guards the book better than I do."

"She is your wife?"

Ardan laughed, holding to his side. He had never heard anything so ridiculous. "I do not mean I know her in that way, Your Majesty."

"This amuses you?" The king slammed his scepter on the hard floor, sending a reverberation across the room, up the walls, and to the windows where pigeons fluttered out. Donal's face turned crimson. "Get to it, man. I have no time for games."

"Forgive me." Ardan bowed, if only to regain his composure. "Let me say that I know what this woman values, how she thinks, what motivates her. I am able to get inside her mind, thus helping your warriors break down the fortress that hides your book, both physical and spiritual barriers."

The king was quiet for a while, no doubt pondering Ardan's words. He motioned to another man, who leaned in close for a consultation. They would take Ardan up on his offer. They had not yet retrieved the book themselves, so obviously they needed assistance.

"What price do you require to depart this intimate knowledge, Druid?"

"What I want is simple." He lifted his palms in a display of trustworthiness. "I have no army of my own. Although my powers are great, there is one thing I need your help with."

The king stood, clearly a man of impatience. "Speak your deal, man."

"After your warriors invade Cill Dara—with the spiritual protection I will summon, of course—I require the safe delivery of Brigid of Cill Dara to me."

"That is all?"

"That is all, Your Majesty."

It was the king's turn to pace. He wiggled his fingers behind his back and stomped across the hard floor, his metal-tipped shoes clacking loudly. "How am I to know you possess great powers? More will be required than just causing a man to fall from his lookout."

Ardan cast out his hand, and the torches on the walls burst into exploding flames. "Apparently your own druids are not of the highest order or you would have taken the book back already."

King Donal held a hand over his mouth. This pleased Ardan to no end. Finally, the royal man spoke again. "The book is extremely valuable. Many a man has wished to keep it for himself. How do we know we can trust you?"

Ardan bowed low in front of him. "If I do not deliver what I promise, you may take my life. Ask your own druids about my words. 'Tis an honor pledge I am duty-bound to keep."

Donal consulted with his attendant again. Then he pointed at Ardan. "Your name?"

When he spoke it, the attendant's face revealed surprise. They whispered again.

"You were exiled, were you not?" the king asked.

"To the Land of the Picts, a place so horrible no one ever returns. No one. Except me."

More whispering, and then the king sent his consult away.

"We have an agreement," the king said.

fifteen

"A lie travels farther than the truth."
Irish proverb

Aine was relieved to learn that Brigid's scouts saw no army thus far. They had gone as far as King Donal's castle and discovered that the king and his army were still in residence there. Now she could focus on her mission.

"Daithi's gone," she whispered into the wash water as she splashed it on her face.

"Is that what you're thinking?"

Aine spun around. Fianna stood with one hand on a broom and the other at her waist, or where a waist would be if she didn't have such a boyish frame. "He's still here, lassie."

"Daithi? How do you know this?"

The sister made a show of sweeping. "Oh, I know things, I do. Heard the abbess speaking to him."

As much as she didn't want help from this nosey woman, Aine wanted to know when Daithi would leave. "What did they say, then, if you know so much?"

"He said you love him, and there's no one here that can say you don't."

"There's me."

Fianna tossed a curl from her face. "Are you saying you're not fond of the handsome lad?"

A twinge of jealousy sparked in Aine. "Just tell me, is he about to leave?"

Fianna turned away and pretended to work. "I suppose he is. Maither Brigid plans to send him and Brother Cillian on their way. Said if they won't help you on your…what did she call it?" Fianna rested her broom and snapped her fingers. "Ah, that's it. Your quest. If they won't help you, she will, especially now that the watches say Cill Dara is safe."

Aine leaned against the doorframe. "And Daithi was satisfied enough to leave?"

"I suppose he was. The Poet told him Cill Dara was your sanctuary. There's nothing he can do about it. The book is not his battle to fight."

Odd choice of words. "Do you think the king will let the book go, then?"

Fianna shrugged. "I would not be knowing that. But you are free to go. And bless the saints, the abbess is determined to go with you."

Fianna seemed almost eager for Aine to leave. She'd get her wish. If Aine could not take the book to her mother's people, at least she would have Brigid with her. Brigid could feed the hungry. The whole island knew about her magic. And feeding them was the first thing to be done. The book was powerful, and eventually Aine would have to come back for it, but she didn't need it right away.

"Are you sure you remember the way, Maither Brigid?" They had just settled into the oxcart and secured their things.

"Oh, aye. I have instructed Brian. Don't worry, Aine. We have the finest driver in Cill Dara. He used to work for my father so he knows the roads quite well."

Aine smiled at the man who tipped his cap to her. "Do we have enough food?" They had packed crates of hazelnuts, barrels of cream, blocks of cheese, and other provisions, but what if there were too many mouths to feed? What if Brigid had lost her ability to conjure miracles in order to feed the poor? Aine closed her eyes and drew in a breath. Somehow she must trust…the gods? Brigid's god? She tried not to think about the things she knew nothing about. Brigid said she would help, and so she would.

"God provided this much bounty." Brigid waved her arms over the cargo. "How much more will He give to those who ask Him?"

"You are going to ask the people to join your community? To pray to your god?"

"Oh, my, Aine. I will have no conditions. God does not work that way. All I am doing is what Jesu asks of me. Feed the hungry. Pray for the unfortunate. Be Christ's hands and feet. What they believe and whom they trust is up to them."

Aine wished she could be sure the people would prosper, but at least some would not starve. She had no choice but to trust the abbess.

They rode on through the day, singing and talking until they had nothing else to say. Then Brigid took up her needle and a vestment she said she needed to work on, although Aine didn't know what for. She'd never seen the abbess wear anything other than unadorned garb. Aine snuggled beneath a fleece and slept.

When she awoke she heard the rushing sound of water. "We are near Aghade."

"Oh, we've a bit to go," Brigid said. "'Tis just the deepest part of the river. We have to wait for the quiet water before we cross. Do you remember this road, child?"

"Of course. You healed me on this road, Maither Brigid."

"God healed you."

"As you say."

Brigid let her needlework fall to her lap, a faraway look in her eyes. "God healed you, and do not take that for granted. Just because God did something in the past, doesn't mean it will be repeated. This life comes with no assurances."

Aine wanted to say something. It was obvious to everyone that Brigid's god had blessed her. A cloud drifted over them and blocked the sun, and soon, sprinkles of rain coated their faces. Gone were the happy songs and assurances that all would be well. Brigid now seemed doubtful. Aine wondered if she had made an enormous mistake by leaving that book behind.

Aine leaned out of the rig and let the wind caress her face. She thought about the Lebor na Uí Náir, Daithi's tribe's book, and the power she felt whenever she held it.

"Worried about your people, are you?" Brigid's words startled Aine.

"I am. I have always worried about my mother."

"I will pray for them."

"Thank you, Maither Brigid."

When they reached the last dwelling before Cillian's hideaway monastery, Brigid urged Aine to wait in the rig. "We don't know what kind of greeting we will get. An abbess will be best received, I think."

Aine squared her shoulders. "I know how to handle myself."

"Aye, but if I'm to help you, child, you will follow my wishes."

Aine dropped back to her fleece and let out a defeated sigh. She watched as a man met Brigid and Brian at the door. "We've no room for travelers. Best move along."

Brigid was not to be deterred. "A word, sir."

He shut the door behind him and came out to the yard, eyeing his hog as though they'd steal it.

"We are looking for someone."

"I don't know anyone."

Brigid let out a frustrated groan. "You live alone?"

"Wife and child, that's all. You should run along now. 'Twill be getting dark."

The sad wail of a child wafted over the thatched roof. Brigid inclined her head toward the sound. "I hear crying. May I help?"

"The child complains whenever her mother works. She'll settle down."

"Is she hungry? We'd be glad to share some food."

Aine gasped. Was Brigid going to give away their store? And after she had just admitted that the providence of her god could not be depended upon? Their driver, Brian, stood soldier still with his hands behind his back. Aine gripped the side of the cart so tightly her knuckles turned moon pale.

The man pulled his straw hat from his head then and lowered his eyes. "That would be very generous. I will fetch my wife." He walked around the outside of his hut toward the crying sound.

Brigid hurried to the cart and began flinging lids off barrels and scooping grain and nuts and cheese into her outstretched cloak as Brian supported the bounty with his hands.

"What are you doing?" Aine squealed, jumping from the cart bed. "That's for my mother. Uh, not her, but her people. Put it back!"

"Trust in the Lord to provide, child. He always does."

"But you said—"

"Never mind what I said."

Aine slinked back and watched. There was nothing she could do but hope the abbess wouldn't give it all away. The man returned with a woman who wore a plaid scarf tightly around her head. A whimpering child nestled in her arms. Brigid approached them and nodded toward the food in the pocket she'd made from her cloak. "Can you use this?"

The woman's face brightened, and the child began squirming. "Why would you give us food?" the woman asked.

"I do Jesu's work here on earth, the things He used to do when He walked here with us. He wants you to have this food."

The woman pointed to the rear of the hut. "I have a large loom back there between two thick oak trees. I work all day, so long as there is sunlight, so my family can eat, and you have brought us more food than I can work for in a week."

The man produced a reed basket and Brigid deposited her gift. She lifted the child from the woman's arms and turned toward Aine. "We know what it is like to yearn for a mother." She turned back to the wee family. "This child only wants her mother's attention. Tell her a story while I work your loom for a time." She handed the child back, and she nuzzled her downy head against her mother's shoulder.

Brigid left with them, and Brian returned to the oxcart.

Aine, feeling a bit humbled by Brigid's words, sunk down low in the back. "How long will this take?"

Brian patted the ox, and the beast huffed. "As long as it takes, I suppose."

Sometime after Aine lifted the lids on the bins and baskets and discovered them still full, the abbess returned. "Maither Brigid, you've done it. What a marvelous thing!"

"What are you talking about?" Brigid's eyes shadowed, and her shoulders slumped with fatigue. She climbed in and spread the fleece over her legs.

"'Tis as if you took nothing from the stores of food. Look for yourself."

Brian lifted the barrel lids, smiled, and then locked them tightly down, returning to his driver's seat.

Brigid shifted until she found a comfortable position. "I do not need to look, Aine."

Aine snuggled in next to her before Brian pulled away. "Of course you don't. You know what powers you have. You will surely bring my family wealth."

171

Brigid sat up. "Wealth? Is that what you think I'm about? Bringing wealth?"

"Of course." Aine laid her head in Brigid's lap and closed her eyes.

Sixteen

"For our struggle is not against flesh
and blood, but against the rulers,
against the authorities, against the
powers of this dark world and against
the spiritual forces of evil in the
heavenly realms."

Ephesians 6:12 NIV

C illian greeted them with open arms. Aine never ceased
to be amazed at how concealed in the woods monks'
huts were, like homes for pine martins. She wondered if that
wee family they'd just left even knew they were there. Philib,
Cillian's oldest friend and fellow monk, greeted her with a

peck on her cheek and led the travelers to the old dining rock where he had laid out bread and broth.

"'Tis been too long," old Philib said to Brigid. "I was engaged in deep study when you were here before and missed you. You must come by more often."

"God willing, I shall do that." Brigid blessed the meal before they ate.

Aine tried to be polite, but she was eager to move on. She could not be with her mother now, but the next best thing had to be her relatives. Somehow, she thought they'd embrace her. She hoped they would. And by bringing them food they'd certainly want her to stay among them. She choked back the emotion that rose suddenly to her throat. Not a foster family, not an uncle who felt obligated, not a husband who had not chosen her. These people would be hers because they shared a lineage. Such things were important. Even the king thought so because he wanted to preserve his printed genealogy. She did not know if she could bear any more delay.

Brigid and Aine finally retired to their old lean-to, the very one Aine had lived in and once shared with Brigid years ago when Brigid brought Aine to live with her uncle. The monks called it the guesthouse now, though they admitted they never had any guests.

They settled in, but Aine could not relax. She tossed back and forth all night, and when morning came, she felt as though she hadn't slept at all. She had fared better when she slept away from everyone that night she'd crept back to Cillian's place alone. No one had known she was there then until the poet spotted her.

Brigid swept out the shelter with a branch broom. "I remember the feeling."

"What feeling?" Aine's fingers shook as she struggled with the laces at the neck of her tunic.

Brigid left her sweeping to help. "Going back to a place where you were not wanted. I returned to my father's home many years after he attempted to give me away to the king of Leinster."

Aine smoothed down her rumpled garment and turned to face Brigid. "I didn't know."

"It was before I founded Cill Dara. The king set me free, of course. That's when I met you." She leaned against the center branch that held the shelter up as though she couldn't bear the weight of the memory without support.

"When you returned home, did you have any trouble? Making the journey, I mean?" Aine wondered what obstacles might lay ahead of them. She wanted to get to her old home as soon as possible.

"No trouble, but well I remember the dread that sank in my stomach like a rock dropped into the middle of Lough Leane. I got through it, though. And so will you."

Aine didn't tell Brigid that she sensed it would be better for her. Her father had rejected her but that meant nothing. There were cousins, aunts, uncles. Plenty of kin waiting to meet her.

They scooted out into the morning mist just as a wolf called in the distance. A bad omen, hearing a wolf call on the morning of a journey. Aine held a damp hand to her cheek, trying to calm herself, but it was no use. "We should not have left the book behind." Aine tugged at Brigid's cloak.

"Now, now, child."

Aine's frantic complaining brought Cillian to them. "'Tis as I feared." He shook his round head. "She trusts the talisman."

"What are you talking about, man?" Brigid pulled Aine behind her as if protecting her from Cillian's accusations.

"Can't you see? She is terrified without it." He leaned over to look into Aine's eyes. "Just what have you seen, child, that makes you fear being without the book? Have you seen dark magic? Or the workings of a druid?"

Aine wanted to refute what he said, but all she could do was stare at him, wide-eyed. She *had* seen magic.

"We won't be staying." Brigid pushed Aine toward the oxcart. She whispered something to Cillian about everyone needing to keep an eye out.

Brian was already waiting, and they rode off, forsaking Philib's meager meal to break their fast. Aine was happy they did not delay, but what had caused Brigid to behave this way?

Cillian lifted his arms as they rode away from him. "Beware! You might not recognize the shifty wizard. Beware!"

Aine whispered to the abbess. "What has alarmed him?" He did not know about the power of the book. If he had, his warning might have made sense.

Brigid put an arm around her. "I had to tell him. The druid he fears has returned."

"The book." Aine bolted upright. "We must get it."

"We have the words we need right here." Brigid pointed to her chest. "I have hidden His words in my heart. Never fear, Aine. The Word goes with us."

The journey would proceed without the book. It had to be enough.

Brian was traveling at a high speed. She wondered about Brigid's belief. Was believing in the power of something as good as holding it in your hands? The page had glowed without the book. Perhaps she too glowed with a magic that had rubbed off on her from carrying it. The reasoning seemed sound. The cattle had been blessed just by drinking water the book had touched. She didn't know, however, how long this fortune would follow her. They must hurry.

After they crossed at the ford, Aine's stomach tightened again. The druid did not much concern her, although she did not wish to anger his gods. Yearning for her mother had filled her thoughts most of her life, but she had buried deep any memories of her father. He had once wished to kill her because of her horrific disease. She had overheard Brigid and Cillian talking about it when she was young, but she had not thought about her father causing trouble today, at least not until they were well on their way.

When Aine was a child, Brigid was forced to run away in order to protect her. The abbess fed the poor back then, and she'd called down powers to heal Aine of her infliction, but she had not stood up to Aine's father, a man whose name she could not even remember. They'd fled, avoiding conflict. Now, with Brigid and the influence of Daithi's tribe's book, there should be nothing to fear, just as Brigid had said.

As logical as that sounded, Aine could not calm her troubled spirit.

As they passed through a tunnel of yews, Aine turned to the abbess who had both hands outstretched, clinging to the sides of the rig to steady herself. "Maire, that was my mother's name, wasn't it?"

"'Twas indeed." Brigid turned sad eyes toward her. "You must understand, child. Your mother was poor and she cared for the ill. Death often takes the finest folks too early.

Your mother is gone. Surely others as well. We must prepare ourselves for what we might find at that village."

Aine pursed her lips and tipped her head. There had to be someone left. She could feel it.

"Even with the worse of outcomes, child, 'twill be an important pilgrimage for you. You will see where you came from, and if God allows, talk to people your mother helped. Such journeys as this often serve to reveal God's purpose for one's life."

Aine didn't know what she meant, but said nothing. She was bringing the famous Brigid to her people, the same woman that the people of the woods had chased after on the day she and Aine escaped to Aghade. Everyone wanted a blessing from her then. How much more so now? With that kind of support, her father or anyone like him, would be outmatched.

Much later, a raven cawed from somewhere beyond the yews. Another bad sign. Aine wished she had asked for a druid's blessing before making the journey, but that hadn't been possible at Cill Dara and certainly not at Aghade. Hopefully the Christian blessing would be enough.

Aine trembled as a cool breeze blanketed her. She crept toward the front of the rig. Brian drove faster now that the sun was beginning to set. "Brian." She whispered, trying not to disturb the abbess, who appeared to be taking a nap. "Do you know the way well enough to avoid the *Sidhe*? We'll not be wanting to traipse over their mounds." The people of the hills who lived underground frightened her and always had. No matter that she'd never seen them. She'd felt them. If bad spirits opposed their journey, they'd be finished before even finding out what her father might try to do.

"Nothing to worry about there, child," he called back.

She sank back to her place and called out under her breath. "Sidhe, grant us safe passage. We bring no harm."

Brian slowed as they approached a narrow passage between two rocky outcrops. A hefty raven sat on one of the rocks, still visible in the low light. When the rig drew close to the bird, it did not move. The creature seemed to stare directly at Aine. Brigid did not stir from her sleep. When they passed by, Aine turned to look at the shiny black bird again. She had never seen one so tame. There was something else particular, a gray streak on the side of its head.

"Turn, back, Brian. Turn back!"

Her ranting startled the abbess awake, and Brian pulled up on the horse's reins until they came to a stop.

"Whatever is the matter, child?" Brigid gripped her by the shoulders.

Tears streaked down Aine's cheeks. "Please, Maither Brigid. I've a very bad feeling. Let's go back to Cill Dara."

"But your quest. 'Twill do you good to complete it. You will not abandon it because you're fearful of what you will find, will you? Did you not hear what I told you?"

"I heard, but I will. I must." She clamped her hands on the abbess's forearms while she still held tight to Aine's shoulders, feeling her pulse pounding in her throat. She forced out words in pant. "Please….I can't…breathe. Take me back to…sanctuary, Maither!"

With a nod from Brigid, Brian turned the rig around and they returned the way they had come. The bird had gone.

Much later, under the stars, they passed safely through the gates of Cill Dara. Aine breathed a sigh of relief. They'd had to drive through the dark forest, but with Brian's persistence, they arrived safely.

She had been foolish to put so much distance between herself and the book. Aine belonged to the book now, as she had once belonged to Daithi. Even if she wanted to flee from it, she could not.

In the warmth of the guesthouse's peat fire, Brigid covered Aine's trembling shoulders with a plaid blanket. "I know how you feel."

"You can't know." Aine noticed the dejected look on Brigid's face. "I do appreciate what you've done for me, Maither Brigid. But I am not you. Things are different. They're just different, is all."

Brigid rose to leave. "Different. Aye." She scooted out into the black night, as quiet as a ribbon of smoke rising from a fire.

Aine breathed in the comforting smell of the smoldering peat. She would find her purpose on a quest, all right, but the book would have to come with her next time.

Ninnidh remained at Cill Dara with a niggling feeling that the abbess would need him. And now that she had returned, he would continue to keep an eye out for Ardan for her sake.

Word had spread quickly, even in the late hour, that the abbess and her young charge had abandoned their journey and come back. From the inside of the guesthouse, he'd heard the iron gates open and the sound of a chariot racing in. By the time he got outside, there was no one about. The rig must have driven directly to the stables. He walked the grounds for an hour at least, hoping to find out if the druid might have had something to do with Brigid's return, but no one wandered about, and he didn't want to disturb those sleeping.

He prayed and hummed and enjoyed the solitude. *If you need me, God, I'm here and willing.*

A raven lit on a branch overhanging the path. Odd to see such a creature in the dark half of the day. A hooded form crouched in the crisp leaves below it. When Ninnidh drew closer he realized it was Brigid.

She turned when he approached. "Ninnidh, that bird…"

The raven didn't flinch.

She stared up at the creature. "It hasn't moved or cawed or even twitched."

He waved his arms, but the bird stayed put. "Come on. 'Tis chilly out. I'll walk you to your dwelling."

She rose with his help, but stiffly. "Ninnidh, the bird spoke to me."

"Did it?"

"I know it sounds ridiculous, but it did. It said, 'You have no purpose here. Leave.'" She heaved like the air had been knocked from her lungs.

"You have purpose here. That much is very plain to see. Do not let disparaging thoughts overtake your mind, Brigid. Is there something else bothering you? Any word about the druid?"

"None. We returned because Aine is more fearful than I had realized. She needs us." Brigid turned back to glance again at the bird and then she turned away, leaning against him as they walked. "You must check on Cillian at Aghade,

Ninnidh. I warned him, but now I feel that Ardan might be near."

"It shall be done. Let's get you to your shelter right now."

Clouds covered the starlight and then rain began to pelt them, growing more intense once her cell came into sight. It was easy to question where God was on such a gloomy night. He hoped that was not what Brigid was thinking. She'd expressed doubts before, and now the odd belief that a bird had spoken to her. She was weary.

Just as he reached for the door latch, she spun around and lifted her face to the driving rain. "Nay. Go away! Get behind me, Satan!"

"Oh, child. Let me help you." The voice belonged to Brocca, although Ninnidh could hardly see her in the darkness.

He edged the door open wider and motioned to the abbess. "Hurry inside." He secured the door behind them by leaning his weight against it, fighting the force of what had become a storm. Catching his breath before he had to go back out and return to the men's guesthouse, he paused.

He heard Brigid's mother's voice from somewhere deep inside the dark shelter. "You are not alone. You are never alone. Has God not ordained you a bishop? Do you not have a calling to teach, guide, and protect His sheep? You shall not run from that, child."

Ninnidh forced open the door and slipped outside, praying that Brocca would be more successful in calming Brigid than he'd been. He shielded his face from the rain until he reached the spot where he had found Brigid. He glanced up at the low branch where the raven had sat. It was gone. A vision? A dream? The bird reminded him of Ardan, a menacing, crafty fellow. The druid did hop about somewhat like a bird as well. Blinking the rain from his eyes, he continued on his way.

As he shook the rain from his hood outside his door, he realized such thoughts served to corrupt. He must not allow them. Saying a blessing upon his entry and again on his nighttime slumber, Ninnidh pledged that, if the druid were indeed near, he would be able to protect the abbess. He was not sure how he might do that and still obey her wish to visit the monks in the woods. Perhaps Brigid had conceived this plan because she didn't want Ninnidh to stay. She could have sent a messenger.

Reclining with his hands folded across his chest, he at last had time to consider the day's events. The sting of rejection was palpable. Why, if she did not want him there, was he so inclined to stay? It would be easier on his heart to leave, to turn his thoughts to work. When he closed his eyes the image of the raven filled his mind. He knew with certainty that his wounded ego was not what mattered. The more light that shone on evil, the less power it would have.

Seventeen

"The lying man has promised
Whatever thing he could,
The greedy man believes him,
And thinks his promise good."

Old Irish saying recorded by Douglas Hyde

Ardan stood in the shadows at the edge of the road and watched the Uí Náir warriors march by, spears straight, iron and bronze heads polished to a shine. Each one wore a long shirt belted at the waist, and some had daggers stowed there. Many carried a long pelt over their shoulders that would serve as a nighttime bed cover in the forest. Most all had stiffened their hair with lime and groomed their beards meticulously. It was a prideful army and a strong one.

A wee clump of meek Christians would be no match for them.

Ardan kept pace with those in front, but hung back in the woods where his black feather cloak would help disguise him. The men had been told a powerful druid would accompany them, albeit from the shadows.

Unfortunately, there were women among the entourage, some warriors, and others serving the army by cooking and tending to injuries. The women made Ardan nervous because they questioned his presence more frequently than the men did, and they talked among themselves. That was the most disturbing. He would know their secrets in time, but now he found their nattering disquieting. Another display of power would be necessary very soon to keep them in line.

He paused to study the army. He made note of their leather helmets, their bull-hide corslets, their heavily oiled leather greaves protecting their lower legs. Most carried shields, although such protection would be unnecessary unless the monastery called in another kingdom's army, and there had been no time for that. Cill Dara had no weapons of their own capable of causing significant injury to these fighters, he knew. No monastery ever did. He glanced again at his palms and then rubbed them together furiously. The memory of blood was ever present. As soon as he had time, he would attempt a spell to get rid of it. He was pleased he now had an army to do the distasteful work.

He turned his focus back to the marching men. No army could be better primed to help Ardan achieve his goal.

"Halt!" came a voice at the front of the line.

Ardan scurried forward, his feathers making a rustling noise against the faded green leaves in the wood. "Why are you stopping?" Ardan shouted at the commander. "We have far to go."

The commander, a man with thick red hair mounded up with lime in the same fashion as his soldiers, glared at him. "We are stopping because I cannot march this army without feeding them."

Women scurried about in the open meadow like mice, gathering firewood and unpacking barrels of food.

Even though Ardan's own stomach rumbled with hunger, he despised this delay. He climbed onto the low branches of an oak that spread over the west edge of the meadow like the arms of a protective grandmother. From there, he observed the activity and listened in on some cooks who hadn't noticed his perch.

"We'll have no trouble getting the book back," one cackled.

A lass with perfectly plaited hair save wiggly strands at her temples stood up and stretched. She placed her hands to her back as though it caused her discomfort. There was something familiar about her. She stretched her long pale arms out in front of her. "Our warriors won't be getting their grimy hands on my father's book."

Her father's book? Who was this lass? Surely the king's own daughter would not be out on a battlefield with hardened warriors.

An older woman wearing a white linen cap pointed a boney finger at the girl. "Listen here, Clare, just because you can sneak behind your father's back and charm the commander of his army doesn't mean you'll be getting into that place and snatching the book up yourself."

The lass turned toward Ardan. "I'll do whatever I please." She winked, nearly causing him to lose his balance.

The others might not have seen him there, but she had known he was there all along and had strutted in front of him like a seductress.

He would not be taken in by this or any woman's charms. He set his mind against it some time ago, but she had obviously seen him admiring her beauty. He wiggled down the far side of the tree and chided himself for letting his guard down.

He found the commander napping in the shadow of some tall rushes. Foolish man. He could have easily fallen into a bed of nettles. How could someone so lazy and careless be leading such an impressive army? Ardan would need to use his skills of persuasion to get this man to do what needed to be done.

The man stirred and held a hand over his eyes to shield the sunlight. "What do you want, Druid?"

Ardan knelt beside him. "You are commanding a fine army. I have never seen such skilled warriors."

The man rolled to his side and closed his eyes again.

"There is one thing, just one thing more, that could make this army indestructible."

The commander yawned but gave no other response.

"The men—and most of the army is comprised of men—are a bit distracted."

The commander, finally aware that Ardan would have to be heard before he could return to his nap, scratched the back of his neck and sat up. "They are finely trained. They will not be distracted by anything."

Just then laughter erupted from behind a lofty cluster of grasses. A warrior stripped of his battle gear was in deep conversation with someone bearing a female voice, but all that could be seen was the head and bare shoulders of the man. The commander scrambled to his feet and ran the lass off.

Ardan held out an arm and shrugged his shoulders. How well he knew human nature. And what perfect timing the gods had ordained.

The commander shook his head. "We needed the women for…other things, not this. We are on a mission. There is nothing more important to our kingdom than our talisman. You speak the truth, Druid. I will order all the women to return home save those who are warriors."

"Are you sure about that?"

He grunted and stomped off.

The rest of the march to Cill Dara was uneventful. Whenever the army rested, Ardan drew pictures in the dirt with a stick, mapping out his plan. *Druim Craig* was situated, as most significant establishments in Ireland were, on the top of a rise, a ridge actually, so that threats could be detected from some distance. Approaching without being seen was what Ardan did best, what this army needed him for. He'd make sure they were cloaked in secrecy. The thick woods would work to their advantage. The army would attack as planned, and Ardan would root out the abbess and steal her away. He knew how monasteries were designed. The dwelling was circular with the innermost ring housing the church, the rectory, and the abbot's dwelling. Beyond that were the cells for the faithful followers, and on the outside earthen ring, the laborers worked and lived. As soon as the outer defenses were broken, he'd rush to the core and find her. He'd learned much from the Christians that he would now use to his benefit.

On the last rest break before reaching Cill Dara, Ardan borrowed a chariot and driver and went in advance. He would be positioned and ready the moment the army broke down the walls. When the great tall crosses came into view, Ardan ordered the chariot driver to return to the camp. He would approach on foot.

The day was remarkably sunny for the season. He would have preferred cloud cover. What creature could he become that could be cloaked in bright daylight? He cursed under his breath. He'd had no time to offer a sacrifice to gain the gods' favor.

His gaze landed on a grassy hill just before the monastery border where several black cattle grazed. When he reached it, he circled around the field, careful to stay to the edges so as not to startle any herdsmen. Finally, when a calf wandered near the trees, he seized his chance and plunged his dagger into its neck. By the time the other animals bellowed out an alarm, he had drug the calf to the forest where he completed the sacrifice.

With the act finished, he hurried to a spring and scrubbed the blood from his hands. Much better. The gods were pleased because a sizeable cloud now drifted overhead, bringing much needed shade and cover.

"I saw what you did."

Ardan jumped at the voice and spun around, blade ready in his hand. The redheaded lass stood there, hands on hips.

"All the women were ordered back. You disobeyed the army commander. You will be severely disciplined."

She tilted her long neck back and laughed toward the graying sky. "Not me, Druid. My father owns the army. The commander will let me do as I wish."

She held her hands out to her side and seemed to float as she did a little dance. Her small feet were bare and her hair, freed from the braids she'd worn earlier, curled from her eyes down to her shoulders. This lass possessed the power of enchantment. If Ardan could not break from her seduction, he would be engulfed in her charms and powerless.

He turned away. "I have business here. Leave me."

"I have business too. I will retrieve the book myself. My father trusts no one else."

A burning sensation rose in Ardan's chest. The king didn't trust him and so sent a woman to do his work—a young one, at that. If Ardan could not prove to the king that his services had been necessary, the ruler would surely renege on his promise to award Ardan the abbess Brigid. He could not have that. He grasped a handful of lovely, long red hair and dragged the lass to his side. She gasped, but otherwise did not struggle. "You will leave me, as I said, or I will do to you what I just did to that calf."

Ardan ran the dull edge of his knife along the girl's soft, white neck and watched the pulsing blue veins throb beneath her skin. He almost bent to kiss her but, when he saw beads of perspiration form on the girl's forehead, he let go, knowing that his message had been received.

She faced him, hair tussled and sweaty. "Get the book then and give it to me."

He sharpened his knife on a rock. "You are hardly in a position to order me, lass."

She rubbed her neck, eyes bulging with frustration. He allowed her to seethe for a moment then stood, returning his blade to its sheath. "I see no reason why you cannot be allowed to deliver it to the king. Stay to the rear of the army. I will find you when the time is right." He glanced up, delighted to see her bite her thin, pink lip. He had frightened her just enough. She marched away.

Ardan continued toward the monastery, glancing back from time to time to look for the girl. He did not trust her to stay out of the way. She could be a spy for Brigid. One thing he was glad of. When she was not in his presence, he did not feel entranced by her beauty. When she was not in front of him, he had no trouble dismissing her from his thoughts. He would keep it that way by not giving her the book once he had it.

He slipped between the bars of the gate. The iron poles had been bent, probably from some accident with a wagon. Foolish Christians, leaving the gate in such disrepair.

Moments earlier, he had changed into his priestly robe, which allowed him to slip in among the residents unnoticed. The book would be in a secure location, the church or the scriptorium, he presumed. Ardan grabbed a waste bucket and headed to the rear of the church. As soon as he rounded the corner, he realized his mistake. The back of this building was not used for garbage. It was a burial ground. A priest would have known this. He flung the bucket away just as a couple of women turned the corner behind him. They nodded and proceeded to wander through the graves.

He watched them a moment as they placed something on one of the graves. The woven object was not of wood or fabric, but common reeds, the type used for cushioning the floor of a house. They crossed themselves from the tips of their foreheads to the middle of their chests and then from shoulder to shoulder, as he knew Christians did. Then they huddled together, reciting what Ardan recognized as one of the Psalms. He pretended to do the same, cursing silently about how long they were taking.

He glanced down one row of graves. A woven object lay on the top of each one, some new and green, and others brown with age, but all identical in shape. Some kind of charm, he supposed, although he had never seen anything like it in the Land of the Picts or even in Armagh. He retrieved one. Twirling it back and forth in his hand, he thought it resembled a wheel. Yet, there was something distinctive about the woven middle and the outstretched arms. He glanced again at the graves, but he could not discern the meaning.

His hand grew warm. He glanced at the wheel cross in his open palm. It glowed yellow and orange. He tried to drop it, but couldn't. Turning his back to the women, he shook his hand violently but could not dislodge it. The warmth spread up his arm toward his heart. He feared for his life and jumped and twisted about, but to no avail.

"Can I help you, Father?"

He turned to find a young nun with sky-blue eyes staring at him. The woven charm dropped from his hand and landed on the grave he had taken it from.

"Was it a bee?" she asked.

He pulled his arm safely up under the sleeve of his robe. "Ah, 'twas. I am fine now. Thank you for your concern."

She dipped her head and then turned toward the other women who motioned for her. "Come along, Fianna."

Ardan drew in a deep breath and tilted his head toward the high branches of the oaks. He had hoped to be unnoticed and instead had drawn attention to himself. He turned to the back wall of the church, rubbing his palms together. Whatever the magic that was, it was gone now. His hands were cool. He examined them. Pressed into his right palm was the distinct image of the charm he had dropped. He rubbed at it with his left thumb but could not erase it. He was permanently marked.

There was a small opening at the rear of the church adequately concealed by a grove of yews. He slipped in and found himself behind an altar. Why the Christians had their altars indoors, he never understood. They did not use them for animal sacrifices, he knew, but even so, if their god was god of the elements, as they claimed, why worship indoors?

Even though there wasn't much light inside, he was thankful to find the place vacant. He wiggled his hands up and down the rough-hewn stone altar, but found nothing but a book shrine, which he quickly determined did not hold the book he sought. King Donal had described it in detail, and this particular book was what the Christians called a missal. He had seen many of them.

As he placed his hands on the altar to steady himself, his right palm began to throb. He turned it over. Blinding rays blasted in his face. He turned his hand away and hurried outside. Thankfully, the burning did not follow him. Just as soon as he found that blasted Uí Náir manuscript, he would invoke his own magic and be rid of the mark.

Convinced that he would not find the book in the church, he backed away and headed toward the scriptorium.

The gods had not smiled on him, just as they hadn't during his captivity on that isolated island. Back then, he'd had to depend on his own good sense and cleverness. He would have to again.

Pausing to look at the sky, he estimated he had less than an hour until the army attacked. If he could discern where it was hidden now, during the confusion, he'd be able to whisk the treasure away.

Hiding behind a tree, he observed monks filtering in and out of the scriptorium with large pockets flung over their shoulders. They transported manuscripts to their cells for study, he guessed. None of them would be carrying the treasured book. It had to be well hidden.

A familiar voice met his ears. He turned to look down the path where two women approached. There was no mistaking the abbess, despite the fact that she was not dressed in priestly robes. Brigid always tried to appear humble, but one's nature does not change despite what god one chooses to worship. She walked with an assured air, causing his blood to sizzle. He despised her more than anyone because she never showed anger or greed. He preferred that those emotions be exposed rather than hidden. He liked knowing what was coming.

If only they were alone. So close.

Patience. Wait for the right timing.

He stooped behind an *ogham* standing stone, a sacred marker that predated the Christians' arrival. He and this stone belonged here, and soon he'd erase all the Christian trappings from *Druim Craig*. From that spot, he could hear well.

Brigid's singsong voice rang out again. "When will he return, Maither?"

Ah, she was with her beloved mother. This woman was still Brigid's weak spot, he was sure. He rubbed a hand across his chin as he thought about this. How much time had gone by? At least seven summers, surely.

They paused just paces from his hiding spot.

"Ninnidh should arrive by vigils, I expect. He went to check on Cillian."

Who was this Ninnidh? He'd be arriving shortly after the army.

"Promise me you will speak to him, Brigid. You need a friend, someone to spill your worries to."

Brigid lowered her hood then and allowed her yellow hair to flow loose. Ardan's body tensed as he thought about how much he despised her. She had outwitted him before, but by the gods, she would not have the upper hand again. His fingers twitched as he tapped the hilt of his dagger. Unfortunately, he needed her alive. She had many followers he needed on his side—a retinue to help him conquer the hearts and souls of other kingdoms. They might not follow him yet, but they would follow her. And she would very soon be under his power.

"Ouch!" A sudden pain made him shout out.

"Who's there? What's the trouble?" Brigid hurried toward him.

He could not let her see him, not yet. With one swift movement he pulled his black feather cloak from his bag and spread a shield over himself.

"'Tis only a bird, Maither," he heard Brigid say.

Footsteps echoing down the stone path told him he'd been successful. They had moved on. He shook his sore hand. She had something to do with the curse that inflicted him. This was yet another thing she would pay for.

Eighteen

"Love hath a language of his own,
A voice that goes
From heart to heart-whose mystic tone
Love only knows."

Thomas Moore

he bell calling the faithful to vigils rang out. Aine watched as several hooded figures passed her on the path to the church. She was headed to the scriptorium. There might be brothers there tending the books, but there was no possibility of them separating her from the book if it called to her. And during prayer time, there would be few people milling about anyway.

She noted the abbess and her mother coming toward her on the path, but they gave her little mind as chattered.

"Shouldn't he be here by now?" Brigid asked.

"He'll be here," her mother answered.

"Do you see Fianna anywhere?" Brocca's mention of the nosey sister gave Aine pause. She had not seen her either for some time. It seemed odd not to have her trailing about watching Aine's every move.

Brigid halted and grabbed Aine just as she was about to pass by. "Come with us."

Reluctantly, she shuffled alongside them.

Brocca grabbed her other arm and they continued on their way. "If anyone knows if he's about, she would."

Brigid clicked her tongue. "Och, that lass. Fianna is a thorn in my side, Maither."

"All the same, she would know."

As they neared the church, they stopped. The young nun was weaving her way through the sacred tree grove although she didn't seem to be headed the same way they were. Brigid called to her. "Fianna, come here, child."

The lass scurried toward them. "I'm pleased to speak with you, Maither Brigid. There is something I should tell you." She gave Aine a sideways glance.

"What is it?"

Fianna tipped her head toward Aine. "She is a guest. We should not bother her with our business."

"Please, just speak what's on your mind, Sister Fianna. We'll be late for prayers."

"I saw a priest in the graveyard earlier today."

"A priest?"

"Aye. He picked up one of the reed crosses from a grave and—"

198

"Fianna! Is this of importance to the welfare of Cill Dara?" Brigid narrowed her eyes.

"I do not know, Maither."

"I will not hear gossip. Have you not learned that?"

The petite lass bowed her head. "Aye, Maither Brigid. 'Twas just so…unusual."

"All I want to know is if Ninnidh the Poet has arrived."

So that's who she had been looking for. They should be glad he was returning to Cill Dara. His placid nature had a calming influence on everyone.

"I have heard nothing of his arrival. Neither has Etain or she would have had me inform the guesthouse servant. But the priest—"

"I've no time for this." Brigid dismissed Fianna and then massaged her temples as if she were irritated, but Aine had never known her to be. Something was amiss.

"I hear a sound," Brocca whispered.

Brigid continued to rub her head with her fingertips. "The bell calling to prayers."

"Nay. 'Tis talking. Soft words. Light footsteps. Someone is sneaking around." She pulled Aine close protectively.

In all directions, worshippers hurried past them and into the church. A dark figure seemed to cross in the shadow of a high cross, but Aine wasn't sure if she'd imagined it.

Brigid put a hand to her throat. "We are all a bit on edge. Let's go along now."

When they entered the church, Aine detached herself from Brocca and slipped into the back row of seated women, perching lightly at the end of a bench. Just before the heavy oak door closed, Aine sneaked outside.

The air filling her lungs carried the scents of holly and moss as she tried to regain her resolve. She'd been startled on the road by an overwhelming sense of dread. She needed that book.

Just as she took a step toward the footpath, someone yanked her back, pinning her against the outside wall. She recognized his scent and the roughness of his beard next to her face.

"Daithi! I thought you'd left."

"I cannot bear to be apart from you, Aine."

"You must go. Why don't you understand? I must have that book."

He pressed her so tightly against the wood-planked wall that she had no choice but to look at him. His eyes drooped, and his face paled. He was not angry, as she had supposed. "The book is nothing."

"Your king thinks otherwise, and so do the people. Look at how prosperous the kingdom has become because of that manuscript."

"If this were true, why would you take the book away?"

"You know why. You were going to destroy it. Now leave me alone." She could not wiggle free from him. She hated being weak.

His stare pierced her heart. "Don't forget what Malcolm thought about it. Your own foster father knew the book was a deterrent to the growth of Christianity."

They heard someone draw in a deep breath and turned to find Brigid standing in the church's doorway.

"Maither Brigid. I…thought…you should be at prayers." Aine realized the position she was in appeared compromising. "He caught me as I was leaving to…get some air. I told him to leave." She tried again to get away, but he didn't move. "Your workers said he'd gone."

"Go to prayers, Aine. I will have a word with Daithi."

Aine broke from the man's embrace just as soon as he let her, but instead ran away from the church as the bell to prayers stilled.

Ninnidh drove his chariot to the Cill Dara stables just as the bell for vigils stopped clanging. When he'd learned that Brigid wanted him to come back, he'd left Cillian immediately. With the news that Ardan may have returned, the monks had busied themselves building new shelters and sharpening stones for spears. Ninnidh had tried to assure Cillian, saying that the druid, if he really was back in Ireland, might not even come near Aghade. Cillian hadn't seemed to listen, though. A terrible slaughter never vanishes from memory, and why should it? Memories, even bad ones, serve a purpose.

Ninnidh greeted Cill Dara's stable hand and said a blessing over his head for his family. Then he trekked toward the church. On the way, he whispered a prayer, asking God to help him shield his heart. He loved Brigid. She was a dear friend. But he couldn't help but ponder whether or not his feelings for her, and his desire to help her, were selfish.

Fianna, the young inquisitive nun he'd met on his last visit, greeted him at the door. She whispered so as not to disturb the others who were on their knees, arms outstretched in prayer. "Maither Brigid will be pleased you've arrived." She shut the door behind him.

"Where is she?" he whispered back.

"Gone to the scriptorium with a male visitor."

Male visitor? Ninnidh's throat went dry. "I will see if she needs help."

The nun glanced to the ground and opened the church door for him to leave.

The scriptorium was brightly lit. A brother let him in, but the building was mostly vacant, as it should be during times of prayer. Brigid sat with someone at an inscription table near the back wall of pegs where multitudes of manuscripts hung in leather pouches. Cill Dara's library was beyond compare. One day, when tensions were not mounting and folks were not scrambling around trying to decide what to do with a disputed book, he'd come back to study.

Brigid stood when she heard the door close. "Ninnidh! A hundred thousand welcomes to you. Please come."

He hurried toward her, acknowledged the stranger, and then turned back to Brigid. "I do not want to keep you from prayers. Shall we go to the church?"

"I'm afraid I have a matter to attend to. Please go yourself." She paused, looked at the fellow and then back to Ninnidh. "Unless…perhaps you'd like to offer counsel." She glanced to the man. "Would you mind?"

"Whatever will get Aine back," the man said.

So here was the man Aine sought sanctuary from. Ninnidh had spoken to the young man before briefly, but he had not recognized him when he first entered the building. The man sat puddled atop a three-legged stool, his head lowered to his chest.

Ninnidh slid the rope handle of his harp onto an empty wall peg and then pulled up a stool. Turning to the man, he said, "You've returned, Aine's betrothed, the man she came to Cill Dara to avoid."

He stretched out his hand in greeting. "I assure you Aine has no need to fear me. I love her."

Ninnidh studied the man's face. He was not too old. His hands showed signs of manual labor. "What is your standing in your tribe?"

"I own enough cattle to have voting rights, but I could never be part of the royal clan. I will always be a commoner."

Ninnidh crossed his arms. "Why is that?"

"I am a Christian. The king does not approve."

Ninnidh was surprised. "Wasn't the previous king a Christian?"

Daithi shrugged. "Aye. The Uí Náirs have been Christians since Patrick came, until recently."

Brigid rubbed her arms as though she was chilly. She might not be comfortable with questioning the man this way, but Ninnidh had no problem with it. He had always asked probing questions of folks. That was how he garnered information to share from kingdom to kingdom. He was used to it.

"What caused this change, Daithi?"

He shrugged again, as though the answer was obvious. "The people began trusting a talisman about the same time prosperity came to our land. They ceased to acknowledge the Creator. When Aine began to believe as the others, I'm afraid I lost my temper a wee bit. I wanted to destroy the thing to convince Aine and all the others that our prosperity was not connected to it." He stood, wove a hand through his dark hair and drew in a long breath. "All that matters is that I get Aine back."

Ninnidh stood also, leaving Brigid to bend her neck upward to stare at them. "All that matters to you, I suppose. But your tribe will want that book back. Do they know she was the one who took it?"

"They suspect because she's taken it before. Her absence casts further suspicion on her. 'Twas all I could do to convince them I'd take care of the matter."

"So they're waiting on you to come back with it."

"I thought so, but I may be wrong."

"Why so?"

"I met a traveler on the way back here who told me the king has assembled his army." He glanced to the abbess, who was wringing her hands. "I'm sorry for this trouble, Maither Brigid. Perhaps the king will be appeased if I bring Aine back, believing the book will follow."

Brigid shifted her weight from one foot to the other. "Nonsense, that. Aine is but a wee salmon in that pond. 'Tis the book they want."

His eyes went wide. "I need to get her out of here, don't you see?"

Brigid let out a long breath. "I'd say we're all in peril."

"He plans to attack Cill Dara?" Ninnidh could not image a king doing such a thing. Cill Dara had the legal right to offer sanctuary.

"I might be able to stop it if I return with Aine *and* the book." He turned to Brigid. "King Donal, even if he himself doubts the book's worth as a talisman, desperately wants it. The manuscript contains the tribe's genealogy, proof that his family has cattle grazing rights. 'Tis a fertile land, and any tribe would be happy to take it from him. Please, Maither Brigid, give the book to me. Bring peace back to us all."

She stared at the rush-covered floor a moment, and then met his eyes. "I do not believe God would want the pagan belief to continue, Daithi."

He bent his head toward her. "Perhaps you can come preach to them, like Patrick did."

Her cheeks reddened. "If they are marching on Cill Dara this very moment, I doubt they will pause to hear me preach. Even if I run out with the books in my hands, they may still hunger for revenge."

"She's right." Ninnidh took a stance next to her. "We will have to discuss this and seek God's guidance."

Brigid tapped her fingers on the table. "There must be a way to petition for peace. If nothing else, we'll call in the Brehons."

He took her arm and leaned in to whisper into her flaxen hair. "We should discuss this alone."

She nodded. "Please wait here a moment, Daithi."

"I want to see Aine."

"Have patience. Aine is fine. Please wait while I summon the guesthouse steward to take you to your bed. You will not want to ride home in the dark and risk encountering warriors alone."

"I appreciate your hospitality, Maither Brigid. I was not leaving without Aine anyway."

Brigid sent the scriptorium caretaker to fetch the guesthouse steward while she and Ninnidh made their way back to the church. Pausing just a few paces from the door, she asked for a few moments before they went to prayers. Torchlight lit her features, a slightly upturned nose, delicate pink lips. She grew more beautiful every day.

She kept her focus on the door. "I do need your advice. This is almost too much for me to bear." She seemed to search the door lock for answers instead of him.

"God gives us friends, companions, for times like this."

She sighed. "Odd, coming from a wanderer like you." Finally she turned her glance to him.

He placed a hand on her narrow shoulder. "You are right. I am learning the value of close friendship." He could no longer separate the closeness he felt to Brigid's soul from his concern and admiration of her earthly person. Wrapped up, body and soul, and he could not deny that he loved her. "I will do my best to help you, friend."

Tears welled in her eyes. "Very well. Please tell me how to handle this, Ninnidh."

Nineteen

"A proud man is always looking down
on things and people: and, of course, as
long as you are looking down, you
cannot see something that is above you."

C.S. Lewis

As soon as the path was quiet again, Ardan stowed his feather cloak in his bag and hurried toward the scriptorium, careful to stay hidden in the shadows of the yews even though the day's clear skies had turned cloudy after the sun set, helping to cloak the light of the moon and stars. The fact that Brigid had almost seen him was too close of a call to risk its happening again.

As he neared the massive scriptorium, he was dismayed to find it lit up inside brighter than a bonfire. There would not be time to wait. The army was on its way. He would have to enter and cast a spell. He bit his lip. He knew how to commune with the gods, how to ask for and receive their favor. He could summon wee bits of wonder to mesmerize the simplest minds, but he was not sure he could invoke a spell strong enough to freeze time and allow him to enter the building and make off with the manuscript. He toyed with his rune sticks, pondering. He needed to use his strengths to his advantage. He was skilled at talking people into doing things they would not usually do. Whoever was inside would hand over the manuscript willingly once he was done with him.

He placed a hand on the latch of the scriptorium door.

"Psst." Someone called to him from somewhere behind a holly.

He stepped back from the door. Leaning from side to side, he could not discern where the sound came from.

"Over here, Father." Just to his right a murky figure held out a curled finger. "Come over here. You don't want them to see you."

He thought he recognized the voice and moved toward it.

"'Tis me, from the graveyard. Remember?"

When he got close, he discovered it was the nun who'd startled him as he held the hot woven reed wheel in his hand. Was she the one who put a curse on him? He reached for his dagger.

"Don't be afraid, now. I know you're a stranger here, but there's no peril at Cill Dara. We must stay unseen, though. Keep low and come over here. I'm standing in a low pit under this tree. No one will see you from here."

The woman might be a seductress, but she was small and he could overpower her. She might even become a convenient accomplice. He inched forward until he slid down a small embankment and landed next to the brown robed, blue-eyed woman. "What are you doing here?"

"What are you doing here?" she retorted.

"I was about to go into the scriptorium. Whom are you spying on?"

Even in the shadows he could see the smirk on her face. She narrowed her eyes. "Not fooling me, you aren't. You've been lurking around Cill Dara all day. Even got a feather cloak to conceal yourself, haven't you?"

Curses! How could she have seen him? Only another…

"You're not really a nun, are you?"

"What else would I be?"

"Nuns are not given to gossip and spying on people. What is your name?"

She didn't answer.

"You will tell me or I'll turn you in to the abbess. You don't know who I am, do you?"

She remained mute, shocked speechless. He grabbed her arm. He waited until she whimpered and then he twisted it. She gasped, tears streaming down her cheeks. He swallowed her scream with his thick hand. "If you don't want me to kill you, you will tell me who you really are. I'm going to release my hand and, if you scream, I'll plunge this dagger into your belly."

She gasped softly when he pulled his hand away. "I…am…Fianna…druidess of the cana degree."

"Only five years of training, have you, Fianna?" He lifted the dull end of his dagger to her chin. "And do tell. What are you doing masquerading as a nun?"

She winced and pressed her limp arm to her side with her good hand. "Same as you, I suppose, Druid Ardan. I tried to warn the abbess you were here, but she would not hear me."

Angry that she had not answered his question, and that she somehow knew who he was, he clinched her arm again. She let out a wail, which he quickly covered by pushing her into his chest. "Obviously, your teacher never taught you about druid loyalty. Whatever curse you've put on me, I'll make you pay, you and the abbess. I will not tolerate those who will not obey me."

She began to struggle, and he realized he was smothering her. He hesitated just a moment before letting go. "Leave Cill Dara immediately, Fianna, if you know what's good for you."

She scrambled out of the pit and darted away through the bushes. He followed to make sure she was leaving and not sounding an alarm. She passed through a hedge of thick shrubs that emitted the glow of a fire. He wedged half his body into the hedge when he was suddenly thrown clear. With his face in the dirt and grime in his teeth, he spat out curses. He lay there, unable to move, and heard a faint whisper as though someone spoke into his ear, but no one was there. "Death to the man who crosses the goddess's hedge. Women alone may come here."

He finally pushed himself onto one elbow and rose to a sitting position. He'd tried to enter a sacred space without realizing it. He was losing his edge. His powers waned. Never had he had so much trouble with his druid dominance as he was having at Cill Dara. Who were all these mysterious women he kept running into? First the redheaded daughter of King Donal, and now this nun or druidess or whatever she called herself.

And of course, Brigid, the woman he detested most. This Fianna lass was somehow on her side even if she was a druidess.

Patting the dirt from his robe, he considered his next move. He'd have to leave, now that he'd been found out, and let the army invade. He'd deal with Brigid away from here, once she fled to a certain cave in a hillside where he knew she'd go. Once a Christian chooses a place of solitude, he or she returns to it over and over. He'd be waiting for her there.

Rather than fleeing out the back during the attack, she'd use a passageway and retreat to her hermitage. He wished he'd had time to uncover the catacombs. All monasteries had them to some degree. Aye, Brigid would escape to plot her next move. Perhaps she'd hide the book there, telling King Donal it had been destroyed. But for whatever reason, she'd go to the cave. He knew her well, better than anyone else. No matter that years had passed. What Ardan lacked in magical powers, he made up for in intuition and divination.

The mountain was a far distance. It would take days to reach it on foot. He could think of no reason to await the army. Waiting at the hermitage was a much better plan. There was meaning for her in that cave, although he didn't know what. What he did know was that it was far from the reach of her god. He'd seen that before. When he'd met her there long ago, she'd been devoid of any power. Sure, she could hide there. She believed no one could find it. He could. He would. Even if it took days to find it. That lair stripped her of her abilities.

That was the place he wanted to meet her again, where he'd have the upper hand.

After days of traveling, he saw the forest give way to a rising elevation speckled with scrubby brush. Ardan could not conceal himself in that kind of landscape, but at least he was completely alone. There were no tracks in the grasses, and the only indication that life had visited lately was badger droppings. But she'd come. Oh, she'd come all right.

With the help of his rowan shillelagh, he made the climb toward a wee opening in the rocks where he'd wait for the abbess. He cursed the walking stick he was forced to use. It was not as fine as his old one. That one had been taken from him during his capture by the Christians and thrown into the sea. The sturdy branch he now used was functional enough, though not special enough to denote his status. Perhaps while he waited, he would whittle it into a better shape and carve oak leaves around the top, marking it with ogham writing. That way it would also function as a rune stick. Why not? Such objects did not have to be ages old, did they? He would have the knob cast in iron and tipped in gold as soon as this task was completed. He had known a proper goldsmith once before. He could find him again. Ardan required a walking stick fit for an *ollamh* druid.

He paused to study the clouds. They were in fine formation, a good omen. Glancing to his hand, he noticed that his scar had significantly faded. Ah, good. He would soon be beyond the reach of Brigid's god.

His foot slipped on his next step, sending him downward. Shards of gravel dug into his hands as he braced his fall. He scrambled to his feet and examined his palms. Only his right hand bled. Red rivulets flowed into the markings on his hand until an image became visible resembling the woven cross he'd picked up at Brigid's monastery. Groaning, he reached for his bag and drew out a length of linen kept for such emergencies. He pressed it into his hand.

"Why are you doing this to me?" he wailed, shaking his bandaged hand at the clouds.

"Why are you doing this to me?" came the reply. An echo? Perhaps, although the voice seemed to belong to a multitude, accusing him, taunting him. "To me…to me…to me?"

He needed to escape the sound. He scrambled to sling his bag over his shoulder and continue on. When he finally spotted the cave, he drew in a breath. *You can do nothing to me now, O God of the Elements.*

Twenty

"Let love and faithfulness never leave
you;
bind them around your neck,
write them on the tablet of your heart."

Proverbs 3:3 NIV

Aine wavered between her overwhelming need for the book and her desire for Daithi. Why wouldn't he stay away? She could think more clearly when he wasn't around.

Yawning, she rolled over on her straw mat. An odd sensation that someone breathed in her face made her open her eyes. She sat up with a jerk. "Fianna! Must you huddle in my shadow like a lost pup?"

The woman held a finger to her lips. She was disheveled and smelled of a wood fire. "I have come to warn you, wee one."

"Warn me? What are you talking about?" Aine pulled her linen sheet over her shoulders like a shawl.

"The one you came to avoid has returned."

"Daithi?" She let out a low breath. "I should have known he wouldn't leave. I should have found another place of refuge," she said, almost to herself.

"I will take you somewhere."

Aine focused on the woman's feet, bare and caked with dirt. Clumps of grass clung to her ankles. "Come, now." She grabbed Aine's arm.

"Why would I go with you? Where have you been? At the goddess fire?"

"Hush. Someone will hear you. Do you wish to escape your betrothed or not?"

"I can't leave Cill Dara."

"Why not?"

"There is something here I need."

Fianna's eyes, dark in the dusky room, grew wide. "The book. I will help you take it."

"Why? Do you think just because I'm young, I'm a fool?"

"The gods told me I'm to help you get away."

So, she wasn't what she seemed. But that did not mean Aine could trust her. Still, if Fianna could lead her to the book, perhaps then Aine could escape the loony woman. Without a word, she dressed and followed Fianna outside.

The trees seemed to stretch out murky and nefarious limbs, reaching, beckoning her to halt. She had a bad feeling about following Fianna, and yet she could not turn back, could not yell for help, could not run. An unseen force compelled her to move forward as she tiptoed behind the odd nun.

"Where are we going?" she finally managed to blurt out.

"To the scriptorium."

"You know where the book is?"

Fianna held on to Aine's elbow to guide her along a hidden path she had never walked before. "I helped Cillian hide it from the druid. Hurry. There's not much time. He is here."

"Cillian is here?"

"Nay. 'Tis that druid."

"Ardan?"

"That's the one."

They wove through thorny bushes and past little huts, the homes of common laborers. When they at last reached the scriptorium doors, Aine planted her feet. "I will not take another step until you explain all this. Why is Ardan at Cill Dara? I thought he was banished."

The nun drew in a breath and stared past her. "Do you want that book or not?"

"First tell me, are the people here in danger from the druid? Is Cillian?"

Fianna groaned and held on to one arm.

"You're hurt."

"Do not worry about me right now. Just get that book and leave. The druid will not hurt you if you have protection."

"You believe in it? Is that why you've been watching me?"

217

Without another word, Fianna tugged open the heavy door with her good hand. Low-burning torches lit the tall walls, casting shadows below. Fianna retrieved one and led the way to a ladder. Scurrying up the rungs, they ascended to a loft and crawled on their knees until they reached a darkened corner where several pockets hung from the rafters. Fianna, panting as though in pain, pulled on one until it gave way. She pushed it toward Aine. "There's your precious book. I care not what you do with it, just do not return it to the Uí Náirs."

"You are just giving it to me?"

"Do not spend time thinking about it. You have what you wanted. Go."

So, Fianna wanted her to take it away. Was she from a rival tribe, tasked to make sure the Uí Náir did not get it back?

Aine's hands shook as she took the pocket from Fianna, suddenly realizing that there might be more consequences to what she was doing than she realized.

"I don't know my way."

The woman pushed her toward the ladder. "I said I don't care where you go, and I meant it. But you will leave."

"Are you going, too?"

"You are going alone, but I'm going to watch you go. Just head south. You'll get there."

A trumpet blast caused them to halt just as they were about to step through the door.

"We're too late. In here." Fianna pushed on a wall and a panel creaked open. After they stepped inside, Fianna yanked on a rope connected to the panel until they were in utter darkness.

"Where are we? What's going on?"

Fianna whispered in her ear. "King Donal's army has arrived to take the book by force. Even if they burn down the entire scriptorium, they won't find us in here. This is the entrance to a dolmen."

Aine's throat felt like she had swallowed sand. "A dolmen?" The spirits of the Underworld would surely punish them for treading on their sacred space. "The dead rest here. We have to get out."

Fianna let out a soft moan, her injured arm obviously giving her pain. "We'll be the ones dead if we're caught in the scriptorium." She turned Aine toward a cold dark tunnel. "Mind your step. Tread lightly. We can find our way if we're careful."

But Aine couldn't move. There was danger just on the other side of the hidden door. She heard shouts and scrambling footsteps. Where was Brigid? Brocca? "Oh, Daithi. Is he truly here at Cill Dara as you said?"

"He is. We can help no one else now. Come on!"

Aine could feel his hand on her arm, smell the damp earth on his shirt, hear him call her name. She didn't want him harmed. She could not leave him in danger. She leaned hard against the panel door.

"What are you doing?" With more force than an injured woman ought to have, Fianna flung her backward. "One thing I will not allow is to have the book you hold fall into Donal's men's hands." She grabbed a fistful of Aine's hair and pushed her through the chamber.

Shards of pain lit up the inside of Aine's eyelids until she finally convinced the woman that she would follow her without coercion.

Voices trailed after them. "We are almost out," Fianna said. "When you see the stars, let the book lead you."

One more push and Aine stumbled out into the fresh air. She lay crumpled on the grass a moment, thanking the gods that she and Fianna had not disturbed the dead and endured their wrath.

Relieved, she sat up and pulled the pocket that held the treasured book to her chest. An unseen force urged her to her feet and led her off through a field. She did not know where Fianna was, but as she'd said, the book directed the way.

When the horns began to blast, Ninnidh knew it was too late for planning.

Brigid cupped her hands to her mouth. "Sound the bell."

Streams of monks and nuns poured from the church, followed by priests in flowing robes. Hoards rushed toward the large scriptorium.

Ninnidh urged Brigid to pause to allow others to pass. "Isn't that where the book is, the one the king seeks?"

"'Tis always been our emergency plan since Cill Dara was built. There is an escape route there to the outside."

They shuffled along with the others until they reached the door. Taking up opposite sides, they urged the people to stay calm as they entered. Brigid called to him over the crowd. "See that they all go through. I will come with the last person."

Ninnidh shouted over the din. "Go through where?"

"They all know. Go now, please. I need you to make sure they all leave. Let no one stay behind."

The people lined up facing an east wall and seemed to be departing through an opening. He drew closer, squinting in the flickering torchlight. Someone had doused the brightest flames. When he got close enough, he saw that there, indeed, was a hole in the wall. He stopped a young priest about to enter. "Where does it lead?"

"Through a dolmen, Poet."

Amazed to see all the faithful daring to go where so many in the countryside would never venture, Ninnidh still feared the army would find them. He motioned to the priest who stepped out of line to join him. "How far away from the scriptorium will they get? Does the passage lead outside the monastery?"

"Aye, Poet. But we must get through and close the opening before the warriors discover it."

A large man Ninnidh recognized as the fellow he and Brigid had been counseling earlier broke from the line and approached them. "Where is Aine? I do not see her here."

Ninnidh glanced around, but in the faint light and crowded chamber, it was impossible to tell if she was there. "Surely she must be here, Daithi."

"I am certain she is not."

Ninnidh studied the crowd again. Spotting the guesthouse steward, he called him forward. "Who is in charge of the female guests?"

"Fianna."

"Do you see her here?"

He glanced around. "I do not. She might have already gone through, though. We let the women go first."

Ninnidh patted Daithi on the back. "You see, man? Do not trouble yourself."

Ninnidh turned his attention back to the priest. "Thank you for your help." He motioned him back in line and then stared in the direction of entry where Brigid stood, murmuring words of reassurance to her flock. Just when he was thinking the line would never end, the door slammed and Brocca and Brigid hurried along behind the others.

Brigid leaned in close to whisper to Ninnidh. "Get my mother in there and help lead her out."

Brocca held up a hand. "I can find my way in the dark better than most."

The trumpet blasts sounded again, this time much closer.

Ninnidh turned in the direction of the entry. "Someone has to seal the door. You go with her, Brigid, and I'll make sure the entrance is concealed."

Brigid jiggled her head. "Nonsense. I've had this emergency plan in place since the monastery was established. I know what to do. You are new here. Please do as I say."

Brocca's hands waved in the air as she tried to find her daughter. "They'll kill you because you're the abbess. You cannot stay behind, daughter!"

"I will be fine. I know what to do. You two must trust me. The people know to flee to Cillian's. No one's better at hiding than he is, and he knows to expect us. Go there. I will meet you with the book when all is safe."

Ninnidh didn't move. She smiled at him. "I have my own hiding place."

Reluctantly, Ninnidh followed Brocca in through the opening. "Even if they found the passage," he said to the frightened woman, "they would not follow. They are fearful of burial grounds. You know that."

She gave a whimper of concurrence as they crept slowly through the passage. When the sound of the door sliding shut behind them resounded against the stone walls, Ninnidh made a silent plea. *Circle her with your protection, Jesu. Keep holiness within and danger without.*

Twenty-One

"I dread the wearying storm and the
game of evil,
That have thrown into slavery the
children of Adam."

from *King of Kings*,
an Irish prayer translated by Desmond
Forristal

ou must go back!" Brocca clung to Ninnidh, and he
knew she was right.

"But I told her I would look after you."

Brocca pinched his arm. "I move around in darkness.
That is my life. I will not have any trouble catching up to the
others. Please, go protect my daughter."

He scrambled away and shoved the door open with his shoulder. "Brigid?"

No answer.

She would be retrieving the book. Now where would they have put it?

He noticed a broom lying at the base of a ladder. A quick glance at the floor told him that she must have swept away footprints. The ladder led to a loft. Stepping on to the lowest rung, he swept away his own prints and then tossed the broom as far as he could, then he made his way up.

Over in the lowest pitched corner of the roof he saw dark pockets hanging like bats. He heard the weeping. "Brigid?"

"Oh, Ninnidh. The book is not here."

He went to her. "Now what? Are we trapped up here?"

Another voice made them both jump. "She has no doubt taken the book and left, Maither."

They turned toward the voice. Daithi, hunched on hands and knees, stared at them. Brigid gasped. "What are you doing here, man? Everyone was to leave through the chamber."

Daithi stretched out his hand although he could not reach her. "Aine did not leave with the others. Neither did her servant, Fianna. I have been looking for them ever since the first trumpet blast."

Ninnidh whispered into Brigid's hood. "I'm sorry. I thought he left."

Brigid accepted Daithi's hand and let him lead her toward the ladder. It was likely Aine took the book.

Before they could descend the steps, the scriptorium door burst open. Brigid scrambled back up and the three of them huddled in a corner, listening. Slowly, Brigid slid her

226

hands along the edge of the roping that roofers utilize for mending until she seemed to find what she was looking for. "We'll go down this way," she whispered. She paused and gripped the wooden cross around her neck in both hands. "Protect us, Jesu. Conceal our presence." Then with the sureness of a mountain goat, she grabbed the length of rope and slipped through a corner ventilation hole. After a bit of wiggling to fit through, Daithi propelled down behind her and then Ninnidh followed. They landed in a heap on the hard ground just behind some vegetation.

Peeking around the holly tree that concealed them, Ninnidh saw that the path was clear. Buildings burned in the distance and the light the flames cast afforded a clear view of their surroundings. "All's clear. Let's get out of here."

Brigid hesitated. "'Tis a long journey where I am going. You two may want to go elsewhere."

Ninnidh scrambled to his feet. "Aren't we going to Cillian's with the others?"

"You may, but I have to go somewhere else. I had hoped to take the book with me, but that's not possible. Not yet."

Daithi stood. "Do you know where Aine might be headed? She has no idea what evil she has unleashed with her obsession for that book. I have to find her. I have to destroy that talisman once and for all."

Brigid brushed the dirt from her hands. "You are not thinking clearly, Daithi. Such action would only bring more violence. Come with me, then. She will be headed to her clan and pass down the same road I'm following."

"I'll go, too." Ninnidh had come back for Brigid. He was not about to leave her now.

They crept from building to building, avoiding attention from the clusters of warriors who wreaked havoc on Cill Dara. Finally they passed far beyond the sanctuary boundary marked by the crosses.

Once they found the road, Brigid spoke to them. "God has turned us into mice, allowing us to flee undetected. Praise be to God."

Daithi hung his head. "Oh, your beloved Cill Dara. I'm so sorry, Maither. Later we will rebuild it."

She laughed nervously. "'Tis been done in other places before, and I suppose 'twill happen again. Like the spider whose web is crushed, we will begin again."

They traveled on foot until the breaking of dawn, only taking brief rest breaks. Ninnidh marveled at Brigid's fortitude. At long last, a wee cottage with a barn came into sight.

"'Tis a widow's cabin," Daithi said.

Ninnidh turned to him. "You know this place?"

Daithi pointed toward a cow and calf that grazed just outside the barn. "Because there's a structure, there used to be more cattle here. Someone has sold off most of the herd. That's all that's left. My guess is a widow lives here."

Brigid pivoted to look at the young man who had been walking behind them. "How do you know 'tis not a man who lives here alone?"

"The path to the house is tidy, and there's lace in the windows, things men care little about when there's no woman at home."

Brigid stepped first onto the path. "Perhaps a man and wife live here with no children. A man and wife could live with so few animals."

"Perhaps, but the barn is need of a whitewash. A man would not let that go, but a woman would not care."

Daithi's remarks intrigued Ninnidh. As a poet, he too had keen observation skills. The young fellow was probably right.

A bent woman in a plaid scarf approached the animals and led them into the barn as they watched. She soon returned and barred the door. Brigid called to her.

The woman waved. "God to you. There is welcome here for you."

The woman led them inside and handed each a blanket. She pointed to a corner under her roof for Daithi and Ninnidh to lay their heads. Brigid was given a cot near the hearth, probably the woman's own bed.

"Rest yourselves. There is a well out back for washing. I will prepare a meal for you."

Brigid cupped the woman's face in her hands. "You are very kind. God will reward you."

After they took turns refreshing themselves at the well, Brigid filled three wooden bowls with water for washing hands and another for cleansing feet. She handed each of the men one.

They entered the house, washed, and then waited. So very different from the public house Ninnidh and Brigid had visited on the way to Armagh. This woman's hospitality was, thankfully, much more typical. Ninnidh did not take it for granted.

The woman was absent a long while. Ninnidh had just begun to drift off to sleep when a whacking sound caused him to open his eyes. The woman was taking a hatchet to her loom.

Brigid jumped to her feet. "What are you doing?"

The woman paused from her work. "I'm preparing the fire for cooking."

"But your loom! How will you weave your cloth? Without cloth, what will you use to barter for food?"

Ninnidh had seen folks sacrifice for him during his travels, but this was a widow with no other means to support herself, and they were three escapees on the run from a king's army. Even though they wanted to help the woman, what could they do?

The woman smiled. "I will concern myself only with this day. 'Tis quite chilly and we'll be needing this fire for warmth as well."

"I'll look for wood." Daithi hurried out the door. Ninnidh followed.

They split up. Ninnidh scrambled down a hill behind the house, but could find no trees. Morning had come, bringing only dim light through a rain-soaked sky, but he could see well enough in all directions. No woods, no underbrush. Even if they'd found wood, they'd need time to dry it out.

He met Daithi at the barn. "Nothing in here either." They returned to the wee cottage and washed up again.

With the fire now burning, the woman set a slab of meat on a spit over the flames. She dabbed it with a wooden spoon that dripped with honey.

Brigid held a hand to her throat and gazed at Ninnidh, then back at their hostess. "You killed your calf for us, didn't you?"

The old woman shrugged and continued with her work.

"As surely as I live, God will restore what you have given us," Brigid said.

The next day as they prepared to leave, Daithi pointed to the woman's barn. "Look."

A wee calf stood where they had seen one before, licking its mother. As they rounded the corner of the house to head back to the road, the woman called after them. "Bless you, Maither Brigid. 'Tis just as you said. My loom is whole and my calf is returned."

Brigid waved and blessed her in return, and they set off down the road.

Ninnidh had seen these miracles before. He should not have been amazed. But the young man was seeing them for the first time.

Daithi pushed between Ninnidh and Brigid. "How did you do that?"

"I did nothing. The woman gave all she had for strangers, and the Bible tells us we will be rewarded when we do that. I simply reminded her 'twas so."

Daithi slung a bag of bread and apples the woman had given them for their journey over his shoulder. "You have no idea, Maither Brigid, how special a gift you possess. God has blessed you greatly, and still you do not know. To you, 'tis nothing extraordinary."

He was right. Brigid seemed unaware. God had not abandoned her, but still she did not see it.

They continued on without further conversation while Ninnidh recited a Psalm to himself.

When at last they reached the place of their parting, Ninnidh didn't want to let Brigid go.

"'Twould not be a hermitage if others came with me," she explained. "I must have time alone to pray and seek answers to why this has happened. My community depends upon it. They will collect themselves and continue in God's way while they await my return."

Ninnidh nudged her away to speak to her alone. "'Tis not a casual journey, Brigid. There is danger lurking about. We still don't know where Ardan might be."

"I am not worried."

"I am. 'Tis not prudent to go off alone."

"There is nothing I can do about Ardan, now, is there? I can also not change, if I would want to, my position at Cill Dara. I have responsibilities to them—and to God. You will go with Daithi." Her words were firm. He wanted to argue but knew it was no use.

They divided the food they had left, and Brigid blessed the young man. "I do not know why Aine needed this pilgrimage to her birth clan, but if you will allow her to make what amends she must, I'm confident she will return with you. You are a caring, loving man. May you have a rich, contented life."

Daithi bowed his head and spoke toward the ground. "I pray God will hear those words, Maither. Aine is quite stubborn. Breaking her attachment to the book will not be easy. She might hate me for taking it from her."

Brigid pointed toward the cliffs of her hermitage. "Bring the book here to me when you get it. Better if you bring Aine as well, but if she will not come, at least tell her I will have the book. You understand that a truce must be negotiated."

Ninnidh touched the abbess's sleeve. "Are you sure that's a good idea?"

Daithi spoke up. "What do you plan to do with it? If I destroy it, you'd be saved the trouble. You would not be blamed for it."

"Do not harm the book, Daithi. I must deal with the tribe's obsession over it. I don't yet know how, but by God's grace I will use the book to show the people the true source of Divine power. We will call a summit, invite the Brehon judge, and the king if he'll come." She turned again toward the rocky outcrop. "I will retreat here to pray and fast until your return."

Ninnidh clapped Daithi's shoulder. "Do you want me to go with you?"

"You should stay nearby in case the abbess needs you. I will go alone."

Ninnidh could not argue.

Daithi kissed her hand. "May I say Maither Brigid has sent me when I meet Aine's clan?"

"Say the One True God goes with you. Inquire of anyone you meet the way to the mountain of *Log na Coille*, should you lose your way."

Daithi returned Ninnidh's strong clasp, and then set off down the road.

"I could sleep outside the cave."

"You will not. They'll need you at Aghade."

"You are not being sensible."

"I am. I told you once to trust me, and you did not, apparently, because you returned to the scriptorium. I hope my mother does not become lost because of it. You must check to see if she made it safely for me, Ninnidh. I need you to do this."

He could not deny her. "As you wish, but I will come back and assure myself you are all right. Depend on it."

As he moved away from the mountain, a chill rose from his feet to his ears. The presence of evil was as real as the black raven that had swooped down and perched next to him. He shooed it away. If he returned, he'd be going against Brigid's wishes. He must believe in her if they were truly going to be trusted advisors to each other.

What now, Jesu? What lurks about me? Where are my spear and shield? May the Three protect her against all evil and grant her wisdom for dealing with kings and pagans…and even druids.

The odd black bird hopped along with him and he marveled at the silver streak on his head.

Twenty-Two

"There are no miracles to men who do
not
believe in them."

Anonymous

Ardan didn't care for Brigid's mountain. There were no trees at that elevation and he bemoaned the absence of wisdom they brought. However, since Brigid's god chose to abandon her there, he would have to endure it. If he were able to change shapes like he wished, he could be a bird and fly through the skies to watch her approach. Curses that he, an ollave druid, could not do that, although he would never admit it to anyone. It was not as if he hadn't tried, hadn't felt himself changing only to be brought back to his original form. He kicked at a pebble, sending a stream of small rocks down the incline. He was a druid of the highest order even without that ability, and Ireland needed to know that.

He held his hands to his mouth, calling out to the raven that spied on his behalf. Moments later, a dark smudge on the horizon appeared. "By the gods, where have you been?" He held out his arm and the bird landed. It flicked its head from one side to another, blinking a black eye at him.

Brigid was soon to arrive, then. He hurried to the lean-to he'd built on the far side of the mountain. The little stick structure resembled the deposit of a stream gone dry. He was pleased with his handiwork. May the gods do their work now.

From what Ardan had heard, Brigid continued to feed the hungry and clothe the poor, as she had been doing when he first encountered her years earlier. Except for the weeks she spent in this cave. That turned out to be a spiritually dry time for her, and he hoped now to make sure the dryness turned into an everlasting desert.

He peered out through his constructed fretwork in the direction of the cave. Before long, he spotted Brigid's cloaked form bending low to look into the cave's opening. His stomach lurched at the mere sight of her, although he should not have been concerned. She had no power here. Ardan glanced to his hand, which had started to throb again with renewed vengeance. He shook it and tucked it behind his back.

Glancing back through his peephole, he noted the abbess kneeling in the dirt, reciting a Christian prayer. Whether chant or a spell, it would do no good. Her words grew louder until he was able to discern them.

"Those who seek God will find Him. There is no such thing as an unholy spot on Earth. God is everywhere."

A cold shiver ran up Ardan's neck. It was as if she'd read his mind, but she didn't even know he was there. He continued to watch as she peeked back in through the black opening. Suddenly she stood, arms wide, beholding the valley below. "Where can I go from your Spirit? Where can I flee from your presence? If I go up to the heavens, you are there; if I make my bed in the depths, you are there. If I rise on the wings of the dawn, if I settle on the far side of the sea, even there your hand will guide me, your right hand will hold me fast. If I say, 'Surely the darkness will hide me and the light become night around me,' even the darkness will not be dark to you; the night will shine like the day, for darkness is as light to you."

A fierce glow more radiant than the sun flashed from Ardan's palm, the one with the mark. He rolled on top of his hand, but the light burst from underneath him. He rolled from side to side until he managed to wiggle his blanket free from his pack, but even that did not hold back the light. He pulled his arm from underneath him and turned his palm upward, bracing himself. The only way to defeat this magic was to confront it. But as he stared at his palm the light gradually gave way to a fading glow. He stared at the mark, Brigid's cross, as his hand cooled.

Sure that the abbess had seen the debacle, he boldly sprung from his shelter. They would battle right then on the mountain. He had defeated her magic before, and he was ready.

But as he came crashing out of his hiding place, all seemed calm. The air was still. Stars were emerging in the heavens. The entrance to the cave was vacant. Brigid must have gone inside, but before or after the light had attacked him?

While Aine cared about Daithi and the safety of the others, she was no longer in control. She stepped through the meadow, holding the book out in front of her. The book clearly did not want to go back to Daithi or his tribe. She was being led southward.

Before long, her legs ached and her outstretched arms begged to be lowered.

"Going to the hills, are ye?"

She craned her neck and spotted a man near a hawthorn sitting in an ox wagon.

"I can take ye. Get in."

Her arms suddenly dropped, and the book nearly tumbled from her grasp. She cradled it like a baby and climbed into the cart, too exhausted to question the wisdom of accepting a lift from a stranger to go…she didn't know where.

The cart lumbered away slowly. "Perhaps you can drop me off at the next cabin," she called to him. "Take this book with you. I don't want it anymore."

She held a hand over her mouth. Had she actually said that? She had been thinking how much trouble this had all been, but as discouraged as she felt, she hadn't actually meant it. Or had she? She stared at the brown leather cover.

She had once cherished it, but now felt mostly loathing. With wealth, it brought despair—maybe worse. There was a cost to it, perhaps more than she even knew.

As much as she longed to be the one to help her mother's family, to receive their appreciation, maybe she had been wrong. If the book were in the hands of some other tribe, perhaps her life would be different. Perhaps Daithi would treat her differently.

She closed her eyes a moment, wondering if her thoughts were becoming a jumbled mess. And yet, when she looked at the book again, she felt it was true. The book really wanted to be apart from her.

The man jiggled the ox's lead, and the cart slowly advanced. "As you wish."

"Do you know a woman named Maire? Or, rather, have you ever?"

"Expect I do. Maire of the forest. Know her, do you?"

Or someone like her. "Is she a Christian?"

"Expect she is." He shook the reins and urged the beast to plod a bit faster.

"Is this Maire you know married to a man, or was she? Someone who, well, someone not very kind?"

"Aye. Maybe ye do know her. Would ye like to go to her house? Two days travel but there's a house you can sleep in just ahead. Know a faster driver there who might take ye. If ye can pay."

She pushed the book to the far corner of the cart. "Thank you. I would like that." Her mother was dead, but her legacy might live on like Patrick's, as the monks she grew up with always maintained. "Oh, but wait. I don't have any…" She felt a heaviness in her left apron pocket and pulled out a half-dozen gold coins, Roman currency. Maybe she'd been hasty wanting to get rid of that book.

Later, she huddled in a bed of straw in the hostel as the new day's sun framed the planked door in an orange glow. Aine thought about her family. How would they receive her?

She sat up and ran her hands through the straw. The book! Oh, no! She hadn't actually said she'd give the man the book. She was sure she hadn't. She thought she'd carried it in. She scrambled to wake a few other lodgers.

"A book, leather cover? Have you seen it?"

Dreary eyed, they'd all denied having seen it. The wee bags they carried were not big enough to hold it. She found the cottage owner in the yard hanging the wash. "You came with only your clothing on your back, lass." The woman wrinkled her nose. "If you're missing anything, 'tis that driver, sure as the saints alive, who took it. I thought it odd you accepted help from a druid. They keep to themselves out here."

Dejected, she went back inside to accept the woman's offer of warm porridge. Druids did not believe in the written word, only the spoken word that they had trained for years to learn. Perhaps it was best the book was gone. First she had been controlled by Daithi and then by the book.

She departed as early as she could, this time in a wagon pulled by two horses. She didn't speak to her driver, a middle-aged man who smelled of honey mead. He seemed to be in a hurry and only stopped when he had to give the team a rest. Later, they slowed down near a shack perched on the banks of babbling brook. "The one you seek lives there."

She thanked him, gave him the last of her gold coins, and then climbed out and headed to the door as he drove off. A voice stopped her short. "No visitors are welcome here."

She would know that voice anywhere—her father! She turned slowly around. He stood a few paces away near a stack of logs, a hatchet dangling in his hand. He'd once threatened her with a tool like that when she asked for bread.

"Off with you, now." He waved it to one side. He looked much the way she had remembered him, except his hair was thinner. "Are you deaf and dumb, lass? Go away!"

He did not recognize her. The last time she'd seen him she was just a girl.

"You won't find another lift here, but there's a lot of beggars there in the woods who would take you in. Go on, now."

She took a step backward and heard the cabin door creak open.

"Are you in need, dear?"

Aine spun around. Her mother, not dead at all, stood before her, clutching the ends of her headscarf in both hands. "Is there something I can do for you?" She inclined her head toward Aine's father. "Don't mind him, dear. If I say you're to come in, then you shall."

Aine closed her eyes then opened them. Her mother was alive, and she was standing right here.

"Maire," Aine's father called out. "Don't be giving that beggar my supper."

"Och." Maire turned her back to him. "Come on in, darling."

Aine followed her inside and shut the door on what was becoming a howling wind.

"Sit there on the stool. I'll fetch you some stirabout."

Tears began to flow as she recognized the hearth, her mother's lone bronze cooking pot, even the stool she sat on. The house was unchanged with the exception of a generous supply of peat blocks. Maire threw one on the fire, and it sizzled and released a heady aroma that sent Aine back in time.

"There you go, darling."

Aine could not find her speech, could not understand how any of this could be real. She accepted the bowl held out to her and gazed into the face she thought she'd never see again. "Maither, don't you know me?"

The woman dropped to her knees. "Aine!" She hugged Aine's ankles. "Oh, my dear, 'tis you. I never thought you'd dare to come home."

Aine set the bowl on the floor and embraced her mother. Their tears flowed together as they laughed and cried at the same time. "They told me you had died."

The door burst open. "Get away from my wife!" Aine's father glared at them, his eyes rimmed red, his knuckles white as he clutched the hatchet in his left hand. When he raised his right hand, Aine noticed the shape of his gnarly fingers, the hand that had slapped her so many times before. *No, not this time!*

Twenty-Three

"A little fire that warms is better than
a big fire that burns."

Irish Saying

A s soon as Ninnidh was convinced Brocca and the
others were secure in a temporary dwelling just far
enough away from both Cill Dara and Aghade that they
could not easily be tracked, he set off to find Brigid.

Brocca detailed the exact location of Brigid's hermitage.
"She went to a cave after I was kidnapped years ago. 'Tis a
wearisome trek, but if you keep to the southward road, you
will find it. She told me about it many times, and I have not
forgotten. Look for a rock on the side of the mountain

shaped like an arrow and weave to the right of it. You'll find the wee opening then."

Ardan roamed about somewhere, although Ninnidh decided not to tell Brocca. She was safe enough being near Cillian.

The first person he met on the road drove a two-horse chariot. "Would you take a song in exchange for one of your beasts?" Ninnidh asked the man.

The fellow eyed Ninnidh's dark green tunic, obviously realizing the status he held as a poet of great learning. He hesitated.

"If you do not approve after you've heard it, you are free to carry on. But if the song moves you at all, you are honor-bound to pay me. Do you agree to this deal, man?"

The fellow's throat throbbed when he swallowed.

"You have my word that I will use no satire." The people feared most poets they encountered for that reason. Ninnidh would not normally take such advantage of his position. "Where do you live? I will return the beast on my next journey to this province."

"The watermill house with the red door. You will pass it on this road."

"I shall not forget your kindness. Do we agree, then?"

"Aye." The man held out his hand, and they sealed their agreement with a handshake.

Ninnidh chose a hymn of the Battle of Ath Dara in which Laoghaire, son of the great O'Neill, was taken hostage. He swore on the sun, the moon, and all the stars that he would never harm the people of Leinster, and so he was freed. He did not keep his vow, however, so God struck him dead with a bolt of lightning. Ninnidh sang.

He gave his word by this he swore,

244

But God's vengeance was the more.

By the time he finished, the man's eyes gleamed with tears. The sad story always caused people to ponder anew the price of taking up arms. He handed the horse's rein to Ninnidh and worked to free the beast from the constraints.

Grateful that he could now travel at a faster pace, Ninnidh easily found the southern road. Yellow-tinged leaves swirled around his head as he rushed on. The elevation rose slightly, giving way to hills and perhaps caves, but he didn't yet see the arrow-shaped rock.

Sometime later, he stopped to refresh the horse at a stream a few paces off the road. He might never have seen the water if the horse hadn't protested so much and pulled to the side. Smart animal.

The vegetation was nearly impervious in that spot. He leaned down and massaged his aching calves. The sound of voices on the road caught his attention. He peered through the branches of a pine tree. Two men stood on the road. One wore a threadbare cap with thick, curly, white locks sticking out the sides. The other was tall and muscular and looked an awfully lot like…well, sure enough, it was Daithi. Ninnidh listened.

"Aye, I took a young woman like that in my cart." The old man held out his hand. Obviously Daithi had nothing to pay him with.

"I am of the Uí Náir clan," Daithi said. "I'm a cattleman. I will give you a calf if you take me where you left her."

"Will you, now? And supposing you never bring me the calf. What will I have then for my trouble?"

Daithi grabbed the man's shirt and pulled him close. "What you'll have is the whole Uí Náir clan on you if you do not help me, man. Do you not know she possesses the clan's talisman?"

"She does?"

He began to shiver and Daithi released him. "Indeed she does. 'Tis a book wrapped in brown leather. Did you see that?"

"I...I'm not sure."

Daithi grabbed him again, this time lifting him out of his shoes. "You better search your memory, man. The wrath of King Donal's men has already been brought down on Cill Dara."

"Cill Dara? The church of the oak? The goddess fire?"

"What was there has been destroyed. Now, did this woman have a book like that? Try hard to remember." Daithi tightened his grip, making the man cry out in pain.

Ninnidh almost leapt from his hiding place, but it seemed more prudent to wait. He had no weapons. Daithi had not seemed to be a truly violent man. He was using intimidation to find Aine.

"She did have it, I believe." The old man coughed when Daithi let him go. "But she has it no more. She sold it."

"To whom?" Daithi's looming figure shadowed the shorter man.

"I...uh...to a merchant on the road. I don't know who he was. Expect 'tis being traded as we speak."

"Forget that. Take me where you left her." Daithi didn't seem to believe the man's story that some other fellow had bought the book, and Ninnidh doubted it as well.

The man picked his hat up from the ground and smacked it on his thigh, sending a cloud of smoke rising to his knees. "Forget that the king's men might be torching our forest?"

246

"Nothing will happen for some time. Just don't tell anyone else you saw that book. Now, let's go." He jumped to the ox cart's driver's seat and held out his hand to help the man up.

Ninnidh retrieved his horse and followed at a safe distance. A few other folks soon joined them on the road, and in the midst of a hog being led by a rope and a wagon full of feisty children, he was able to keep his presence concealed.

After a long journey that had given Ninnidh plenty of time to worry about what the young man was up to, they arrived at a hostel.

"This? This is where you took her?" Daithi jumped out and although Ninnidh was now in plain sight, he paid him no mind. "Is she still here, man?"

"I doubt it. She hired a driver. Can't say where she went."

"You're lying." He started to lunge at the man but stopped when he held his hands up in surrender.

"I can tell you this. Said she was off to see the clan of Maire of the forest, she did."

"And is there such a person?"

"Oh, aye."

He propelled himself back onto the seat next to the man.

"Hold on now. I did not take her there, and I can't take you either."

"And why not? I'll pay you two heads of cattle."

"Mighty tempting, that. But ye can't drive this ox into the thick woods. The young lass got a horse driver. That's all I can tell you. Don't even know who he was. I just know they hire out to folks sometimes."

247

Daithi reached for the man's shoulder. "I will repay you for this information. Come to this hostel owner in one moon. I'll leave the calf here for you. You have my word."

The old man grinned, exposing gums with few teeth. "I will appreciate it."

When Daithi approached the hostel door, Ninnidh met him.

"What are you doing here?" Daithi began to push past him. "I'm in a hurry, Poet." He shifted from side to side, eager to get through the door.

"How do you know Aine cannot take care of herself?"

"She never has. She has no clue what danger she's in."

Ninnidh put his hand on the man's boulder-like shoulder. "Suppose you tell me about that over a jar of mead."

Together they entered a large room. A hostess wearing a white linen apron led them to a table board where a man reclined with a mug of ale. "Are you the driver for hire?" Daithi asked him.

Ninnidh wondered if the man was sober enough for conversation.

"That I am," the fellow said. He pushed himself up on one elbow. "Where do you want to go?"

"Did you recently take a young lass into the deep woods?"

This brought a whoop of laughter from the men lounging in the room.

"What's it to you if I did? 'Tis my own business."

Daithi's face grew scarlet. "Please, God, help me control my temper," he whispered, almost to himself.

He did not call out the name of a pagan deity or speak the words of ritualistic incantation. From what Ninnidh could tell, Daithi was Christian.

The driver turned and took a long swig of his drink.

Daithi pounded his fist on the table. "You know what I mean. A young lass with golden hair. She was on a quest. Recently. You remember. You will take me where you dropped her off."

The other men in the room rose from their seats and surrounded them.

The driver wiped his lips with the back of his hand. "You have silver?"

Daithi leaned down and stared into the man's glassy eyes. "You stay with your cup, man. I'll not be hiring you to take me anywhere. Just tell me where you left her."

The man snorted and wiped his nose on his sleeve. He motioned to the others until they backed away. He glared at Daithi with glassy eyes. "I'm telling you this to get you out of here. We were having a fine time until you showed up."

"Happy to let you go back to it," Daithi said.

"Maire the Merciful, that's what we call her. Aye, I took a lass there, though she could have walked from here. There's a path out back. Follow it to the split boulder. Turn left and continue on 'bout two hours on foot. You'll find it."

Daithi turned to the door. The driver shouted after him. "Any harm come to Maire, and me and the lads will come after you."

Ninnidh followed on Daithi's heels, calling to him once they were outside. "Wait! I have a horse. What kind of danger do you think she's in?"

Daithi turned around. "Get your horse, then, before these beggars take off with it."

249

When Ninnidh returned to the path on his horse, carrying a torch a kind lass from the hostel had given him, he found Daithi lumbering through a patch of nettles.

"Come on," Ninnidh called to him. "Get up here. We don't have two hours of daylight left."

Once they were settled on the horse's back and Ninnidh handed the torch off to him, Daithi began to speak. "Thank you, Jesu, for squelching my anger. Now get me through this journey into the arms of my love."

A brother in Christ. Ninnidh asked him about his quest. "Why is she in danger? Does it have to do with the druid Ardan?"

"Who?"

"The once-banished druid who would do anything he could to diminish Brigid's influence on the people."

"I don't know about that. All I know is King Donal would go to war over that book, and foolish Aine thinks she needs it to feed herself and her birth clan."

The forest was so thick that the fading daylight could barely penetrate. Moisture dripped from the leaves overhead and fell sizzling onto the torch. If they'd come after Samhain, the way would have been clear since most of these trees would have dropped their leaves. But now the leafy canopy made traveling dark and treacherous. The path was barely wide enough for a horse, as the man in the hostel had said.

A wolf howled from a distance. A pack might be tracking them.

"Hurry, man." Daithi waved the torch to one side.

Ninnidh heard the sound of a dagger sliding from a sheath. "Don't panic, Daithi." Easy to say. If danger lurked out in the forest, they couldn't see it.

250

When they reached the boulder, they steered carefully to the left.

"Do you think your horse can make it traveling in the dark, Poet? If we stop, we'll become prey for sure."

"I don't know. Has not been my horse for long." He feared for Brigid. Was she alone in the dark? Did she know how to light a fire? Could she fend for herself? *Please let her be safe.*

Twenty-four

"A man will not be found where he lives,
but rather where he loves."

Irish saying

hen he first saw the fire blazing at the cave's
entrance, Ardan crept out and hid in the brush
below. Brigid appeared with her arms raised over her head.
He'd seen country people do the same thing, as if they could
summon the gods without the help of a high druid. Her
heard her melodic voice, calm and strong.

Sing to the LORD, you saints of his; praise his holy name.

She murmured something and threw a stick into the
fire. She repeated this two times. Then she paused and sang
again.

For his anger lasts only a moment, but his favor lasts a lifetime; weeping may remain for a night, but rejoicing comes in the morning.

Ah, 'twas night now, and she'd surely be weeping. And if suffering did not come of its own accord, he would make it happen. But first things first. He must get the book. If he alone brought the tribe their talisman, he'd gain their loyalty. One step at a time, he would gain control of the fertile lands—first in Uí Náir territory, then in Cill Dara.

He laughed softly to himself. The Christians may have subdued him for a time, but that was over. Now it was his turn to seize the opportunity the gods presented.

He skulked slowly up the mountain, careful to stay in the encroaching shadows. He would come to her like a dream, one that she'd believe she'd conjured up. Drive her mad, that's what he'd do.

Circling his black-feathered cloak around himself, he clung to the ledge just to the right of the cave opening.

"I left you before at this cave, and I am leaving you again, my child," he softly called out.

"What? Who's there?"

He heard scrambling and the lighting of a torch before she emerged in clear view. He stepped back, squeezing his feathered body behind a rock formation. "I am your god, Brigid. Do you not recognize my voice?"

A silence followed, and he waited. He was patient. He always got what he wanted when he was patient.

"Don't leave me," she whispered into the twilight.

"Seek me again at twilight next," he said. "I will instruct you."

"I will."

He projected a raven call out against the side of a hill and his bird friend appeared and landed at Brigid's feet. She bent to touch him, but the bird took flight, cackling in the ghastly way ravens do.

She retreated back into the cave, freeing him to scramble back down to his dwelling.

Twenty-five

"What is a friend? A single soul
dwelling in two bodies."

Aristotle

Ninnidh had heard people say that they sometimes feel
the need to be in two places at the same time. He'd
never understood that until now. Normally, he took his time
when he traveled, always listening for God's direction. Now a
panic rose from his gut to his throat. He needed to be at
Brigid's hermitage, and yet he could not abandon Daithi and
Aine. There was danger everywhere he turned his head.

"Would you like me to take a turn driving the horse?"
Daithi asked.

"Let's just keep on."

His legs ached and throbbed, but they could not be far from the destination. No sooner had he thought that than a waft of smoke met his senses.

"There's a cabin near," Daithi said. "I can smell it."

Ninnidh eased up on the reins, and the horse whinnied, grateful for a slower pace.

Moments later, the dark form of a wattle and mud hut came into view. They both scrambled down from the horse's back. A hunched figure sat outside the house, sobbing.

"Aine?" Daithi ran to her.

She stood and embraced him.

"Oh, Aine, my love. I'm here. Everything's going to be fine." He rubbed his hand over her head and she buried her face in his chest. "Are you hurt?" He pushed back at arms' length to look at her.

"I am fine. Oh, Daithi, my mother lives here. We were just reunited."

"Your mother? The report that she'd died was false?"

"It seems so." Her voice crackled with sobs.

"There is more. Tell me."

"My father is here too." Her voice broke again. "He put me out. Like before. I tried to stand up to him this time, let me know that I am not that weak child anymore, but he is so strong. He pushed me out."

"Are you hurt?"

She shook her head.

Someone approached from behind the house. Ninnidh stood on Aine's other side as Daithi retrieved his dagger.

"Aine. Oh, Aine. Come here, daughter."

Aine ran to the woman, who was carrying what seemed to be a traveling bag. Snatching her daughter's hand, she led them away from the house before she spoke again. "'Tis good that your friends came for you, but please, daughter, consider going with me."

They stood in a small clearing where moonlight cast a glimmer on a meadow so sheltered by the forest only someone who knew where it was could find them.

"Is there danger?" Daithi asked Aine's mother.

"Maither, this is the man I've been promised to." The way Aine said it, Ninnidh had to believe she had not wanted the marriage at all. A divergence from how she'd greeted the man moments earlier.

After brief introductions, the woman named Maire waved for them to follow her deeper into the woods. "Aine's father is slumbering next to an empty whiskey jar. Tonight we'll rest at Sorcha's house. A wee hut, but she'll have us in and my husband won't follow. He thinks she's a sorcerer. She's, in fact, a healer who likes songs. Trained for years with the druids."

Ninnidh had met women like this Sorcha before. Some folks feared mysterious healers who lived in ivy-covered cottages so deep in the woods that the dwellings blended secretly into the trees, but he found such women intriguing. Some had been receptive to hearing about Jesu, and in time, they trusted the supreme source of healing. God uses people where they are, but only those who traveled as much as Ninnidh had that understanding.

After traipsing through brambles and looping their way around trees with branches spread out like arms, they found the healer's home. They were welcomed inside by a woman about Ninnidh's age and her gray cat.

Sorcha's snug would have been more spacious had there not been such a festoon of herbs dripping from the rafters and so many wooden boxes stacked about. "Winter's coming," the woman explained, tossing her dark brown hair over one shoulder. "Must harvest while I can."

Maire accepted a blanket from the woman. "Thank you for giving us shelter." "You are most welcome here. You've done so much for me and for others, Maire the Merciful. Besides, as you've taught me to understand, I do Jesu's work."

Daithi declined Sorcha's offer of a hot drink. He took Aine by the arm. "Does your father have the book, then?"

"What book?" Maire asked.

Aine's face drained of color. "He does not, and I don't either. You got what you wanted."

The healer's face brightened. "A book? With pages of written language? I haven't seen one of those in years." She handed Ninnidh a bowl, and he readily took it. It had been a long time since he'd had anything to eat.

"What happened to it?" Daithi still nudged Aine's arm.

"Let her go." Maire's voice crackled with emotion. "I will not have my daughter mistreated. One mistake like that in a family is more than enough."

Daithi let his fingers fall away. Tears streamed down Aine's face, mirroring her mother's.

Maire stroked Aine's hair. "I'm so sorry, Aine. That's why I sent you to live with Cillian. I could not bear what your father might have done to you. He has the demon of strong drink in him."

"Someone hurt my Aine?" Daithi's eyes bulged. He felt every emotion deeply.

The healer held both palms up in the air. "Quiet, everyone. There is much confusion here. We will sort it out one question at a time."

CINDY THOMSON

"A wise idea," Ninnidh said. "Let's start at the beginning.

"I gave the book to a trader," Aine said, biting her lip.

Daithi huffed. "Don't you know the king will hunt you down? And now you don't have it?"

"I, uh, I did not mean to give it to him. You do not understand that book, Daithi. I have tried to tell you, but you don't listen."

He crossed muscular arms across his chest. "I am listening now, *mo chroí*."

Aine twisted her fingers in her skirts. "It, well, it decides where it will go and who will carry it."

"Preposterous. Superstitious nonsense." A vein in Daithi's neck bulged.

"Hold on, now," Ninnidh said. "Suppose we start with you seeking out the abbess," he said to Aine. "Why did you steal Daithi's tribe's book and bring it to Cill Dara?"

"Hmm." The healer raised her eyebrows and turned to Aine.

Aine focused on her betrothed. "Daithi wanted to destroy it."

"To keep pagans from worshipping it." Daithi raised both hands in the air and then dropped them to his lap.

"A book is a valuable thing," the healer mumbled.

Aine knelt at her mother's feet. "I wanted to bring it here for you, Maither. Cillian said you had died, so I wanted to bring it so your starving clan could survive."

Maire sighed and gave her friend a glance. "We thought it best if you thought I was not living. I knew you would eventually ask questions, and when you did, we agreed it was best this way. Then you would not seek me out. You are in

261

danger here, child. I…I am overjoyed to see you again, but you should not have come. I am truly sorry."

"But I'm a child no longer. I can help."

Daithi shook his head like the suggestion was preposterous.

Sorcha waved an arm in the air. "Cillian says we're starving, does he? If we are so bad off, what are you eating now?"

Ninnidh had to admit that the broth was thick and flavorful, enhanced by the healer's fragrant herbs and loaded with chunks of lamb's meat. A feast even a king would approve of.

"We have plenty to eat," Maire said. "We stay in the woods in order to help people and to teach them about Jesu." She turned to her daughter and held her face in her palms. "You know Patrick's God? I am sure Cillian has taught you well."

Daithi cleared his throat. "She knows, but she chooses the old ways."

Tears continued to run down Aine's cheeks. She lifted a shoulder to wipe them.

"Do not be fretting, child," Maire said. "He knows you." She kissed the top of Aine's head.

Ninnidh was nearly moved to tears himself, but he swallowed hard and attempted to bring the conversation to the immediate matter that needed to be dealt with. "The Uí Náir army must be met. Brigid is surely the one to speak with them, but without the book…well, if we had it, we would surely gain audience with King Donal."

Maire did not acknowledge him. "Aine, you must be truthful. If you truly do not want to live with this man, leave with me. I will build us shelter in the hills, and we will speak

God's peace to all who seek us out. Not even your father will dare oppose us."

"Why not?" Aine's hands trembled.

"Because Jesu will not allow him."

"If you believed that, why didn't you come for me, Maither?"

Maire shook her head. "I truly believed you were better off where you were."

"But you weren't better there. Why didn't you leave?"

Ninnidh caught Sorcha's eye and inclined his head to the door. They should let them work this out without an audience. But Sorcha shook her head insistently.

"I should have left that house long ago, but I had the false hope that your father's heart would be changed," Maire continued. "Uh, no one wants to be alone. I know it sounds foolish."

Daithi stood, wringing his hands. "'Twill be your choice, Aine. No one wants a love that must be forced, either. I'll not stand in your way if this is what you want. You will surely be safe from the warriors back here in these woods." He nodded at Maire. "In your mother's care."

Aine's eyes were as wide as goose eggs. She did not speak.

Maire looked from Aine to Daithi. Then she suddenly cast her attention on Ninnidh. "You are a high poet, aren't you?"

He inclined his head. "I am. And I serve Jesu."

She clapped her hands. "Then you must know."

He raised his eyes while keeping his head bowed. "I know many things. What do you speak of?"

"You travel. You meet lots of people. Surely you have seen injustice and justice alike. Compassion and neglect, anger and kindness."

"I have."

"Have you loved deeply, Poet? Not as a husband loves a wife, but as one soul loves another?"

Brigid's sea green eyes flashed into his thoughts. "Indeed I have."

"I longed to have my husband love me that way, but his heart is hardened. For far too long, I thought he would change, but he did not."

Aine squeezed her mother's hand reassuringly, but she had a look about her that seemed to suggest she'd rather jump from a cliff than be part of this conversation.

Ninnidh wasn't sure what was going on, but as Maire kept talking, Aine's face turned even paler. "Tell us, Poet. Do these two before you, Daithi and Aine, have a soul love like that for each other?"

"Well, I do not think it is for me to say."

"You must," Maire insisted. "'Tis extremely important. You know so."

"They do." The words slipped so quickly from his mouth that he could not even remember beckoning them.

Aine, now trembling, threw herself to the dirt floor on top of Daithi's feet, weeping. "Don't throw me to the wolves, Maither."

Twenty-Six

"Love rules without a sword,
Love binds without a cord."

Anonymous

Aine felt as though the breath had been knocked out of her. Her head spun as voices from the past vaulted in and out of her consciousness.

"You won't," her father bellowed.

"I must," her mother said.

She remembered that they often quarreled over her mother's acts of charity. But it was not the arguing that shot thunderbolts through Aine's heart now. It was the memory of seeing her usually strong and confident mother cowering in a corner. Her father picked up a shovel, lofted it above his head, and then whisked the musty cottage air with it. He had been about to bring the shaft down on Aine's mother's head when…Aine did something. She couldn't remember. What did she do?

Aine pulled at her hair, suddenly aware that Maire was speaking to her. Voices from the present—Daithi, Maire, the Poet—rang far off on some distant cliff. She resisted leaving her memory. She wanted to know what had happened that day in the wee house in the woods. Despite it all, Aine lost the battle as those in the room succeeded in bringing her back to the present.

"I would never hurt you, child." Maire attempted to lift Aine's chin. Aine pulled away. "You must know that, daughter."

"I do know. But the man you call my father—he would hurt me, and you too."

Aine glanced at the others. They stared like stone statues in a churchyard—deaf and mute, powerless. Aine had come to bring wealth, a way out of a desperate situation. But alas, she had arrived without anything of worth. Except perhaps Daithi. If Aine married him, he would be duty bound to help take care of Aine's mother.

She covered her face with her hands, finding it too difficult to think in that small room, smoky with peat. Daithi had a temper she wasn't sure she could live with. Her mother should not have to tolerate that all over again.

Maire's pleading look, all of their stares, told her she needed to do something.

The most distressing revelation of all was that the Poet had been right. Aine did love Daithi. Her fear of his becoming like her father held her back.

"Come, now." Her mother urged her to her feet. "Never was there a more harrowing day. Sleep at my side, daughter, and we will sort all this out tomorrow."

Daithi hadn't moved a shuffle. Aine longed to feel his arms around her again, to relish the way he had touched her hair when he found her outside her father's house. But he did not reach for her or even say her name. He was angry, and the one thing she could not endure was a man's rage. She wished she didn't long for him. How much easier it would all be if that were so. Aine's whole body tensed as she willed her heart to obey her.

As she took her mother's arm, she watched Daithi open the door and step outside. "Wait. Where is he going? I must—"

Her mother urged her back. "Let him go, child. A man needs his space. I'm afraid you've wounded his ego. He'll not venture far on foot. There are no other dwellings for some distance."

"I will check on him later," Ninnidh offered.

"And bring him a blanket," Sorcha added.

A heavy weight landed like an anchor on Aine's chest. The mention of a soul partner, a friend so close that you shared the same heart, had sent him running away from her. She hadn't helped matters by saying that her mother was throwing her to the wolves, but that was what she feared, being discarded, unloved.

Aine glanced to the Poet, who was silently making up his bed on the opposite side of the hut. He must be a diviner to say that she and Daithi loved each other. Aine had even hidden the truth from herself. Love did not need to be acted upon, however.

"I don't want to be married."

Maire gave her a puzzled look. The Poet tried to pretend he didn't hear, shaking out his blanket.

"He seems like a nice man," Maire whispered.

Aine opened her mouth to respond but stopped as visions of the past buzzed around her head like before. She blinked and found her tongue. "We must not let anyone control us, Maither."

"Control? Certainly not. Jesu is my only master, Aine. You're not thinking every man is like your father, are you?"

"And you know Daithi's not?"

"I have helped many people over the years by bringing them food and providing shelter. I've met many travelers, men, women, and children. Most folks only want to be treated kindly, and if you do so, as Jesu would, they respond with kindness. Now tell me, what has Daithi done to you?"

"Done? Uh…'tis not what he's done."

"What is it then?"

Her father's voice reverberated through her mind again, and all Aine could do was drop to the floor and cup her hands over her ears.

Moments later, she composed herself. Everything was happening so quickly.

"'Tis been too much to comprehend in such a short time, daughter. You should rest." Her mother helped her to the sleeping board the healer had collected from under a shelf. Then she covered her with a lavender-scented sheet and lay down beside her. Aine whispered into her mother's ear. "The problem is my heart is so deeply entwined with his I fear I'll be trapped."

"I never let your father keep me from doing acts of goodwill. If I did not feel trapped, you should not either. I do not wish you to live with violence. If that is what is keeping you from marrying, then you are wise to escape it. But if it's something else, you must examine your heart. You cannot run from God…not for long."

The healer began murmuring something Aine recognized as a Psalm. Cillian's teachings had not all been forgotten. The familiar words were both comforting and convicting, as though the Christian God himself was wooing her. *God, I will praise. In God, I have put my trust.*

She soon drifted off to sleep.

When she awoke sometime later, she heard whispering. Her mother and the healer still slept. Aine wrapped herself in a blanket and stole outside. Although the sky was shielded from her sight by a mass of tree cover, the underbrush carried the glow of sunrise. She had left her shoes inside, and the dew on the mossy ground dampened her feet. She glanced around for a place to sit. Morning always felt like a sacred time. She supposed that was because there was little activity to occupy her thoughts.

The whispering was louder now, coming from the behind the hut. The voices she heard belonged to the Poet and Daithi. She sat on a log that the healer apparently had used for popping seeds out their pods. The remains lay scattered all around. She pushed the crinkled husks across the ground with her toes as she considered moving closer to listen to what they were saying. Finally, she decided to stay put.

What did it matter what Daithi said about her? Her mother was her main concern. Maire had finally broken free of the abusive man she'd married. She had an ally in the healer woman. That was good. Perhaps she didn't need Aine, had no room in her life for a grown woman who most people thought should be married by now.

She watched two robins fight over a worm. Daithi would do whatever he wanted, stay or go. And so would she. Perhaps she should return to Brigid once the book trouble had all been settled, if the woman would indeed forgive Aine for having causing it.

Shouting made her jump.

"I won't do it!" Daithi's voice boomed.

Aine hooded the blanket over her head.

"And what then?" asked the Poet.

They were coming her way, so she scooted back into the house. Her mother and the healer had been awakened by the noise and started for the door. She blocked their way, holding a finger to her lips. She left the door open a crack.

Daithi stood with both hands on his hips, facing the house, and the Poet stood in front of him.

"If there is a soul connection, what can you do to deny it? To run away will only cause misery, both to her and to you," the Poet said.

"But she follows the old ways, Ninnidh. God will not bless such a soul match."

"And a marriage is different?"

"A marriage is for convenience and for children."

Aine's heart sank. He did not love her. Her first instincts had been correct. She had been right to run away.

She had been right to steal the book away from him. He alone deserved the wrath of his clan over that book.

She bit her lip, threw open the door, and marched toward the Poet's horse. Because she was small, she was swift. Daithi's attempts to snatch her as she whisked by were futile. She was atop the horse and galloping down the path before anyone had a chance to call out her name.

Unfortunately, she glanced behind her just as a tree branch crossed the path. Shards of pain lit up her head as she smacked up against it. She felt herself falling from the horse, sucking in air as she struck the ground.

Ninnidh saw the girl fall, slowly as though floating through coagulated air. He reached out both hands to catch her, but he was too far away. Daithi now held her limp body in his arms.

"Let me see her." The healer pushed past Ninnidh and Maire. Daithi relinquished his hold on the girl, and Sorcha lay her down on the dew-damp ground. "She's breathing."

Maire breathed relief. She cried out to Jesu to save her only child.

Ninnidh was reminded of songs he'd sung, tragedies about ill-fated lovers. He prayed he would not be composing another sad ballad about this.

Moments later, Aine blinked her eyes.

"Squeeze my hand," Sorcha commanded. "Good, lass." She looked up at them. "Had the breath knocked out of her for a moment, but her eyes are clear and she can move. She'll be fine, though her head will ache mightily. Got something for that, I do." She pointed at Daithi. "Carry her inside."

Inside the hut, Sorcha began brewing a concoction that sent smoke billowing toward the hut's ventilation hole. Aine rested with a rag on her forehead, speaking quietly with her mother.

Ninnidh turned to the healer. "May I ask who taught you about the herbs? Has your knowledge come from ancient sources?"

"Ah, it is so. An old druid. Bram of Ennis Dun was his name. He learned much about Jesu from the abbess Brigid, before she was called Maither."

"So I have heard. What happened to the old man? Does he live?"

"I cannot say. Perhaps Maither Brigid knows. He is one with the earth wherever he is. God alone knows who rules Bram's heart, but I am grateful to pass on the things he has taught me."

"You have an apprentice, then?"

"I will one day."

A thunderous bang resounded at the door. Since he was closest, Ninnidh opened it. A dusty leather bound book lay at his feet. He looked up at a man on horseback.

"A curse, 'tis," the man said. "The blasted thing led me here, burning my hands until I dumped it. Woe to he who possess the book!" His horse reared up on its back legs and then carried the man away until they disappeared into the woods.

Ninnidh, not believing in curses, picked up the book. It was warm, like it had been in the sun all day. When he turned around, the thing flew out of his hands and landed at the foot of Aine's cot. No one spoke for a moment. Then they all spoke at once. Daithi wanted to tear the book to pieces. Maire wanted to shield her daughter from Satan's curse. She flung herself onto Aine's bed.

"It owns me. It controls me," Aine cried.

Ninnidh snatched the book before Daithi could get his hands on it. "Calm down, everyone. We will do nothing until there is peace in this house."

Sorcha waved a pot of burning incense. "Listen to the man!"

Daithi paced the small room. "That man will lead the army here, no doubt. We've got to leave at once."

Ninnidh shoved the book into his traveling bag. "Brigid asked me to take this book to her, and that's what I'll do." He turned to Daithi. "Everyone must stay here until I return."

The large man motioned toward the door. "'Tis not safe here. You know that man found us, Poet."

Ninnidh had to get to Brigid immediately. He felt it strongly.

Sorcha set her incense pot on the table board. "Mine is not the only dwelling deep in this forest."

Maire spoke. "Don't, Sorcha."

"Are these not the people you trust, Maire? You know the evil greed that drives men to kill for such books, aye?"

Maire put her hand on Sorcha's shoulder. "Very well. 'Tis time."

Sorcha took a step toward Ninnidh. "I know someone not far from here. He will hide us if we ask."

"Good." Ninnidh put a hand on the door latch. "What is this man's name so that I may find you when 'tis safe again?"

The woman's beaded locks rattled as she nodded. "Conleth, although it won't do you any good to know his name. No one will tell you where he lives. No one knows but Maire and me. We will find *you*, Poet, if need be. Do not worry."

He backtracked and took each person's hand in turn. "If we do not meet again, I wish you the peace of God."

Aine pinched her lips, seemingly restraining herself. It was clear she was not happy with the arrangement, but she had said she wanted to be free of the book. What power she thought it had, he could not be sure. Perhaps she had not realized the consequence of her decision to steal it and was now remorseful.

With the book snug in the bag he tied securely to his waist, he set off in the direction he remembered. There was a bit of trail to follow before he arrived in the mountains. From there, he would retrace his previous path to Brigid's hermitage.

"I want to stay with you," Aine whispered to her mother. She glanced toward Daithi, who wove his fingers together as he sat on a stool near the hearth.

"Remember, dearie, if you send him away, you'll live with that decision for the rest of your life."

"I remember the terrible fights." Aine tried to hold back her tears, but her face was wet before she knew it.

Maire wiped Aine's cheeks with a cool cloth. "Daithi isn't like that."

"You just met him."

"Cillian is how I know. He promised me he would protect you. He'd never send you to an abusive husband."

"He might if he wanted to get rid of me. He's so consumed with avoiding that druid Ardan that he hardly noticed me."

Daithi picked his head up when he heard Aine raise her voice.

Maire turned toward him. "Do you know of Ardan?"

"An evil druid, that one. Rumor says he seeks to stomp down Christianity wherever 'tis found."

Aine groaned. "I think 'tis all foolishness. My uncle is afraid of a man who is nowhere to be seen."

Maire gripped Aine's shoulders. "Daithi's right. Everyone knows the trouble Ardan has caused in the past. You are too young to remember, Aine."

Sorcha brought more of her terrible-tasting elixir, which Aine swallowed because her head was beginning to pound and every muscle in her body throbbed.

Sorcha smacked her lips as though trying to convince Aine the syrup was tasty. "Good, lass. The medicine will help. And do not worry. This Ardan cannot find us, and even if he could, the prayers of Old Conleth are enough to shield us."

Daithi stood, dusting his hands. "I won't go with you if you don't want me, Aine."

Oh, his worried brow, his pleading eyes. Aine closed her eyes against the pain in her head. When she opened them again, she found everyone staring at her. "Maither, Sorcha, would you mind very much if I spoke to Daithi alone?"

Pausing at the door, Sorcha pointed a long finger. "Do not be wearying yourself, child."

As they left, a chilling blast of air washed into the cottage.

Daithi dropped to the floor beside her cot. "I do not know how I'll go on without you, Aine, but I will if that's your choice, God help me."

"There are things I must know."

"I have no secrets, Aine."

"Why would this god of yours allow you to marry me but not be my soul friend? I heard what you said."

"What are you talking about?"

"I do not seek such a union, Daithi. A mate but not a match for the soul. You said your god would not approve of me as your soul friend."

"'Tis only your preference for the old ways, Aine. These things, they can be worked out. I will teach you."

She turned away so he would not read the disappointment in her face.

"Hear me, love. I confess I am a passionate man, speaking before my brain has a chance to catch up with my tongue. You know how I am. I'm sorry. I did not mean that as it sounded. God has not given me the gift of eloquence."

"You didn't mean it?" Hope rose in her heart. He was short-tempered, but perhaps there was a way.

"I didn't mean it *exactly* the way it sounded."

"Exactly? What did you mean, Daithi? Speak clearly." Her words were sharp enough to let him know she wanted nothing but truth.

"I do love you. I want to take care of you and live with you for the rest of my life. But…you see, we do not share a spiritual…" His gaze darted all over the cottage. He tapped his fingers on his knees. "That is, we do not have a commonality that would permit us to be soul friends, not while you follow the old traditions, Aine. My ways are those of Jesu, the God of Patrick. I had thought that because your uncle helped raise you and you lived among the monks, you held different beliefs. I was surprised to find…well, let me say this: we can be married, but so long as you deny the One True God, 'tis simply not possible for us to be soul friends, though I would like nothing more."

"I could do both."

He shook his head. "You cannot serve two masters. And there is something else."

Christians had too many rules. "What?"

"If you change only for me, 'tis not the same."

"What other reason is there?"

He closed his eyes a moment as if forming his words carefully, not something she saw him do often. "You know about Jesu. You've copied verses from the sacred Bible. You have gone to prayers with the monks, and yet you still do not believe?"

"I did not say that."

"But you coveted that book."

"There is scripture in it."

"Oh, there is, but that is not why you held it dear, now, is it?"

She let out a frustrated breath. "By the stars, man. The book is gone."

"The reasons remain. You believe in false gods, in fairies, in unknown forces."

"I have seen them!"

"What you've seen, Aine, if 'tis wondrous power—"

"Aye, it is. You must believe me."

"If you have seen a miracle, it came from the One True God—nowhere else."

She thought about the magic the book held. The way it glowed. The way the absent page had led her back to the original manuscript. The book had even floated on air to return to her. There had been no doubt its magic blessed the cattle of Daithi's lands. Anyone could see that. It was much easier to believe when you saw the things she had. "I believe in the magic of the talisman and also in Jesu."

"Nay. You cannot serve two gods." He backed away from her.

"But Daithi, you saw it too. I mean, some of it. You know the cattle grew in numbers after the book visited them. You saw that the book made its way back to me. You must know what I say is true."

He stared at her a moment. Unshed tears sparkling in his eyes. He backed away and left the cabin.

The pain in her chest pulsated, growing with each inhaled breath. But it was no physical pain. She knew the feeling well because she'd felt the same way the day her mother sent her away with Brigid. A groan rose from her throat, sounding as though it came from somewhere beyond herself. Dropping to her knees atop Sorcha's sheepskins, Aine sobbed until her well of tears was completely dry. She had no will to rise from that bed ever again.

Twenty-Seven

"Insomuch as any one pushes you nearer
to God,
he or she is your friend."

Anonymous

N innidh prayed for the people he had just left. *Please,
God, let this Conleth shield them from all harm.*

Surely the man the healer spoke of was not the same
old bishop that Ninnidh and Brigid had visited many years
ago on their return from Armagh. So much time had passed,
and the man had been ancient then. He couldn't still be alive.
Whoever this man living deep in the forest was, Ninnidh
prayed that he would provide shelter and safety.

His thoughts returned to Brigid, the woman who filled his mind most of his waking hours, as he guided his horse along an overgrown path—a shortcut. He'd seen such trails before in his many travels, so he'd had no trouble picking up this one. Local folks often blazed their own roads to get where they wanted to go. The way was quicker than a king's road built to guide travelers to hostels that helped pay the king's taxes. He knew the danger of taking such paths, though. Without maintenance, the trails were wrought with pits, hidden bogs, and sometimes thieves. It was a risk to save time that he hoped was worth it.

Moisture dripped from the tree limbs, making the undergrowth slippery. The horse adapted well and carefully plodded along. Soon, they entered a meadow where Ninnidh let the horse loose to graze. Taking his harp from its bag, Ninnidh found a soft spot to relax. He would tarry only a short while. Brigid needed him.

As he watched the horse nibble and wander, he sang a tune about the abbess. He'd been practicing it in his head almost since the last time he saw her. The tune wasn't romantic, as he'd at first anticipated. The words spoke of her duty to God and her compassion for hungry beggars. Brigid's generosity is what should be remembered, passed down to future generations. Never would he speak of her doubts.

Brigid's desire to escape to a hermitage probably meant she was now fraught with misgivings. He'd seen too many Christians fall away from the faith when tested severely. Hard times always come. There could be no escaping it. Those that prospered turned to an *anamcara*. He'd seen life-long friends, foster parent and child, teacher and student, hold each other up. God's design was for his children to live in close company. Ninnidh should be, wanted to be, her soul friend. He prayed she would understand one day. In the meantime, he would be ready.

The sun cast shadows on his corner of the meadow. He'd tarried long enough. Ninnidh called to the horse and mounted. He was turning the animal toward the path when a flash of color met his eyes. An old man, hunched and leaning on a staff, stood near a hawthorn at the meadow's opposite end.

Ninnidh called out to him, thankful he'd encountered a harmless old man instead of a rogue with a spear. "Greetings, my friend."

The old fellow held up one hand and Ninnidh trotted over to where he stood.

"Welcome in the name of Jesu." The man's voice was gravelly. "I do not get many visitors out here."

Ninnidh noted that the man had a mule tied to the hawthorn. "Jesu's blessing to you. I am just passing through."

The old man winked a watery eye. "Whether the road is crooked or straight the shortcut is the best way."

"Aye. I am abiding by that old proverb." Ninnidh had never been comfortable with identifying himself, but Brigid encouraged him to tell others who he was, so he would follow her advice. "I am Ninnidh of Lough Erne."

The old man nodded. "I have not seen you in a very long time, Poet." He wrinkled his brown-spotted nose. "Don't you know me? By Jesu, son, I'm Bishop Conleth."

Ninnidh dismounted. "I am honored to find you well, Bishop."

"As well as can be expected, thanks be to Jesu. Eighty-two summers the Lord has blessed me with."

Ninnidh glanced to the rear of the bishop, noting the bent grass in the direction the man had come. "Do you live far from here? Travelers will be looking for you."

"Truly? I haven't had a visitor in five summers, maybe six, save for the healer woman. She comes by wanting her potions blessed." He smiled. "And brings me stew and apples."

The man kept talking the way older folks are prone to do. Despite himself, Ninnidh grew impatient. "Please, Bishop Conleth. 'Tis an urgent matter. Three people, including the healer Sorcha, are seeking refuge at your home right now."

"Ah." He tapped his fingers on his staff. "By Jesu they will find it. Sorcha knows my place well. I do not need to be there, but I will return tomorrow." He chuckled. "I used to dread those seeking me out for spiritual training. Hid from them at times, I did. But now that I am older, I realize that I grow closer to Jesu each time I place my hand on one of the young one's heads."

"Go in peace, Bishop Conleth. And pray for Abbess Brigid, would you? I am on my way to her hermitage now."

"Brigid? In a hermitage? I must be getting old. Never thought I'd ever hear of that. The blessing of the Three on her, son." The bishop prayed for Ninnidh's journey and then they parted ways.

The sky was pink by the time Ninnidh rejoined the road. The hills spread before him. He would soon arrive at Brigid's cave. He didn't know if he would find her distraught and afraid. He hoped not but was sure his hope was ill-placed. *Please, God, let me find her in residence.* God forbid that Ardan had kidnapped her or…worse.

At the base of the mountain, he tied the horse to a tree and began his climb. The book added extra weight, soon causing his thighs to scream for rest. All the riding he'd done over the last few days took a toll. Foot, hand. Hand, foot. He climbed with determination. If he would be Brigid's *anamcara*, God would expect no less of him.

A momentary flash of blackness caught the corner of his vision. He turned his head sharply. Nothing. Whatever moved, a wolf or beaver or a large bird, was gone now. He quickened his pace the best he could. Finally, he stood at the cave's entrance. He bent down and called into the hollow. "Brigid? Are you in here?"

"I'm here, Jesu," a weak voice replied.

Ninnidh smiled to himself. Surely anyone who sought God for days in a lonely place would imagine the voice they heard was God's. "'Tis me, Ninnidh." He retrieved his harp and examined it in the fading sunlight. Miraculously, it had survived the journey without a scratch. He strummed it, hoping the music would draw her out.

Moments later, she still hadn't come to meet him. He called again. "Brigid? Shall I come in?"

"Come," she whispered. "Come, Lord Jesu."

Puzzled by this reply, he entered. Brigid sat with her cloak across her lap, a wee fire burning in the middle of a ring of stones. Her tangled hair lacked its usual golden sheen. She lifted her gaze. "I told you God would abandon me, Ninnidh. It has happened. You should flee this place."

He placed his harp on the dirt floor of the cave, careful to avoid the dampness dripping from the cave's roof. "You are not well, Brigid. Let me fix you something to eat."

She didn't answer as he pulled his stash of oats from his bag. A small bronze pot with a lid stood near the fire, and he picked it up. "Do you have water?"

She pointed behind her. "There is a spring at the back of the cave."

"I'll return shortly."

Later, after he'd coaxed her to eat a bit, he strummed his harp, hoping it would soothe her as it had so many others. He'd stoked the fire for more light and gazed at her. She was not herself, but a hollow shell. She, a consecrated sister of the church, now believed God had left her. He could scarcely grasp the idea. How could sleeping in a cave bring about such a change?

He chose one of his favorite Psalms that he had set to music and let his voice echo off the cave walls.

Why are you cast down, O my soul? And why are you disquieted within me?

Hope in God, for I shall yet praise Him for the help of His countenance.

She turned to him. He had finally gotten her attention. "I heard God speak to me, not once but several times. He hates me, Ninnidh."

He took her hand. "God doesn't hate you, Brigid. Listen to me. Your, uh, *anamcara* would not lie to you. God is in your very breath. He is close. He made you and knows you best."

"He made Satan too, didn't he?"

"And he was good until Satan turned that goodness into evil. He was one of God's best angels, and he took his talent and corrupted it. You have not done that."

She shook her stringy hair.

"Right now. You have not."

284

He thought about Old Conleth. The old man had said that he began to enjoy life once he started blessing others. "Brigid, you do not wish to be away from your work, do you? Think of the hungry children, the lonely mothers, the pagan women of the fire. You don't want to turn your back on them, do you?"

She shook her head. "But I do have to seek God. A war might be waged against my people. Is there any hope in convincing God to hear my prayers?"

"There is." He withdrew the book from his belt and set it down next to her. "There is always hope. Just as the psalmist said."

He withdrew to the spring again to collect water for her bath. Then he left her to examine the book alone. He hoped she would also search her heart. He would sleep next to his horse.

Ardan cursed his luck. Just as he was gaining ground in convincing Brigid that she had no power, her green-mantle-clad poet friend had shown up. He could not spook them both. He had almost convinced himself to give up the game and return to King Donal. Getting that king on his side, like the king of Leinster had been before he eventually turned to the Christians, would be more productive anyway. Book or not, he would cast his power of influence and win the kingdom's trust. They would credit Ardan with the prosperity of their lands. But then he noticed the Poet exiting the cave, the bulge in his belt no longer evident. He could have been delivering food, but why would he tie it to his belt when he had a traveling bag. Nay, 'twas much more likely that he had transported the book. Ardan's luck was turning around after all.

He waited until the cloak of night had rested on the earth for several hours before approaching the cave. He had hatched a plan to sound more god-like this time. Ardan was skilled at changing his voice. Other druids might be able to change shape, but disguising his voice would prove more valuable in this endeavor.

He snared a deer and struggled with it until he maneuvered it far from the cave. He wasn't sure where the Poet went, but it seemed he'd gone far enough away. Even if the singer heard the death cry of the animal, he would suppose it to be the law of nature on this mountain—nothing out of place.

Ardan drew his dagger across the deer's neck and collected blood in the ceremonial half shell he always carried with him. Ardan would need the gods' blessing before he began his task. He decided to examine the animal's entrails as well. Knowing what the future held would be most valuable.

He was not happy with what he saw. This animal had a diseased liver. Very bad luck. Should he abandon his plans? He gazed at the sky. The moon was full, a good time to begin anew. He stared up at the bright constellations, a glorious sprinkling of light prickling across the dark woolly blanket of the sky. This was a good sign. He had just chosen the wrong animal to study. Would the gods accept this sacrifice anyway? They had to. He had no time to search out another. Daylight would come too soon.

Ardan washed his hands in the deer's blood and then rinsed them in a stream. He hurried back to the cave. He called out in his best deep voice but there was no response. Had she crept away while he was worshipping?

He ducked his head into the cave. There she was, lying in front of a dying fire. He cloaked himself and entered. Not even the rustling of his bird feathers stirred her. He placed a hand on her forehead. She was burning with fever. His gaze landed on lump under her blanket. Carefully, he peeled back the fleece back to reveal a leather-covered book.

Brigid groaned and rolled to one side. He let the covering slip from his fingers. When it was clear that she would not awaken, he snatched up the book and hurried outside.

"Where do you think you're going with that, man?" The Poet stood in his path.

"Wherever I chose. I am a high druid, an ollave. I suggest you back away."

The Poet pointed the sharp end of a dagger at him. "You hold no higher status than I do."

"Nonsense."

"I am Ninnidh of Loch Erne."

Blasted. He was right. There was no treachery Ardan could do that this man could not cast off. He would have to rely on pure grit. He picked up a rock and struck the handsome young ollave squarely in the middle of his forehead.

Twenty-Eight

"For what is faith unless it is to believe
what you do not see?"

St. Augustine

N innidh stumbled toward Brigid who had come outside
to investigate. She hefted a brass cooking pot over her
head and brought it down with a thunk on top of the druid's
head. Ardan staggered a bit, gazing at Brigid as though his
own mother had struck him. Wobbling like a pottery bowl
on the edge of a table board, he eventually landed in the fire.
He franticly rolled to one side, smothering the flames that
singed his ebony cloak. The druid rolled with abandon,
haphazardly striking his head on a rock formation near the

cave wall where he passed out. Wee wisps of charred feathers jumped from the fire.

Ninnidh went to the man. "He's alive. I'll tie his wrists before he wakes up."

Brigid moved as though sleepwalking. She went to her bed and lay down on a fleece, pulling it up to her chin.

When Ninnidh finished with the druid, he went to Brigid's side. She opened her eyes. "Words are swirling around my head, Ninnidh."

He touched a tear on her cheek. "You are exhausted. Sleep. I will take care of everything."

She continued talking. "At first it was random letters on a page that made no sense, but soon they joined and spoke to me." She opened her eyes wider as though she'd just remembered something. "I read those pages, Ninnidh. Right before falling asleep."

"Shush. Do not worry."

She lifted herself on one elbow. "Nay, listen. I remember those brown marks on calfskin. I've seen books like that many times in my studies. Some of Cillian's manuscripts are similar, but…" She rubbed a hand across her forehead. "This is different somehow." She glanced around the cave. "Could I have read them somewhere else? Where?"

He moved his hand to her forehead. "You're hot with fever." Ninnidh supported her shoulders until she sat all the way up, leaning against his chest. He tilted her head and drizzled spring water into her mouth until she managed to swallow it.

Refreshed, her sea-holly eyes stared past him. "Cry out for insight and ask for understanding. Search for them as you would for silver; seek them like hidden treasures."

"That's what you read in the stolen book?"

"Ninnidh! Have you looked at the book?"

"Brigid, please calm down. You are ill."

"I'm fine." She threw the fleece from her lap. "There's not a thing wrong with me."

"Still, you should rest."

"There is no time."

He stretched out his hand to gauge the temperature of her skin. She was right. The fever had vanished. Praise God.

"For now, drink the water and lie back. I will take care of this vermin."

A deep moan came from the druid as he slowly lifted his head.

Brigid whispered. "We had better talk about this now while we have the chance. Tell me, did you read the Uí Náirs' book?"

"I did not. What is so urgent?"

She took a long drink of water and then reached for the book when he held it out. "There are genealogies, as Daithi said, and many stories about various kings. 'Tis true that the book establishes the Uí Náir as rulers of their kingdom, and as such, the book holds great value for them."

"This we knew."

"There is more." She waved her hand for him to come close.

He leaned over her shoulder and stared at the page she held open, his long hair brushing against her back. The writing was faded and seemed to be hurriedly written, making interpreting it difficult. After a time, he understood. "Incredible. I knew that this tribe once had a Christian king. He or his scribes, someone versed in Latin, must have written those words in the book, among the pages of the other information."

"And they are more valuable than anything else in here, whether the people realize it or not."

Ardan howled and turned toward them. He wiggled but could not break the restraints.

Brigid rose and stood over him. "I'm sorry I hit you. You gave me no choice. I could not sit by and see you attack my friend. It is well known an abbess needs her *anamcara*, Druid."

Ninnidh's heart raced.

Brigid glanced back to her blankets where she had gingerly laid the book. Then she turned back to her nemesis.

"Untie his hands, Ninnidh. He isn't going anywhere with his ankles bound like that."

Ninnidh obeyed and Ardan seemed grateful to be able to rub his head.

"That explains it." Ardan slid a hand over the tender spot on his head. "This man defends you."

Brigid smiled. "He certainly does, and I, him."

"Evidently. Untie me. There is no need for this."

"No need, you say?" Ninnidh reached a hand to his own sore head. "You tried to kill me."

"Enough. Just give me the book, and I'll be on my way."

Brigid stood at Ninnidh's side. "Certainly not. We will hold a council with the Uí Náir king and the Brehon to decide the fate of the book."

"Brehon? What need do we have for him? Just give it to me, and I'll return it. When the king has the book, peace will come again."

Brigid would never trust the druid again, Ninnidh knew. She had believed him once, years ago in this very cave. The druid had convinced her she had no worth without the power of miracles. She had even bargained with him, so Ninnidh had heard, promising not to use this power, and he had promised to return her mother. Ninnidh had rescued Brocca himself.

Brigid drew in a long breath and placed her hands confidently in front of her. "God, not me, sent you away from here years ago. You remember, aye?"

The druid narrowed his eyes to slits. Ninnidh was sure that if the man were freed now he would strangle them with his hand hands.

"You, and Christians like you, did that to me, woman."

Brigid did not back down. "Nay, you're wrong. A band of pirates carried you off to a far place, now didn't they?"

"You had something to do with that." The druid snarled.

Brigid pursed her lips before responding. "I certainly did not."

Ardan spit on the clay cave floor. "A lucky coincidence for you, is that what you're saying?"

"'Twas not that, either."

"You are mad."

Brigid began to pace around the bound man, much the way they'd seen the druid do during the previous encounters. "You are a spiritual man. Surely you understand that there are forces outside of our control."

Ardan groaned, grasping his right wrist. "I do know that. Whatever curse you put on me, take it off!" He began to wail.

Brigid knelt low to look into the man's eyes. "I have done nothing to you. I did not even know you were back in Ireland until recently, and I believed you were in Armagh. That's what folks said. I had no reason to put a curse on you, even if I would do such a thing, which I wouldn't."

He continued to moan and opened his palm. Ninnidh saw nothing that should have caused him pain.

Brigid placed a hand on the man's shoulder. "I think I understand. God has touched you, Ardan, and good cannot dwell in the midst of evil."

Ardan spat again.

A realization seemed to dawn in Brigid's eyes. "'Twas your voice speaking to me, wasn't it?" She went back to pacing around the druid, tapping her fingers together. "You pretended to be God."

Ninnidh saw the truth in the man's face. What had he done to her?

After she'd marched around him several times, he beat his fists on the ground. "You're mad. Always have been. As lame as the church is, I still would never have thought they would have consecrated you a bishop."

"Know about that, do you? Well, let me tell you something you don't know."

Ninnidh crossed his arms and tilted his head to one side, listening.

"There is nothing you, abbess, can tell me. I am an esteemed druid, an ollave, a master."

"Oh, you hold knowledge, certainly, but you have not used it for good. Nay, just the opposite. I wonder what the Brehon will say about that."

The druid's intense brown eyes held Brigid's. "I will not stay for the Brehon."

Ninnidh opened his mouth to speak, but she beat him to it. "You'll stay even if we have to keep you tied up." She lifted the book. "Are you afraid?"

Ardan's bottom lip trembled. He stared at his palm. "I bear your mark, the same one that is on that book. Remove it!"

There was nothing on his hand, and the book's cover was only smooth, brown leather with no tooled symbols.

Ninnidh stood. "Who's mad? I see no mark."

The druid pointed a finger. "That wheel thing the sisters put on graves. You've seen it."

"What of it?"

"'Tis there." He held his hand toward Ninnidh. "You see it, man?"

Ninnidh shrugged. There truly was nothing.

Ardan rubbed his hand furiously as though trying to remove an invisible mark. The abbess showed pity on him and retrieved a finished rush cross from her traveling bag. "This?"

Ardan bobbed his graying head franticly. "That's it. 'Tis here on my hand. Why doesn't anyone see it?"

The abbess stowed the cross in her bag. "God has marked you."

"The gods hate me today, it seems."

"I used to think the same thing of myself, but a wise friend showed me that God doesn't hate anyone."

Ninnidh winked at her.

She patted the book with an open palm. "This will explain. May I read it to you?"

He grumbled. "If you must."

She snapped the cover shut, sending dust into the dank air. "If you do not want to understand the mark, man, so be it."

"Nay, nay. Carry on."

She opened the book again and turned toward the back. Her hand rested on a crinkled page. "Cry out for insight and ask for understanding. Search for them as you would for silver; seek them like hidden treasures."

"No surprise, that." The druid shrugged his shoulders. "I have done so my entire life—searching. 'Tis the work of a druid. If you were wise, you'd know that, abbess."

"Aye, if I were wise. I have been quite foolish until now, but Jesu has opened my eyes."

"Fine. Your epiphany, if that's what it was, has nothing to do with me. I beg of you, remove this mark. I will leave you *and* your precious book." He gritted his teeth.

Conceding defeat did not come easy for an arrogant druid. Ninnidh had met many a man who struggled against the Christian concept of surrender.

Ardan lifted his chin. "This island is big enough for me to go where no one will find me."

Brigid clicked her tongue. "I said you will stay here and you will hear me out. There is something you do not know, ollave druid."

"What?"

Brigid patted the leather binding again. "Your name is in this book, Ardan."

"Impossible."

"Your father was a fisherman."

"How could you know that?"

"'Tis all in this book, your history. And once you hear it, I pray to Jesu that your heart will be changed."

Ninnidh took the book from her. "Is his name really in here?" He began thumbing through the pages.

"In the genealogy."

Ardan stared at the rope binding his feet. "This book has marked me as well. Others have bemoaned its power. If you are wise, you will cast the book away. I offered to take it from you, as you may remember."

"The only way this book has marked you is if its words have convicted you."

He narrowed his eyes. "'Tis your mark, woman, that burns my hand."

She drew in her breath. "We will let the Brehon decide what needs to be done."

A commotion coming from the side of the mountain caught their attention. Ninnidh handed Brigid the book and left to follow the sound. He soon returned. "More visitors. It seems, Maither Brigid, that your hermitage is not the quiet retreat you had hoped for."

She scrambled to their bags and began to search out grain and herbs to cook over the fire. "I do not mind at all."

Twenty-Nine

"What paints the heart must be
washed away with tears."

Irish proverb

ine hadn't wanted to go, but once again, she'd been
given no choice. At last they arrived at an unoccupied
house. Dark with the smell of age. "Let's not go in there,"
she'd complained.

"Be grateful, Aine," her mother had scolded. "'Tis more
than a wee bit better than sleeping in the wild."

It had not been a matter of gratitude. She feared going
alone, without the book and without Brigid. She wondered
aloud if the old man might be a sorcerer.

Sorcha laughed. "I expect he knows less about healing and herbs than I do. What he does know, child, is how to intercede with prayer."

When the old man returned to his secluded hut, Aine learned that he had been expecting them. Apparently he'd encountered the Poet, who told him they were coming and that Brigid was in trouble.

"We must go," Maire declared. "If Brigid is in danger, we cannot delay."

Aine was happy to have found her mother, but she complained about the journey. "What we must do is keep Ninnidh from bringing her the book."

"One step at a time," Maire said. "First we must tend to the abbess, bring her food, herbs, and clean clothing."

On the road, they found Daithi, who was happy to contribute his muscle to the quest. Now the wee troupe of travelers included Aine, her mother, Sorcha, Daithi, and the feeble old man referred to as Bishop Conleth. What a band of ill-fitted companions.

"Maither," Aine whispered from the rear of the caravan. "I am not comfortable with Daithi being here. All I can think about when he looks at me is how he wanted to marry me for sole purpose of bearing children."

"Comfort has nothing to do with this journey, Aine. We must think of Brigid."

She did think of the abbess, but not as someone who needed rescuing. She would be the one who would make them all see that she'd been right about Daithi. She'd be an advocate for Aine after all this business about the book was resolved.

Aine forgot all that when they arrived at the hermitage. The man called Ardan had been tied up and the Poet was standing guard.

Aine rushed to the abbess's side. "Oh, Brigid. I am so sorry for the trouble I've caused." Her gaze was immediately drawn to a fleece blanket where the book rested. "You've got the talisman, don't you? See? The book has kept you from harm."

Daithi sighed and found a seat on a boulder. She ignored him and turned back toward Brigid. "All will be well now. We've brought you supplies."

Brigid blessed her, passing a hand over her hand.

Aine felt at ease knowing the greatest powers she'd ever seen were right there with her in that cave. The book, as unpredictable as it had been, could be controlled by Brigid.

Maire led Aine to a seat near the fire as the druid's gaze followed them. It was a good thing Cillian had not been with them. He'd have gone mad with the druid so near.

Brigid patted the leather cover. "The book gives no comfort, child. It has no power on its own."

"But the cattle. Even Daithi saw how they prospered in the presence of it. What about—"

Brigid interrupted her "The herds flourished with the blessing of Jesu." She passed around a pot of stirabout, and they all ate. Still, the pot remained full—another miracle wrought from Brigid.

The abbess curled up on the fleece as the others crowded around the fire. Even the druid, partially restrained, was a part of their circle.

The abbess opened the book's cover. She did not seem alarmed by it, and for some reason the book was not unleashing searing heat into her hands. "Let me read some of the words that were copied into this book."

Aine curled up next to Brigid, and as Maire joined them, Aine laid her head on her mother's shoulder. The men on each side of the miserable druid perched like watchmen guarding a castle gate. Aine had read parts of the book, but the words were insignificant. Perhaps Brigid would tell stories instead, like the Poet. With the day slipping into night, Aine didn't mind postponing a return trip to the dreary old man's house. She wanted to stay with Brigid.

Brigid ran a finger down the script. "Ah, listen to this." She waited until all eyes were on her—all except the druid's, who seemed to be pouting about his circumstance. "'Tis a prayer I have heard uttered but have never seen written down before. This book is quite a marvel."

Maire stroked Aine's shoulder. "Please, read it."

"I am bending my knee in the eye of the Father who created me, in the eye of the Son who purchased me, in the eye of the Spirit who cleansed me, in friendship and affection. Through Your own Anointed One, O God. Bestow upon us fullness in our need, love toward God, the affection of God, the smile of God, the fear of God, and the will of God to do in the world of the Three, as angels and saints do in heaven; each shade and light, each day and night, each time in kindness, give us Your Spirit."

"So lovely." Ninnidh strummed his harp as though he were about to compose a song.

The words relaxed Aine until the druid Ardan barked an objection. "I see no need to bend my knee to anyone. 'Tis the weakness of Christians, submission."

Daithi inclined his head toward the druid. "Want me to stuff a cloth in his mouth?"

302

Brigid chuckled. "'Tis not necessary. I supposed he'd not like it. But I promised him there was something here for him, besides his name in the genealogy."

This time the old bishop spoke up. "His name is in the genealogy, is it? The wonder of Jesu!" He clapped his wrinkled hands together.

Brigid smiled. "Aye, he is of Daithi's kin."

Daithi made a face. "Everyone knows the evil perpetrated by this druid. He's no kin of mine."

Brigid got to her feet, the book cradled in her arms. "Every clan has a black sheep or two. But he could come around. Jesu has some words for him." She paused. No one spoke. Aine wondered if the abbess might be making it up. Few people knew how to read. If she made something up, who would be the wiser?

Brigid cleared her throat. "Many are saying of me, God will not deliver him."

More silence. No one expected this god or even any other to deliver this druid. He was surely bound for punishment.

"But you are a shield around me, O LORD; you bestow glory on me and lift up my head."

Well, looking at the pitiful man right now, he was certainly not bestowed with glory.

"To the Lord I cry aloud, and he answers me from his holy hill. I lie down and sleep; I wake again, because the Lord sustains me."

Ninnidh lowered his voice and stared at Brigid. "Are you sure these words aren't for you, Maither Brigid?"

"These are King David's words. A scribe wrote them down for all of us. Ardan just doesn't recognize that yet. He will."

All of us? Aine was puzzled. Were the words for her as well? She gave Brigid all her attention.

"I will not fear the tens of thousands drawn up against me on every side. Arise, O Lord!"

A wind began to howl outside the cave and then a current swooped into the cave and swirled about them, tossing Aine's hair into her eyes. She clung to her mother, afraid of being swept away. Brigid was still as powerful as ever to conjure up such a show of force.

Brigid raised her voice over the wind. "Deliver me, O my God! Strike all my enemies on the jaw; break the teeth of the wicked."

The wind left Aine then and seemed to entirely surround the druid. He was caught in a storm and lifted off his feet. Then, just as suddenly as it had appeared, the wind died, dropping the druid on his face with a thud.

"Ow!" He clutched his left cheek.

Sorcha ran to him. "God has broken his jaw!"

The raging storm pushed out the opening of the cave, leaving only the guttural cries of the once powerful druid.

Brigid lowered her voice and whispered, "From the Lord comes deliverance. May your blessing be on your people."

They were left awestruck. Time passed in silence. The old bishop snored. Sorcha placated Ardan by wrapping a cloth around his jaw and tying it atop his head. Eventually, everyone settled in to sleep, but Aine could not rest. She approached the abbess. "Brigid, who are your god's people?"

"Anyone who believes and calls on the name of Jesu, Aine."

"Surely your god is greatest."

Brigid brushed her grimy hair from her face and smiled. "My God, the God of Patrick, the God of all the fathers written about in scripture—you remember Isaac, Jacob, and Joseph?"

"I do remember."

"He is the only God. There are no others. The display of power you saw here tonight is from Him, not from me or any mortal being. He created all the elements of the universe. He set the stars and moon in the sky."

"He is all-powerful."

"He is, but there is more to tell." She hurried to her pile of belongings and returned with a woven figure, holding it up in the firelight. It was a symbol, much like those carved into doorposts and on the face of high crosses, but this one was woven from rushes. Four arms protruded from a diamond shaped center, like the spokes of a wheel.

Ardan began wiggling back and forth. He could not speak because of his injury, but he held out his hand. "What's wrong with him?" Aine asked.

The noise startled the others. Daithi stood in front of the druid and held his hands up like a shield. "Stay clear."

"Let me see what's wrong," Aine insisted. She was strangely drawn to the druid at that moment and could not keep herself from peering around Daithi's massive shoulders. What she saw made her gasp. Ardan's palm glowed orange, just like the page of the book had done. But on his skin glowed the shape of the wheel cross that Brigid had just shown to her. Tears streamed down the druid's face and bounced about on the hard dirt floor of the cave. Sorcha tried to comfort him to no avail. "Why is he marked like that?"

The others looked at her like she had spoken a language they could not comprehend. "His hand has the symbol," she explained, pointing to the rush cross Brigid held. "That. That is burned into his hand."

"Nonsense," Daithi said.

The others agreed there was nothing there, but Aine saw it plain as day.

"I think I know what is happening," Brigid finally said. "Please, brothers and sisters, be at peace. Sit down." She disappeared to the dark part of the cave and returned moments later carrying a shell full of spring water, which she mercifully poured on Ardan's painful burn. "God is speaking to the unbelievers, calling them to him."

Aine still stared at the druid. "Why?"

"Let me explain with this cross. I'll tell you what I told my earthly father when he was dying. It made a difference for him, and it should for you too."

The bishop reclined near the druid and snored loudly, undisturbed by what was happening. Probably hard of hearing, Aine assumed. But the others were attentive. The poet sat crossed-legged to the right of the prisoner. Sorcha continued to tend to the poor druid, dabbing his perspiring forehead with a cloth pulled from the bag of cures she wore around her waist. Daithi, finally convinced the ailing druid was no real threat, retreated to the Poet's right. Aine sat down next to her mother on the fleece close to the fire.

Brigid stood in the midst of them and cleared her throat. "When I first wove one of these, I was thinking about Jesu dying on a cross."

"Torture," Daithi added. "Our Lord was tortured on a cross and He died."

"True enough," Brigid said.

"Your god is dead?" Aine could barely believe what she was hearing.

"Listen to the story, child," Ninnidh said as he added his music to Brigid's telling.

"Why did someone kill him?" Aine could not be silent. This made no sense.

"They thought he was a king who would one day rule over them all. They didn't want him to have so much power."

"Your god was a king?" Aine felt more confused. None of the prayers she'd heard the monks recite spoke of this. None that she could recall.

Brigid fingered her woven cross. "Ah, a king he was, but not the kind they expected. He was kind, gentle, and forgiving, but fierce when someone broke God's laws."

"Fair enough." Aine wished for people to be reasonable, not overpowering. Perhaps this god could be real, if he had not died.

Brigid pointed a finger at her. "Now, you might be wondering why anyone would kill a king like that and why he would not seek to save himself. He had many followers who might have come to his aide."

"Why didn't they? Why did he have to die?"

"He went willingly to his crucifixion, telling his friends, 'He who lives by the sword will die by the sword.'"

Aine thought about the army pursuing Brigid and the book. This was why Brigid had sought out a hermitage. She wanted time to make a plan rather than to fight a war.

"I still don't know why your god died and what good he can do us now."

"You should believe, Aine, because he did this for you."

"Me? I do not know him."

"He knows you, Aine. And he knows Ardan." She looked in the druid's direction. "He is the very breath you breathe. Without Him, you have no life in you. You know this. Think about it. Concentrate on what I am saying. Turn it over in your mind like a farmer plows a field."

Aine closed her eyes and tried. Listening to her own breath—in, out, in, out—she felt the rhythm of life and heard the name of Jesu with each exchange of air.

After a few moments, Brigid spoke again. "Nay, our God is not dead. Death did not destroy Him. He rose above death to life everlasting, and not just in the Otherworld, but in our world too."

Brigid's words settled in Aine's mind.

"Give thanks that He died so that you could live. Forgiveness comes at a great price."

Aine had more questions. "What price?"

"The price of opening one's heart. When you see his body hanging on the cross, you know what it cost."

"But why? Why did he do that?"

"Because he loves us, each one of us, more than his own life. To offer the heart is to offer the self, nothing held back."

Aine looked back to Daithi, tears streaming down her cheeks. She didn't know if she could love him like that, but she understood that was what she had been scared of all along, the cost of opening her heart.

She asked more questions as the fire burned low, and then she willingly allowed this Jesu into her heart to be her only God.

Thirty

"God does not refuse grace to one who does
what he can."

Medieval Latin Proverb

Aine and the others returned to Cill Dara the next day. Aine kept close to the abbess, sensing the presence of God. Surely he was with Aine as well, but Aine felt joy radiating from the abbess, and she wanted to soak in that warm sunbeam of strength.

Brigid seemed happy to get back to Cill Dara and find her flock waiting. Etain met them at the gate. "We hid until it was safe, and we prayed for your safe return." She kissed Brigid on both cheeks.

"You have done well. Ninnidh has gone to summon the Brehon, and Daithi has returned to make a request to his king. We will have a great feast in two days. There is much to be done. Where is Fianna? We have guests to take care of."

"I do not know, Maither. She has disappeared."

"She was not harmed?"

"I have no word of that."

"At least we have that. Would you take Maire and Aine to the guesthouse? I trust it still stands."

"It does, indeed. Would you like me to take that book to the scriptorium or will you have the brothers take charge of it?"

Brigid gripped the book to her chest. "I will deliver it myself. Please tend to the needs of my mother and our guests. We also have a healer visiting, Sorcha. She lingered in the stables to see if the horses need care. See to her needs as well."

Etain blinked her faint eyelashes. "She won't find any beasts there, Maither, other than those you brought with you."

Aine knew what Brigid would say, and it was amazing.

Brigid whisked a hand through the air. "The army may have stolen our animals, but God has restored them. The beasts seem to have left their captors and returned to us."

The nun bowed and did not seem as astonished by this news as Aine had been. "Come, please." She nodded to Aine and Maire.

"Wait a moment." Aine saw the old bishop approaching the abbess. He padded toward her, leaning on his staff.

Brigid held out a hand. "I hope the journey has not been too hard on you, Bishop."

"Not at all, Maither Brigid. I have become quite fond of travel, praise Jesu. My body may not favor it, but my spirit does."

"Well, you are welcome here. I hope you will stay for as long as you want."

He winked. "You will need my services soon, and I will be here." He accepted Maire's arm and hobbled away with her toward the guesthouses.

Aine lingered behind. "I want to help you, Maither Brigid. May I accompany you?"

"As you wish."

When they entered the scriptorium, Brigid greeted the brothers who had been working diligently at their tasks, sweeping and sorting. The destruction of such an important part of the monastery was heartbreaking. Burnt timber smell permeated the walls. Many books lay scorched and worthless on the floor.

"The faithful will rebuild and transcribe more books." Brigid patted Aine's arm and raised her chin as she proceeded to stroll through the rubble.

As Aine followed, she wondered why God had not prevented such destruction.

Brigid pulled an intact book satchel from a high shelf, shook cinders from it, and slipped the Uí Náir book inside.

Two days later, just after Lauds, Aine heard a brother calling from a lookout near the gate. "Visitors approaching, Maither Brigid."

Aine had been walking with the abbess, listening to her prayers about the upcoming proceedings. Brigid smoothed her hands along her cloak. "Do not worry, child. All will go as God has planned."

Brocca came up behind them and placed a hand on Brigid's shoulder. "A big day."

"'Tis indeed, Maither." She gave Brocca a quick kiss. "I treasure you."

"One needs people, Brigid. 'Tis how God made us, to be in relationship with Him and with others."

A trumpet blared, but with a sound much more inviting than the war cry Aine had heard when Cill Dara was attacked. When the army had first approached in a show of force, the trumpets mimicked the sound of ravens, harsh and piercing. The noise had made her shiver. Now, however, she was filled with anticipation. Her newfound faith gave her a sense of contentment that was just as amazing as the things she'd seen from the book. What it all meant, she did not know, but the summit that was to soon take place could hold answers.

Brigid and her followers formed a line to allow the king's entourage to pass. Aine hung toward the back, but the elevation of the ground she stood on allowed a view of the procession. When the king drew closer, Aine's excitement waned. The royal man scowled as though he wanted war and not compromise.

He stopped in front of Brigid. "Abbess Brigid."

She bowed her head, allowing him the respect his position called for. He in turn was polite, though in no way affable. Etain led the way to the refectory, the only building at Cill Dara large enough to hold them all that wasn't charred as the scriptorium was.

Aine scrambled to keep up. "Where's the Poet?" she asked a sister walking near her.

"I'm sure he and the Brehon are on their way."

"Is that druid still here or did the abbess let him go?"

The lass giggled. "She wouldn't do that, not before this convening."

The sister, with long legs and long strides, paused to let Aine catch up. "The druid Ardan is at the hospital with a healer they call Sorcha. He is mending nicely, so I hear."

"It would be a pity to allow him to disrupt this."

"Oh, don't be worrying. He won't."

"How can you be sure? He's a powerful druid." Heat rushed to Aine's face. "I mean, I know God is stronger, but, he should not be underestimated."

Another sister joined in the conversation. "I would feel better if the Poet were here. Everyone knows his influence. What could be taking him so long? The Brehon's residence is not so far."

The crowed filed in and clustered close to the walls. Those who could not fit waited outside along with many of the king's men.

The king spoke. "I am here to personally receive my property, Abbess. Because you administer a spiritual establishment here on lands properly granted by the king of

Leinster, we will require nothing of you. Give me my book, and we will depart."

Aine was appalled. This man sacked the monastery and he sounded mighty self-righteous. Not even an apology.

Brigid reached out and touched the king's scepter. Surely she despised this show of granting her the right to speak in her own refectory. "All in good time, King Donal. We are awaiting the arrival of the Brehon."

The king's deep voice bellowed against the timber walls. "To what end? I am the rightful owner of the book. You are a learned woman. Surely you have deduced my ownership by reading its pages."

"There is that, but I have discovered something else."

He blustered on about wasting time, tugging carefully groomed strands of long brown hair from under his jeweled headpiece.

Brigid remained undeterred. "Surely you owe me this consideration after what your warriors did to Cill Dara."

He sniffed. "I owe you nothing, save what you've already gotten."

A slight grimace crossed Brigid's face. "Well, King Donal, if you will not admit you owe me the courtesy of allowing me to speak a few of the words from the book to this assembly, I will wait because I imagine the Brehon will."

The king shifted on the stately chair brought into the building by his royal servants. "A few words, you say? And then you will return the book?"

The room grew silent with this bargain. Had Brigid anticipated the king's acceptance? How could a few spoken words resolve this conflict?

A whispered announcement made its way across the assembly. "The Brehon is here."

When the king heard it, he nodded.

The Brehon entered, followed by the Poet. Aine felt her shoulders relax. Brigid had the support she wanted. Aine couldn't help but wonder if the book was in agreement. Or, rather, if God would allow this bargain to be made. She'd seen the book go its own way before.

The Brehon, his silky beard rivaling the king's in both length and splendor, touched the king's scepter and then greeted Brigid with a kiss on her cheek. "You have summoned me, Maither Brigid?"

"I have. Thank you for coming. We have a dispute about a book." She explained the situation to him.

The Brehon stretched out both arms. "I have seen the damage done to your beloved Cill Dara."

King Donal piped up. "I have been offered terms. All here heard before you came, Brehon. The abbess is honor-bound to see it through and give us our book back."

Brigid tapped her staff on the floor. "I do not deny it."

"You agree that the book will be returned?" the Brehon asked her.

"I do. But I ask something first."

The Brehon glared at King Donal. "I believe you are entitled. What do you want?" The judge tented his fingers across his chest. Then he bent low to speak in a hushed voice. Fortunately, Aine was perfectly situated to overhear. "Does this have to do with the *élúdach*?"

Aine wasn't sure what an *élúdach* was, but she supposed it was a legal term. A sudden dizziness overtook her. Could they be talking about her, the renegade taken in at Cill Dara? She had instigated all this, after all. She stole a look at Daithi, who stood among the men in Donal's entourage.

Brigid held her head higher. "There is no need. The king has not asked that the person who took the book be held responsible."

The king bellowed. "I have already held you all responsible. You've paid a great price, and that is enough for me if the book is returned."

Air escaped Aine's lungs. Those crowded around her gave her annoyed looks. She wiped her brow with a cloth she pulled from her waist bag. She alone owed Brigid restitution. She would pay the best she could.

The Brehon nodded. "Then we shall move ahead." He raised his voice. "What is it, Maither Brigid, that you want in exchange for returning the *Lebor na Uí Náir*?"

She turned to her assistant. "Bring him in, Etain."

Etain stared at her with a face white and eyes as big as platters and did not respond.

Brigid grasped both of the nun's arms. "What's wrong?"

Etain's voice trembled. "He's gone. He overpowered Sorcha and he's gone."

A rumbling began where those close overheard and quickly spread around the room.

"Is the healer hurt?" someone asked.

"She is not," Etain managed to say.

Brigid turned first one way, then the other, her face white with panic. While the druid might pose a danger, he was surely not needed in this meeting. The abbess's reaction made no sense.

The king stood. "What is the delay? I demand my rightful property. I warn you, Maither Brigid, if you don't hand it over immediately, we will take it by force. Here in the witness of the Brehon, we are entitled."

"Bring the book," Brigid said loud enough for everyone to hear.

Etain stood frozen.

"I said—"

"Maither Brigid, the book has vanished as well."

Chaos broke out. One of the king's men took Brigid by the arm. The Poet lunged to her defense.

The warrior holding on to the abbess shouted back. "Ask the Brehon. We have the right to take the abbess with us until the book is found."

Terrified, Aine looked to the Brehon. He frowned but made no objection.

The Poet's voice escalated. "This is a travesty."

The warrior urged Brigid along. She resisted.

"Do something, Daithi," Ninnidh called.

What would he do? With his temper, he might make the situation worse. Aine wove her way over to the Poet.

Daithi joined them but to Aine's surprise he only shrugged. "What can I do?"

A bell clanged with force, piercing through the bedlam. Old Bishop Conleth stood on top of a table board, striking a bronze bell with a hammer. The expected sound hushed the crowd. All stared at the old man—even King Donal. Astonishingly, the king removed his crown and dipped his chin toward the floor.

With the room quieted, the old man spoke. "Maither Brigid will stay here at Cill Dara. King Donal, we Uí Náirs will continue to defend Cill Dara, as we have done since ancient times when the site was home to the fire worshippers alone. We will cause no further harm, whether the book is found or not. Let this be known: I will oversee the search for the book and send news to the king."

We Uí Náirs? Bishop Conleth was a clansman. Aine recalled the old man saying that the abbess would need his help. He must have known that King Donal would be difficult to deal with. His connection seemed to have been unknown to others. Certainly Daithi and the Poet had not known.

The king, however, fully acquiesced. He quickly departed with his entourage, marching out the front gate, ignoring the regal feast that had been spread on tables under the vast oak tree.

The crowd dispersed, but Aine remained, feeling terrible about what she had caused. Maire stood silently by her side. What had Brigid planned to say? And why had she given up on her speech the minute she learned Ardan had escaped? Brigid had protected Aine more than once. What had Aine done to show her appreciation? She could have been jailed for theft, subjected to an honor price that she had no way of paying, but Brigid had somehow gotten the king to dismiss the matter, and the bishop had convinced the king to return home without the book. She could scarce take in all that had occurred.

She was torn from her reverie when Daithi took her arm. She turned away.

"Aine, my heart, don't—"

"I can't."

"Aine," Maire said. "Please."

Etain pushed her way toward them. "Come with me, Maire and Aine. Maither Brigid wants you both to sup with her. No sense in letting all this food lay waste."

Aine couldn't eat, but she and her mother went with the nun, leaving Daithi standing alone.

Later, as Etain served boiled lamb and bread dripping with sweet honey to the Brehon and Bishop Conleth, Aine sat at Brigid's side as they discussed what should be done. Again, Maire was beside her but said nothing.

The bishop pierced a piece of meat with his knife. "The Brehon should investigate. There are no other Brehons near that we could summon quickly. He's already here and he can rule without council."

"'Tis true." The Brehon crossed his arms on the table board. "I will do whatever I can for you, Maither Brigid. You have shown so much kindness to others, 'tis the least I can do."

Brigid touched the wooden cross hanging from her neck. "'Tis the work of Jesu I do."

Ninnidh sat at her right elbow, but did not join in the feast. It was as though her guests were his also. Aine wasn't sure what entitled her to be in this company. Perhaps Brigid needed her silent support. She couldn't imagine, however, why the woman hadn't pushed her out of Cill Dara's gates. Aine's own mother had nothing to say to her.

The corners of the Brehon's mouth drooped, as he seemed to contemplate his next words. "However, if we do not find the book, you will be held responsible, Maither Brigid. An honor price will need to be paid, and for a tribe's book of genealogy, it will be great. 'Tis the law. I cannot do anything about it."

Aine glanced to her sweaty palms in her lap.

"But she did not steal the book," Ninnidh protested.

Maire squeezed Aine's hand.

Hot tears formed in the corners of Aine's eyes. She sucked in a breath.

The Brehon stroked his beard. "Be that as it may, Maither Brigid was the last to have possession of it. Therefore, she is responsible."

The Brehon's words hung in the air as Aine watched the others chew their meat thoughtfully. Did Cill Dara have enough cattle to pay this price? And if they did, would the sacrifice cause the residents of Cill Dara to starve? Doubt about the new faith she'd accepted crept into her mind. The book could fix things. Or could it?

A headache drummed at her temples. She closed her eyes to ask for strength and then opened them. "I cannot allow you to pay the price for what I have done, Maither Brigid."

Brigid put an arm around her. "You cannot pay it yourself, child. But God can make a way."

Ninnidh leaned across the table and whispered, but Aine heard. "Brehon, the honor price. Could it possibly be the abbess's life?"

"I'm afraid so, Poet. May God protect her."

Thirty-One

"The wisdom of the prudent is to give
thought to their ways,
but the folly of fools is deception."

Proverbs 14:8 NIV

Ardan winced at the pain in his jaw and the throbbing of his palm. He pushed yew branches away from his face as he hurried with the book under his arm. He wheezed, sucking in breath as he ran. Foolish Brigid to believe one weak woman could keep him captive. He paused in the shadow of one of the towering crosses to catch his breath. Once he departed Cill Dara and made for the deep forest, no one would find him, not even that arrogant king. Traveling alone, he'd be able to enter Uí Náir territory long before the king and his mighty but slow entourage returned. With the talisman in his possession, he imagined the people would have no hesitation in declaring him king.

"Where do you think you are going?"

The tip of a spear grazed the skin just under his ear. He slowly turned around, ducking away from the weapon. As he faced his adversary, he gripped the shaft and snapped it in two. A lovely blue-eyed nun, the one he'd encountered before, stood before him. She may have lost her spear, but her other hand deftly aimed a short-handled knife at his head.

He chuckled, hoping to defuse the situation. "Well, now." He let out a breath. "You believe that will stop me?"

She flipped her wrist and the knife winged into his ankle. He cried out, pulling the blade from his flesh.

She snatched the book away. "You should die right here for what you've done to the sacred land of the oak, Druid."

"Perhaps you are the one who should die," came another female voice from somewhere behind the first.

The bright-eyed one spun around. With her eyes diverted, he crouched low and began to creep along the ground, but he was so painfully wounded he could not get far.

The king's redheaded daughter grabbed the nun by the wrist and wrenched her arm behind her back. Two warriors flanked the women but did not intervene. "This book belongs rightfully to my father and my clan," the royal daughter said.

"The book has powers you will never understand," the nun blurted through clenched teeth.

Another sister, this one older and long-limbed, hurried toward them, followed by a woman Ardan well recognized:

the blind mother of Brigid. A hefty monk flung open the iron gates at that moment and confusion swirled like a wind tunnel.

The next thing Ardan recalled was the aroma of herbs. He was back in Brigid's hospital. "What's going on?" he called toward the rafters. His words were garbled, and when he spoke, pain shot from his teeth up to his temples.

The healer who had taken care of him before came into his line of vision. "I'm fixing you up so you might hear the words from those pages, don't you know. Hear *me*, man. The sisters *will* get that book back."

Her face was bruised and her left arm wrapped in a linen bandage. He had caused her injuries, yet she was helping him, albeit it with a grimace. He would never understand Christians. No matter how much misery he managed to inflict on them, they rebounded and grew even stronger. Never in all his time as a druid had he seen anything like it. Most people responded to brutality with more of the same. Certainly that was true with the Picts. These Christians! Only a superior god could…He quickly dismissed the thought. Pain brought disturbing and irrational thoughts.

He squeezed his eyes shut. What had the healer said? Something about Cill Dara not having the book? He pushed words out through his swollen lips. "What happened to…b-book?"

She dabbed at his head with a smooth cloth, wiping away the perspiration that his effort to speak had brought. "I don't suppose you remember because you fainted dead away."

Impatient, he grunted. It was all he could do.

"Hold on. I'll tell you, man."

She dipped the cloth in a pan of water. The water splattering in the pan, as she wrung it out, brought an anticipation of comfort.

"As soon as everyone discovered the druid at the gate and carrying that book, as you were, a quarrel broke out."

A quarrel? Who did this woman think she was speaking to? A foundling? A silly child?

"Well, the king's daughter managed to be holding it somehow. I'm sure there'll be a logical reason for it, though no one can manage to explain it right now."

He raised his eyebrows to indicate that she should continue.

"Well, somehow, she turned into a dove, that one. Others say 'twas a rodent. Something happened for sure because she got away, and sweet Fianna disappeared as well, though they did not seem to be on the same side of the matter."

Oh, how Ardan despised woman talk. Just get on with it. Where was that book? She had no idea how perturbed he was becoming, however, because she kept on, providing more details than necessary. Who cared who was at the gate? Who cared what time of day it was and what the metalworkers and cooks were working on at the time. Those two beautiful young women were shape shifters. No wonder he'd admired them so. They could make themselves very appealing if they chose to.

The words he wanted to say stuck in his throat like sour kernels of wheat.

How would the gods judge now? Who would win the book? And most importantly, how would Ardan benefit from the matter?

He leaned his head to one side. He needed to get out of that place. Everyone knew by now that he had no shape shifting powers himself.

"As I said," the healer continued, "Maither Brigid insists that when the book is found, you must sit for a reading."

He groaned again.

"Don't be that way. You are an obstinate child if ever there was one."

So, she did think he was an imbecile.

All his plans had failed, and now, he would be forced to listen to a speech by another Christian, and the worst one of all—Brigid.

Aine was in the woods before anyone awoke in the guesthouse. As many times as she'd done this, she had become proficient. Once she heard that Brigid's life might be in danger, she knew she had to go searching for the book. She was the cause of it, after all. Daithi had warned her long ago that there could be consequences for her actions, but she had never imagined it would come to an honor price involving the abbess.

An owl called from thick tree branches above her head. Shape shifting was a myth, she told herself. She stared up, trying to bring the dark shapes into focus. No one had been able to explain where Fianna and the king's daughter had gone. They'd vanished. Like magic. Or…perhaps the One True God had caused it to happen—a miracle. He'd done it for Patrick. The *Fáed Fíada*, The Deer's Cry. She'd heard the story many times from Cillian's monks. When an evil king sent chariots of soldiers to murder Patrick because he'd dared to light a Paschal fire before the great lights of the festival of Beltaine had been lit, God had turned Patrick and his followers into a herd of deer to pass by the army safely. He could have done the same thing to protect the book. But where was the book now? Aine couldn't leave it to chance, no matter how desperately she wanted to believe that God was in control.

This time, she'd remembered to bring a torch. Wolves were a threat, but they'd not come near fire. She held the flame toward a matted down place in the grass. Etain had pointed in this direction when the two women fighting over the book had disappeared. Fog was rising. Perhaps that was what had hidden their disappearance.

She glanced to her feet. The path had turned muddy in an overnight rain. She lowered the torchlight. A footprint? It was. And another. And another. She crept slowly forward. A wolf howled, much closer than she would have liked. Swallowing hard, she continued along the trail. The tinge of a wood fire met her nose. She was approaching the pagan flames near where she had once buried the book. Perhaps the firewatcher had seen the missing women.

She soon found the hedge, but it was much too thick to squeeze her torch through without lighting the whole of the vegetation. Best not to put out her torch in case relighting it from the sacred flames was forbidden.

The sounds of singing sprang forth—two voices, maybe three. She recalled the cycle of the moon, deciding it was not yet fest time. Why would more than one person watch the fire?

She prodded the handle of her torch into the muddy ground until it stood erect. Then she wedged her way through the bushes.

One of the pagan women watched the fire, dancing around, elder leaves woven through her hair. The leaves, Aine had learned from her time among these women, were believed to bring bounty and health. She had since learned that while God made the trees, and He could be found even in the most dense forest, He dwelled among His people. The trees were not gods, therefore the leaves brought nothing. God was the source of all good things. Her stubbornness— or had it been fear?—had given in to superstitions, and she had clung to them like autumn seeds on a newly woven shawl. But now her eyes were open, bringing back the stories she'd learned as a child from Cillian, stories she knew to be the truth. Not that the old beliefs didn't call to her from time to time. Throwing out all tradition seemed wrong, somehow. But she would not worship trees, fire, or the stars. The Creator alone was worthy of praise.

She glanced back to the pagan fire. She had heard other voices. She looked to the shadows and spotted two dark forms. One rose and came toward her. She immediately recognized her. "Fianna! What are you doing here?"

"Shh, Aine. The abbess and I are praying."

She heard harp music but could not tell where it came from. Fianna noted her puzzled look. "The Poet. He's sitting on that side of the circle." She pointed in the opposite direction.

"I don't understand. What's going on? Where have you been?"

Again, Fianna placed a finger to her lips. "What are you doing, little one? Why are you here?"

Still confused, she turned toward the direction she'd come. "I am the one who lost the book, Fianna." She stared at the ground. "I gave it away too easily, and that allowed the druid to get his hands on it." She glanced up at the nun just in time to see her flinch at the mention of Ardan. "I came out here because I wanted to find you and the other woman, the one who fought you and Ardan for the book. I suppose she got it away from you. I want to find the book and give it to Brigid. This is all my fault. Do you think that woman will give the book back to the king? Perhaps that's best. He'll drop the matter."

"I do not think it will be so easily resolved, but now is not the time to set blame."

"So she did get it away from you."

"The king's daughter escaped with it, aye, but for her own gain, I'm afraid. Not for the people."

Aine sighed and turned toward the fire. "Why are you here, Fianna? You, who chastised me for coming to this place."

Fianna put an arm around Aine's shoulder. "I was only trying to protect you. You came to us confused, and this was not the place for you to find answers. Druids are drawn to special places like the oak. I had been expecting him to show up here. And I was not pleased, but not surprised, that you were drawn here as well. Didn't I tell you I knew you were coming?"

"You said the gods told you."

"Well, I suppose I did. Whether the gods told me or no doesn't matter now."

"But Brigid was away. How did you all come to be here?"

"Shh. We will talk of this later. Right now we are praying for God to deliver us from this predicament. If you'll be still, you may come pray with us."

This woman still spoke equally of the gods and the One True God. Like Aine once had. It seemed Brigid had not rejected her for it.

When they approached the fire, Aine found not only Brigid, but also her mother and Etain. Aine sat on the ground with Fianna, just behind the others. They had all come to petition God. Even the Poet, whom she could hear but not see. Men were never allowed to draw too close to this fire. The women wanted to avoid distractions, she supposed. Remembering her own distraction, she asked, "Is anyone with the Poet out there?"

Fianna whispered in her ear. "I am not sure. He and Daithi share the men's guesthouse. He might have come, too, but don't worry, they won't come any closer."

"I'm not worried." But maybe she was. She had to get the book and Daithi would try to stop her.

"I can't just sit here," Aine said to Fianna.

"We are not just sitting," she snapped. "We are praying." The old Fianna was back.

"Even so, I have to go. I'll leave quietly." She rose, squeezed Brigid's hand in greeting as she passed by, and wormed her way back through the hedge. When she emerged on the other side, she realized the darkness had caused her to lose her bearings. Instead of arriving at the place where she left her torch, she found herself standing in front of the Poet and Daithi. The music stopped. The air grew calm.

Daithi rose. "Where are you going, my heart? The guesthouse is the other direction."

"I…uh…" She didn't know what to say. He would try to stop her. She could not let the gracious, generous Brigid be sacrificed because of her. She backed into the hedge and scrambled past the women. Then she flung herself through the other side of the hedge, scraping her limbs painfully and landing with a thump on her backside. She lay still for a moment, trying to focus her eyes by staring at the stars. How would she ever track down the king's daughter? She could be halfway to anywhere by now. She thought about the red-haired king's daughter, a lass she'd never seen in all her time with her foster father's tribe. Who was she?

Why hadn't she thought of it before? Her foster father would help her. She stood slowly, willing her scraped arms and legs to stop stinging.

"Looking for this?" Daithi held the torch out to her.

"You won't stop me."

"I learned that long ago." He took a step toward her. "Let's go now, so we don't disturb the prayers."

"I'll not be going back to the guesthouse." She planted her tender feet the best she could.

"Neither will I."

"Where are you going, then?"

"With you, back to the Uí Náir. We will petition the help of your foster father."

A gravelly voice came from the darkness. "I'll go, too. I knew that man long ago. I came to help." She hadn't noticed Bishop Conleth standing behind Daithi until he spoke. "We best be going, young people. Time is wasting. Hitch my mule to one of the nuns' carts, young man, and Jesu be praised!"

Thirty-Two

"Cry out for insight, and ask for
understanding.
Search for them as you would for silver;
seek them like hidden treasures."

Proverbs 2:3-4 NLT

B y the time they reached Daithi's green pasture, the sky
had pinked. Wiping their dew-covered feet on the
stone outside the door of his dwelling, they entered
silently—first Aine, and then the bishop who said a blessing
upon their arrival.

Daithi shut the door behind them and pulled up a stool
for the bishop to use to remove his shoes. "There's been no
one in here since I left," he said. "Place is a bit damp."

Aine had never before seen the inside of the house where she was supposed to live once they married. A large central hearth was rimmed in stones carefully shaped with masonry tools. There were no leftover ashes. She was impressed with Daithi's fastidiousness. She accepted a stool he offered and bent to untie the laces of her shoes. The floor was not earthen as she would have expected, but laid with the same fine stones as the hearth.

She glanced around as Daithi carried peat blocks to the fire ring. A long table board rested against the east wall under a shuttered window. She had gazed upon the outside of that window before when Cillian first told her this was where the man she would marry lived. No one had known she was there at the time. Curiosity had brought her. She still remembered gazing at the tree near the window where the rooks were roosting and wondering if Daithi laid his head down just on the other side of it. In the months that followed, she became acquainted with him and his servants, and shortly thereafter, Daithi remarked that she followed the old ways too closely. She, in turn, had decided he was too demanding. Then she had stolen the book and set events in motion.

She rubbed her chin as she thought about it. He had been right all along. She had placed too much trust in the book, and she hadn't known what her actions would cause. Tears came to her eyes as she prayed that God would forgive her, and that Brigid would as well.

She focused again on her surroundings, blinking away tears. A finely carved wooden chest graced the opposite wall where she assumed he kept blankets and other household goods. A rush mat was rolled and placed beneath a sleeping shelf. Besides the stools she and the bishop sat on, the only other chair was a wee bench drawn up to the hearth. Her gaze landed on the wall opposite the door, and she gasped. A porcelain cross trimmed in gold caught the light from Daithi's fledging fire.

He glanced up at her. "Like it? 'Tis the only thing I have that my mother owned."

"What is it?"

The bishop crossed the room to have a better look. "'Tis in the shape of the cross Jesu died upon. I have never seen anything like it, but I've heard such treasures exist in other lands such as Byzantium."

"Could be from that far away," Daithi said. "My father bought it for her from a trader. Cost him fifty heads of cattle, so he said."

"And you left a treasure like this in your house where thieves could take it?" Aine asked.

Daithi shrugged. "Wasn't thinking about that when I left." He wiped a hand across his brow and stood up, admiring his smoldering fire. "All I was thinking about was getting my Aine back."

Her eyes moistened again. Why did he always melt her heart this way? She answered his gaze with her own. "Why then, Daithi, don't you want me as your soul friend? Please, tell me."

The bishop looked at them each in turn. He seemed embarrassed to be part of the conversation.

Daithi stared at the fire again. "My soul friend must first have Jesu as her soul friend." He turned to her. "I have decided I will wait, Aine. I will not marry. I will wait for you, even it takes forever."

Her cheeks grew hot. "You do not have to wait, Daithi. Jesu is my very best friend, and you will be my husband if you will still have me."

When they embraced, the bishop cleared his throat. "A marriage is a fine thing, but we are on a mission, do not forget."

They dropped their arms to their sides as though they could make the man forget what he'd witnessed. Daithi turned in a circle, his hand on his chin. "Wait here. I will collect Fergus, Aine's foster father."

"Shouldn't we go to his dwelling?" the bishop asked.

"I do not want to anger him. I will go to my caretaker's cottage and have him ready a steer to take with me. This will be payment for the time Aine has been gone."

The bishop bobbed his head. "Aye, she departed without proper permission." Conleth turned to her. "An insult to the man, my dear."

She held out her hand to Daithi, wishing she could feel the warmth of his arms around her again. "Send him my apologies, please." Tears flowed freely down her cheeks. "Tell him I have been a foolish young lass, but now I have mended my ways."

"I will tell him." Daithi kissed her hand, leaving a scent of peat and smoke and fragrant forest grasses in his wake.

She stared at her hand for a long moment.

The bishop napped while Daithi was gone. Aine went outside to pace around the house. Where was the book at that moment? Were people dunking it in the cattle troughs or was that woman evoking evil magic with it?

She thought about Fergus and his wife, Nessa. They had been kind to her and had tolerated her childish rants. She had worried them with her nighttime wanderings, but they had never reported her to the clan leaders or tried to return her to Cillian. Would they forgive her for running away? Would they accept Daithi's peace offering and agree to help them petition the king?

She glanced toward the house, where the old bishop rested. He was connected somehow to the tribe, he'd said. If that were true, why hadn't he gone directly to the king himself? Knowing her foster father in years past would give him no special favor she could think of. Perhaps he was a bit demented by age and Daithi was showing grace by allowing him to think he was helping.

The sound of trickling water led her to a spring, where she splashed water on her face. Taking a comb from the pocket at her waist, she began plaiting her hair. If Fergus did decide to come, she wanted to look her best and not like a child who had been climbing trees all day. Her fingers shook as she groomed herself. *Hurry, Daithi. God's precious servant, Brigid, needs us.*

As she was finishing up, she heard the old bishop calling her name. "I'm here," she answered, stepping into the clearing near the house.

He smiled and waved.

"Do you need something, Bishop?"

"You need something," he said when she got close enough.

He is crazy. Hurry up, Daithi.

He held the door open for her to enter with the bucket of spring water she had drawn. She didn't bother responding to his remark.

Light filtered through the house. The old man had thrown open the window shutters, and to her surprise, there was not just one, but two windows facing each other. The cottage was quite nice. She didn't know if Daithi had built it or if it had belonged to his parents, but obviously someone had lovingly cared for it.

She poured water into a bronze pot hanging over the fire and then set the half empty bucket to the right of the door. "How long do you think Daithi will be gone?" she asked.

"A few hours or all day, depending on how much trouble Fergus gives him."

She gulped back tears. "I should have gone. This is my fault."

"Nonsense." The bishop rose from his seat and stood next to her. "I said you needed me, and 'tis true."

"You? You didn't go with him."

"I am a bishop in God's church, as you know, but I have not always been. I was once chief druid of this clan, in line to be king."

Old folks liked to relive the past and sometimes embellish it. She wasn't in the mood. She busied herself sorting through a barrel of dried beans she found on the window ledge, thinking she might throw them into the caldron.

The bishop would not be ignored, however. "You are the daughter of a pagan. Surely you understand of what I speak."

She didn't look up. "I was raised by a Christian monk."

"Indeed, but one who lived in fear of a druid, am I right?"

"You are." She had two handfuls of beans now in her apron, which she deposited in the simmering water. She moved to a row of wooden boxes stacked in a corner that she had overlooked before and began to search for herbs to season the soup. She found a tiny linen bag of fennel seeds and added a few. Turning back to the bishop, a thought came to her. "How is that you and this evil druid Ardan come from the same tribe?"

The bishop ran a hand over his smooth head. "I was wondering when you were going to ask me about that."

She turned back to her searching to keep the man from seeing her irritation.

He grunted. "'Tis a long, long story, as most are."

Oh, dear. She was growing tired of this.

"Let me just tell you that Ardan was never in line to be king. His mother was Uí Náir, but his father was not."

"How do you—?" She stopped herself. This had nothing to do with their mission, and she really didn't want to know.

"How do I know?" He chuckled. "Don't understand much about druids, do you, lass? But then, you wouldn't, having grown up as Cillian's charge and then sent to fosterage with a family who would never teach you such things."

First he blamed her pagan upbringing and now her Christian one. The man was truly confused.

He continued. "But as you came closer to the Uí Náir, being promised to Daithi, things were set in motion."

She looked at him. His piercing stare unnerved her. What secrets did he know? He seemed determined to tell her, so she sat dutifully on the rush mat and gave him her attention.

He licked his dry lips. "It seems to have all started with that book, and I suppose 'tis where it will conclude."

She crossed her arms. Now that he had her rapt attention, he cast his gaze away as though it made him uncomfortable. "When I was a younger man, long before King Donal was born"—he chuckled—"and before anyone else who is still alive can remember, I suppose, I was chief druid and keeper of the books."

"There was more than one book?"

"Oh, five or six, I believe. Most druids would have burned them, but I didn't."

"Why would they burn the books?"

"The druids hold all the knowledge, all the stories, all the tales of the past. They don't want those things written down because, the more they are recorded and people learn to read them for themselves, the less the druids will be respected and needed. They feared losing their influence." He raised his shoulders as though this didn't make much sense to him.

"But not you? You were a druid who kept the books?"

"I was. I have always loved books. What magnificent wealth words can possess, my dear." He smiled at her.

"Only one survives? What happened to the others?"

"Ah, some fell apart. They were not well crafted. Others were loaned to friendly tribes, and after I left, I cannot say what happened to them. But the book that endured was special." He pointed a finger at her. "I knew 'twas, even back then."

She rubbed her arms, smoothing out her crinkled mantle. "Because it held the tribe's genealogy?" She wondered if he'd seen its magic. Daithi and Brigid had not.

"That's right, the tribe's lineage. I knew no one would part with it for that reason. That's why I recorded the information there."

She sat up straight. "What information?"

340

He grinned. "I learned to read and write from an old saint named Ciaran of Saighir. I learned to follow Jesu's ways at the monastery. 'Twas not a small task to get there. I had to travel beyond the Kingdom of Ossory, but I was a chief druid with many privileges that allowed me to do what others could not."

His mind was wandering again. She would have to get him back to the topic. "Bishop Conleth, what did you write in the book?"

"Ah, most folks copy from the gospels: Matthew, Mark, Luke, John. And the Psalter. But I had access to some rare proverbs and scriptures, and I copied some of the wisdom into that book, knowing that it would never disappear because the genealogy was too valuable. After the king, the one on the throne when I was a young man, adopted Christianity, I no longer feared the book's demise. 'Twas about that time I grew weary of my duties. I left to live the life of a hermit. Fine life it was for me, at least after I got used to it. You know, lass, when you are all alone, you must face yourself and your sins. Can be a frightening experience."

"I'm sure." He had something important to tell her. She would have to work hard to get it out of him, it seemed. "Bishop, how does this concern me? You said I needed you."

He tented his fingers. "Well, two things. First, King Donal does not actually own the book. I am the rightful owner. In light of that, you did not steal it from him. He was only holding on to it for me. And you did not pilfer it from me if I do not accuse you, which I do not."

"How can you claim ownership?" She was skeptical. If it were true then the king had no right to an honor price and no reason to have burned Cill Dara in the first place. It did not make sense."

"I told you I was in line to be king?"

"You did."

He tapped a finger on his forehead. "Nay, that's not it exactly." He glanced up at her with eyes watery with age. "I did own the book. Donal is unaware. But now the codex is the property of the church. The details do not really matter, child. I represent the church, you see."

"The book belongs to the Christian church?"

He nodded. "Before Donal was even a glimmer in his father's eye, I granted possession of the manuscript to Patrick's church. There is a record of it in Armagh. I will testify to this, and rest assured, the Brehon will concur. But it won't come to that. The king will drop his case against the abbess, and he will even help me get that valuable book back where it belongs."

She remembered how she had seen King Donal acquiesce to the bishop instead of taking Brigid away. She still didn't understand that exchange. "Why would he do that?" They had veered away from what she had to do with this, but at least they were getting somewhere. She hoped to have it all figured out before Daithi returned with Fergus.

"Because he is my son. I am his earthly father."

Aine had heard of men leaving their families to devote their lives to the church or to find God in isolation. She suspected some of Cillian's brother monks had done so. But still, this news surprised her. "So why don't you go resolve this? Why do we need Fergus? Why did I need to come at all? Daithi would have gladly brought you here if you would have told him."

He rubbed the back of his neck. "Most matters like this are not so simple, and so it is with this. King Donal may not

342

trust me, truth be told. Children seldom understand the decisions their parents make in these circumstances."

She had to agree.

"Fergus has kept this truth to himself, as he is honor bound to do. I do not doubt his loyalty even after all these years. We are brothers in Christ, Fergus and me, former foster brothers. Fergus, a well-respected tribesman, will vouch for me with the king. At least I hope he will," he said, contradicting his previous assertion. "By the grace of Jesu, we shall find out."

"But…you two are…" She wasn't sure how to put it.

"Not the same generation? Perhaps he is older than he looks or I am—by Jesu, I don't even know my own age." He shook his head, and strands of his white hair fell across his forehead. "Ah, well, we were soul friends, just the same. My deepest regret is that I abandoned him. For many, many years I mistakenly thought that to follow Jesu meant to leave all others behind." His eyes twinkled. "I was wrong. Jesu is to be found in the hearts of fellow men and women. This certainty I have learned, and not so long ago."

She knew his words to be true. Hadn't she seen Jesu through Brigid? Through Daithi, too?   [[Comma added before "too".]]

"You weren't sure if Fergus held this against you? That's why you sent Daithi on ahead? To make clear your path to reconciliation, Bishop?"

"Ah, astute you are."

"So when the king is presented with this information, he will have to drop the matter?"

"He will."

"Does your son know anything about you?"

"Other than that his father is a hermit? I believe he does not. 'Twill be a difficult reunion for us, I suspect."

She glanced to the door, longing for Daithi to return. "Did you love the king's mother?" The question might be intrusive, but she couldn't help but wonder if he left her because she didn't follow Patrick's God.

The morning light showed every wrinkle in the man's face. "That was a long time ago, but I did love her once."

"Is she still alive?"

"Ah, she is not. Died in childbirth."

She went to him and took his hand. "That must have been hard for you."

He wagged his head. "A long, long time ago." He glanced up at her, tears in his eyes. "Might have been why I went away by myself."

As the hours passed, Aine continued cooking while the bishop took several naps. As night began to fall, she lost hope that Daithi and Fergus would return that day. She ladled two bowls of bean soup and handed one to the bishop when he finally stirred from his slumber.

"I hear something," the old man said. "They are returning and I haven't told you the other thing yet."

The sound of whinnying horses and the squeal of a cart's wheels were unmistakable.

"What thing?"

"What you have to do with this, you and the druid Ardan. And why that red-haired demon wants the book."

She had been so taken with the bishop life's story that she had forgotten he had not told her everything. She flipped open one shutter. The flicker of a torch and two dark figures moved steadily toward the house. "Quick, tell me."

The bishop lowered his voice. "Ardan comes from a long line of fishermen on his paternal side with a genealogy that goes…" He hesitated. "Well, the important thing for you to know that is you are connected. God sent you here for such a time as this, just like Queen Esther."

"Who?" There wasn't time to figure out what he was talking about. Daithi opened the door and ushered in Fergus.

Thirty-Three

"The Lord opened the understanding of
my unbelieving heart, so that I should
recall my sins."

Saint Patrick

When Daithi entered, Aine and the bishop must have
had stunned looks on their faces. He smiled at them
both. "No need to worry, my friends. Fergus is happy to help
us."

Old Conleth rose gently to his feet, and Fergus
embraced him.

Fergus carefully tapped the bishop's back with an open
hand. "By the saints, I thought you'd be dead by now."

The old man laughed. "Jesu still has use for me so long as I am breathing. Praise be to Him that you have not turned away from me."

They stood staring into each other's eyes. Fergus wagged his furry head. "Never, my friend. I have always prayed for you."

The exchange amazed Aine. She knew her foster father to be a passionate, outspoken man, but she had never heard him speak of the bishop. Evidently this relationship with the old bishop was a dearly personal one.

Fergus turned his attention to her and let out a whoop. "God be praised, lass. You're safe and under Daithi's protection." He lifted her off her feet and planted a wet kiss on her forehead as he lowered her back down to the floor.

Fergus was nothing if not passionate about life. "You're not angry?" She tried not to look into his pale blue eyes.

"A wandering one, you are, wee Aine. A free spirit. Warned Daithi 'bout that, didn't I, man?"

Daithi shrugged.

"Finished with my wandering, at least alone." She exchanged knowing glances with Daithi.

"Glad to hear that." Fergus slapped his knees. "Now, on to business."

The three men sat around the peat fire. She retreated toward the sleeping shelf to await their plan. *Hurry!* She silently prayed. *Brigid needs us.*

"Talk is, the king will keep possession of the book if he can get it away from that lass, and he'll do it by force," Fergus said.

The bishop's raspy voice rose. "He will not."

"He might," Fergus insisted, "if we do not act swiftly. He is not of the mind that blood matters, other than you,

348

Bishop Conleth. But his reverence for you, I believe, is due to his fear of a curse. The lass being his daughter makes no difference to him. And impatient, he is."

The old man sighed, cradling his chin with both palms. The red-headed lass was his granddaughter.

"Fergus has told me the tribe's leaders plan to visit Cill Dara in two days," Daithi explained. "We should return to the church of the oak tomorrow."

Aine heard them discuss the Brehon and the king and how they would get everyone together at Cill Dara. The discussion went on long into the night until the desire for sleep blazed at her eyes and she could hold them open no longer.

Somewhere in her dreams, Aine remembered what the bishop had said. She could not be related to the evil druid, could she? Her mother's family resided in the kingdom of Leinster for as long as anyone knew. But her father? She knew little about him and cared not to.

A cloud seemed to hover over her as she tumbled in and out of sleep. A black bird descended from the fog and rested a hand width from her nose. Its talons clamped around her arm and it blinked a black eye. She wasn't afraid. "Speak," she cried. "I've no time to waste."

The bird began hopping around her and lifting its wings.

"I am not afraid of you," she said.

The bird spoke in a human voice. "We are the same, you and I, like hatchlings born to the same mother."

"No we're not."

The bird cawed and squawked as though she'd hit it with a rock.

"You cannot run away," the bird mocked, cawing as it flew away.

"I'm new. I'm different," she insisted.

What had the creature meant? She was nothing like the bird. The skin on her forearms crawled. She glanced down to find wee black feathers sprouting from her arms.

Aine woke with a start. She wasn't sure if the odd dream roused her or the sound of the others preparing to leave. She rose and hurried to the well to refresh herself. When she returned, she declined to break her fast. A haunting mist of guilt drifted over her. Her own sins or that of her forbearers?

When they returned to Cill Dara, they found workmen tying fresh thatch on roofs and painting newly hung doors. The place buzzed with activity much as it had earlier when they'd prepared for a feast that never happened.

"God's blessing on you all," Brigid greeted them. "Welcome home. We are preparing to meet God here as we do every day. Most times 'tis through our prayers and our daily chores, but now we are preparing for a council and then, of course, a feast. This time, I believe it will happen even without the book."

The bishop clapped his hands. "Jesu be praised."

The Poet joined them, looking less confident than Brigid. "Has anyone heard from the Brehon yet?"

"We have," Brigid answered.

"Any troubles?"

"Not so far."

They walked off with the bishop, jabbering away.

"I need to find my mother," Aine told Daithi.

"Of course. I will…" He glanced away. "Uh, check on the bishop's horse at the stables. You can find me there if you need me."

She gripped his large hand. "Thank you."

After scouring the refectory's kitchen, the outdoor spinning wheels, the blacksmith's hut, and the herb garden, she finally found her mother just outside the monastery's hospital.

"Oh, Aine." Her mother's eyes widened, and she ushered Aine away from the building before giving her a hug. "There is plenty of trouble, as you know. Why did you run off? Are you all right?"

"Do you know where I went?"

"I do. Somehow Fianna knew and also Etain, who spoke to the bishop before he left with you. Why did you not leave this business to the men, daughter?"

"'Tis done, Maither. This will soon be over. Do not worry over me. As you can see, I am fine." She glanced back to the hospital. Normally the doors were open on both sides to allow air to flow through to the patients. The only reason the doors would be closed would be if… "Maither, has something happened to the druid?"

"Nothing new. Let's go for a stroll." She pushed Aine toward the path.

"Why are you so insistent? Is there some reason you want me away from here? Are you afraid I'll learn that druid is blood related to me?"

Maire froze. "What...are...you...talking about?"

"The bishop told me."

"What did that old man say?"

"He only said that Ardan and I are related. Is he your kin or my father's?"

Maire let out a slow breath. "'Tis not what you think, daughter."

"I'm a grown woman ready to be married. Tell me."

"Married?" Her face brightened.

"Just as was arranged, Maither."

"That's good."

Aine's jaw tightened. "Tell me."

Maire nodded and led Aine to a grove of yews where they sat on a log bench. "There is a connection, not through me. Though truth be told, the connection is likely my fault."

"You are not saying that man fathered me, are you?"

She jerked her head back and forth rapidly. "Your father is the man you know. I have had no romantic relationship with any other, and while I'm forever regretful that I yoked myself to an unbeliever, I'm thankful our union produced you, daughter."

"Then what?"

Her mother kicked at a pebble with the toe of her shoe. "'Tis not blood, like I said."

Aine was confused. In her dream the raven, a symbol of the druid she believed, said that they were the same. "Are you sure, Maither?"

"Do not question me, daughter."

The sharp tone of her voice startled Aine.

Maire urged Aine to resume walking as they talked. "Ardan is of the dark side. Surely you know that."

"I know many people are scared of him."

352

"And well they should be. The connection he speaks of…what he means is…" Her hands began to tremble.

"Maither? What's wrong?" Aine bent her head low to look into her mother's eyes. "I need to know." Aine didn't want to admit the man scared her, but truthfully, even the mention of his name made her skin crawl. The book even seemed to shun him, preferring to be in the hands of the king's daughter.

"What's wrong with him, Maither?" She was trying hard to give up her old beliefs, but if she couldn't blame the druid's evil essence on the fairies, then how could she explain it?

Maire put a hand on her daughter's shoulder, allowing the distant owl cries to fill the silence. Aine waited, nervously, for her mother to say something. Maire let out a long slow breath and then spoke. "What is wrong is that he has allowed himself to be so corrupted that the light of God is nowhere to be seen in his eyes."

Aine thought about that and the other things the Christian sisters had been teaching her since she returned to Cill Dara. God was with her—she felt that truth, breathed it, and carried it with her now. Thinking about God's light being completely hidden made her squirm. "Maither, are you saying the blackness around the druid is caused by an absence of God's light?"

Maire sighed. "God cannot be absent. To think such a thing is to lose all hope. God is there, but like I said, Ardan covers up the light. He has decided to do that, and it's that choice that releases the presence of evil."

A cold shiver ran up Aine's arms. "He can turn from it, then?"

"Aye, he can. So far he has not."

Aine took her mother's hand. "I still don't understand what it has to do with me. What were you trying to tell me?"

The sound of a bell broke through the conversation. A sharp, incessant clanging sounded alarm, not a call to prayers. People burst from every building and barn. "What's happening?" Maire called to two monks passing by.

"The king's army approaches. Run for safety!"

Thirty-four

"God gives the gifts where He finds the
vessel empty enough to receive them."

C.S. Lewis

I n the midst of all the confusion, Aine spotted the old
bishop waving his arms at panicked passersby. "I will
speak to them. By Jesu, I will speak. Do not fear!"

No one paid attention, no one but Aine and her
mother. "Foolish man," Maire whispered. "Let's get him to
the refectory."

"Wait, Maither. What if he is right? He is from that
clan. He has a connection that no one else has."

Maire cupped Aine's face in her hands. "You know
something. Tell me."

A monk whizzed past them, wielding a shield like he was carrying a shovel. Aine pointed at him. "These people don't know how to fight. Old Bishop Conleth can help because the king is his blood son."

Maire dropped her hands and rushed to the old man's side. Aine followed along behind. The bishop smiled. "The people must listen. I have no practice at this, I'm afraid. I'm an old hermit."

Maire glanced around, and Aine tried to follow her gaze, wondering what she was might do. "Well, then." She turned back to the man and patted his outstretched hand. "We will find someone who will halt this madness. Someone with a strong, loud voice."

"May I be of service?" Fianna seemed to appear from nowhere. Others said she had the druidess power of shape shifting, but Aine was beginning to understand that a busybody like Fianna was able enough to pop up anywhere she wanted.

Maire took the young nun's arm. "Do you know where the abbess is?"

"She's gathering the flock to safety."

"Is she near, then?"

"She is not close, but would you like me to take you to her?"

Aine studied the bishop's face. His cheeks were the color of cold ashes. He muttered softy to himself.

"No time." Aine dragged Fianna over to the man. "Shout whatever he tells you to say."

Fianna cast her gaze toward Maire, who held up her palms as if to push Fianna along. The nun bent low to hear what the bishop said, then cleared her throat and placed her hands alongside her mouth. "Do not be afraid. There is no need to take arms."

She had to shout the message a few times, but eventually those around them halted and listened. "The bishop will speak to the king. A man gives ear to his earthly father. The king will hear Bishop Conleth. Make no mistake!"

Aine spotted Brigid at the edge of the crowd. The abbess approached the bishop and touched her forehead against his. They conferred for a moment, and then Brigid spoke to Fianna, who related the message in her booming voice. "Assemble in the field near the wall of hedges surrounding the sacred fire. We will hold counsel."

The mood of the monastery morphed from one of panic to purposeful chatter and activity. Aine was amazed at the effect Brigid had. People trusted her. God used this trait in the woman, just as he used Fianna's nosiness and loud voice, and the bishop's connection with the king. Well, at least Aine hoped God would use it. Would the king really listen? Even Conleth had expressed some doubt that he would. *Please, God, bring peace to Cill Dara, and destroy the people's worship of a powerless book.*

She had spoken her prayer aloud. A firm hand gripped her shoulder. "What about that book do you think is powerless?"

She turned to find the Poet standing behind her.

"The book is not a god," she answered.

"True, that is. But powerless? The book contains pages of words, and words speak to the soul." The Poet drew a crowd, as most poets do. Standing behind him was not only a cluster of monks, priests, and nuns, but also Daithi.

357

Brigid put her arm around Aine, and Maire stood to her left.

"Tell the lass what you mean, Ninnidh," the abbess said.

He smiled at her, his eyes brightening. "Words have power." He spun around to make sure the others knew he was addressing them all. "We all know that the spoken word can be entertaining, educational, and sometimes, thankfully, even humorous."

Murmurs of agreement rose up.

"But the written word has the power to influence apart from the one who writes them. Even after the writer has died."

Roses returned to the bishop's cheeks. A few monks led him to a lattice chair near the Poet.

"There are words in that disputed book, meaningful, powerful words that have not yet been heard by most of you." The Poet pivoted as he addressed a growing crowd. "We will meet the king and his army in the field in front of the oak and invite them to our newly restored church. By God's miraculous power, the book will be returned to its rightful owner in peace, and the words will be read aloud for all to hear."

Cheers erupted as the Poet and Fianna urged the crowd to move on toward the open meadow beyond the round huts and newly thatched buildings of the monastery.

Daithi took Aine by the arm and then reached for her hand. He held her palm against his cheek, and his tender touch sent wiggling shivers up her arms. He whispered into her hair. "God will use the book for his purposes."

She nearly floated on air as they followed the others to the gathering spot.

Thirty-Five

"All that mankind has done, thought,
gained or been: it is lying as in magic
preservation in the pages of books."

Thomas Carlyle

Ardan was escorted to a large building. The smell of bread filled his senses. He had taken only broth for nourishment. It would be a long while before he would be able to chew bread and meat again.

The building overflowed with men and women, commoners and monks, nuns and royal members of the clan. A brown-robed monk everyone called Michael gently guided Ardan to a bench near a raised podium. Ardan's ankle still troubled him, but at least he no longer depended upon the monks to carry him whenever he needed to relieve himself in the woods. Despite the humiliation, those who cared for him had been kind and patient. No one forced him to pray, like the Christians had in the Land of the Picts. No one cursed him either or called him evil. He no longer wished to bring down the gods' vengeance on Brigid's Cill Dara. He merely wanted to be released to go live alone, to recoil to some distant wood like a maimed animal. He was defeated and he knew it.

Men congregated on long benches to the right of the podium. King Donal was there, and to Ardan's surprise, so was the thick, muscled monk he'd seen at the gate. He'd seen him before. Where? He searched his mind. He was not as astute as he once was. Age had caused his memory to fray a bit. Ah! Now he had it. This was that weakling who lived in the woods. Ardan had easily frightened him years ago. Others had murdered some men in the bog and this monk— Cillian, wasn't it?—had blamed Ardan.

Ardan's palm throbbed, and he realized that he wasn't being completely honest in that assessment. Well, sure enough, Ardan had sent the murderers there. He was responsible even if he had not been present.

The pain diminished a bit.

Music murmured from behind. He turned to find the Poet, Brigid's constant companion of late, strumming a harp. Suddenly the harp was accompanied by horns, and then Brigid entered, not donning a ceremonial white robe as he would have thought, but clad instead in simple brown clothing. She carried her head high and spoke in a clear unwavering voice. "The book of the Uí Náir is missing."

King Donal bolted from his royal chair and began waving his arms in front of the Brehon's face. Foolish man.

If the book was lost, the Brehon could do nothing about it. Rumor was the king's own kin had snatched it, that red-haired lass, so there would be no theft for the Brehon to rule on.

After a few moments, the king, consoled oddly enough by an old bishop and a ruddy man with huge forearms, returned to his seat. The two men seemed to be having an intense conversation with the king. At long last, Donal raised both arms in surrender. They had somehow convinced Donal not to leave the meeting.

Just as he sat down, a rush of wind came from the west, sending crumpled leaves and twigs dancing around the crowd. From behind a line of chariots came that lovely auburn-haired woman. She seemed to be tugged along by an invisible force as she clutched what appeared to be the infamous book. "Take it from me," she cried, even though her arms were clamped tightly around it. The leather cover glowed orange just as Ardan felt his hand warming. The lass's voice carried through the assembly as though it came from the heavens. "…while some coveted after, they have erred from the faith and pierced themselves through with many sorrows."

The book fell from her arms at the feet of the abbess, and the glow vanished, although the mark on Ardan's palm continued to ache.

A curse obviously rested on that object. Why Brigid didn't willingly give it back to Donal, he couldn't understand. *Just be done with it and let me go.*

The wind blew again, this time with more vigor. The petite woman, now without the talisman, sailed backward in the gale toward the setting sun. She grew smaller and smaller until Ardan could no longer make out her form. She fled or else was flung away. He couldn't tell.

Brigid scooped up the book and climbed the podium. Opening the cover, the abbess smiled directly at Ardan, making his stomach lurch. He would endure this in order to be set free.

Brigid nodded at the king. "Your daughter has returned the book."

"I have no daughter."

"The woman who was just here, she is not your kin?"

"I saw no one woman. The book was already on the grass when we arrived."

Brigid tilted her head skyward. "Praise Jesu."

Sorcha the healer leaned over to Ardan. "If God had not arranged that, you would have taken the book away and not heard its words."

"Senseless woman. There was another. There was a battle between that woman and your Sister Fianna. Fianna would have stolen it back for you if she had been able."

The healer shrugged. "Let's just say Fianna is a Doubting Thomas."

"A what?"

"She does not fully believe, and no one can say what she might have done with that book. I believe God sent that other one to protect the book until it could arrive here in this gathering."

Ardan rolled his eyes toward the sky. These Christians. Nothing they said made sense.

"Finish, and let's be done with this," the king ordered. "My chief scribe will take charge of the book when you are done."

Brigid paused and stared at Ardan. "These words are for you."

He nodded to let her know he heard.

She glanced to the book. "Our Lord Jesu chose disciples. Some were fisherman, such as Peter, Andrew, James, and John. James, son of Alphaeus, came to our island and some of his sons remained here." She looked up. "There is a genealogy written here that descends to Ardan. It seems the druid is blood-related to one of the apostles of Jesu."

Gasps rose up from the crowd. Arguments erupted. What did Ardan care? While it was fact that he'd come from a long line of fishermen, his father had not been a Christian. He pulled his special fire rock, a family gift from his father, from within his cloak. Every time the Christians captured him, they had amazingly allowed him to keep it.

"Look there." Sorcha pointed to the etching on the rock. "That is the *ichthys*."

Ardan turned to her. "What are you blabbering about?"

"The Christian fish symbol. The rock has it. Early Christians used it to identify themselves to each other during times of peril." She laughed. "You've been carrying the mark of the Christian, man, and you didn't know it. I wouldn't be surprised if that had belonged to James himself."

He shoved the thing deep into his cloak pocket. The Christians would not claim Ardan because of this genealogy. He would not allow it.

The abbess held up her arms, and the crowd quieted. "There is more."

He could stand it no longer. He jumped to his feet, longing to cry out, "Get on with it and let me go!" But he could only utter nonsensical sounds, and no one understood. Defeated, he sank back down on the grass.

Brigid turned one of the vellum pages. "'Tis written here, copied from a rare manuscript attributed to the ancient scribe Paul writing to his friend, Timothy, 'The Lord knows those who are his,' and, 'Everyone who confesses the name of the Lord must turn away from wickedness.'" She glanced again at Ardan. "Jesu is calling you. Do you not now feel it?"

Ardan's right hand burned hot coals, but this time he did not jump about. He held it out to her. "You...cursed...me, Bri...gid...uh...Cill...Dara."

She smiled. "I utter no curse. What you sense is Jesu's all-encompassing power. As the pages say, 'The Lord knows those who are his.'"

His? Ardan turned to Sorcha, who nodded. The surrounding Christians sent approving looks his way. Could Ardan, a man full of pride with a lust for power, change because he was called by God? He felt it deep inside. He silently prayed to the God of Brigid, the only one proving to be true, and asked forgiveness.

A hand touched his shoulder. The young woman who had once coveted the book gazed at him. "I was like you. I thought the book was calling to me, but 'twas God doing the calling. My mother has explained it to me. We who love Jesu are kin. The light is there in you. Search for it."

He closed his eyes. Aine was right, and he knew it. When he opened his eyes, she laid a woven cross, the kind Brigid's nuns made, into his hand. When he shifted it to his left hand, he noticed the burning mark was gone. His hand was white and supple as though there had never been anything wrong with it. "What's happened?"

Aine continued to grip his shoulder. "The light has come through, and you are whiter than snow. 'Tis the power of the words on those pages spoken by the Creator to you."

Thirty-Six

"He wanted to cry quietly but not for
himself: for the words, so beautiful and
sad, like music."

James Joyce

Dispirited, Ninnidh knew the time had come for him to leave. It pleased him that much had been accomplished, things he could never have foreseen. Ardan was redeemed. Aine and Daithi were reunited. Maire would move to live with Daithi's clan. King Donal had his book back, but with the understanding that any abuse of it would result in forfeiting it to the church in Armagh. The old bishop had a reunion of sorts with his son, although still strained. What took years to erode could not be mended rapidly.

Brigid stood outside the stables to bless his departure. "I wish you were not leaving," she said, shading her eyes from the sun with her hand. Or was she shielding tears from his view?

"I do not want to leave, either, but my father's school requires my presence."

She approached and patted the nose of his mare. "I wish sometimes things were different."

"'Tis a great responsibility to oversee such a grand monastery."

She smiled, tight-lipped.

"Come with me," he whispered, his words binding to the breeze.

She looked up at him, her eyes ocean pools nearly overflowing.

He did not know when he'd see her again. It was time to say what he felt. "If things were different, I'd have you as my wife."

She leaned against the horse's neck. "And there is no one I would want more if I chose to marry." She backed away. "But I am blessed to have you as my friend, my closest friend who gives my soul a home."

He leaned down to kiss the top of her hooded head. "We shall meet again, my friend. While we are apart, I will write many pages of encouragement to you."

She took in a breath. "Please do." She tucked one of her woven crosses into his traveling bag.

"I give you my vow, Brigid. I will find a courier when I can, but either way, I will write. You shall have my prayers day and night, and you shall be in all my songs."

"'Tis more than I could hope for, Ninnidh. And you will remain in my prayers as well." She sucked back a sob and squeaked out the words, "And also in my heart. For all time."

"We do not know what the future holds for us."

She smiled. "We do not. But we know who holds the future."

He trotted away from the monastery, certain he would return one day, and when he did, he would find nourishment for his soul.

Acknowledgements

I confess that when I wrote *Brigid of Ireland*, over a decade ago now, I had no plans to write a sequel. But readers told me they wanted to know more about the mysterious poet, the evil druid Ardan, and even the kindly druid Bram. What kind of monastery did Brigid establish? Was she always faithful? Did those she touch make any long-term changes in their lives? I realized the characters had more to tell, so I thank those of you who asked me to write the rest of the story. I enjoyed revisiting ancient Ireland. It's one of my favorite places!

I want to thank the members of my street team who help spread the word about my new releases (contact me if you'd like to be a part) and all the readers who visit my author table at Irish festivals to purchase autographed copies and ask when the next book will be available. You encourage me more than you know.

A special thank you to Sandy Beck and Cris Carnahan for your continued support in so many way.

Thanks to Laurie Tomlinson and John Pierce who helped improve this book with their amazing ideas and sharp eyes while reading the *Pages* manuscript.

Thank you, Kim Draper, for your artistic input and for creating such a lovely cover.

Thank you to my Wednesday night prayer group: Tom, Viola, Judi, Gina, and Mary. Life is about more than books and writing. Your support and faithfulness boosts my spirit each and every week we meet.

Thanks to my family for asking for updates on my writing, sharing Facebook posts, and encouraging me. A shout out to Dan, Jeff, Kyle, Kelsey, Aryn, Eileen, Cindy K., John, Scott, Dawn, Kendra, for helping spread the word.
And finally, to Tom my husband: thank you for your love, cheerleading, and frequent gifts of flowers. And for sharing my joys and disappointments, and telling me to keep writing. *Tá mo chroí istigh ionat.* My heart is within you.

Author's Note

While little can be documented about fifth-century Ireland, there are stories, fables, and high tales to spark the imagination. Brigid of Kildare (Cill Dara)—according to the accounts of her written down much later—did found a duel-monastery, consult with a male bishop named Conleth, and experience a close friendship with a man named Ninnidh. She lived from approximately 451-525 A.D. Many of the legends about the saint are so wrapped up in the tales of the goddess Brigid that untangling them is as impossible as unraveling a Celtic knot. My story was created by using what we know about ancient Ireland's society, the legends surrounding St. Brigid, the spread of Christianity in Ireland, and the rare and cherished books.

For a narrative history of St. Brigid and other Irish saints, and a historical look at this time period, please see my book *The Roots of Irish Wisdom, Learning From Ancient Voices*. You can learn more about all my books here:
http://cindyswriting.com/books/

For free reading, contests, and other fun, please sign up for my monthly newsletter at:
http://cindyswriting.com/newsletter-sign-up/

I'd love to hear from you. You are the reason I write!

Made in the USA
Monee, IL
23 June 2023

36893014R00218